Praise for Amanda

Humbug

"*Humbug* is the Christmas cuddle we all want and need this festive season. Once again Amanda Radley has given us characters we can love, a gentle romance and a setting we never knew we needed."—*Kitty Kat's Book Review Blog*

"This is a classic Christmas rom-com, with holiday cheer and a predictable storyline. I would vote for *Humbug* as my favorite Christmas novel of 2021."—*The Lesbrary*

Under Her Influence

"Light, sweet, and remarkably chaste, this sapphic love story will make as enjoyable a vacation pick as it is an armchair getaway."—*Publishers Weekly*

"My heart is just…filled with love and warmth! Finally, I have found an author who does not rely on sex to make a book interesting!! I'm probably going to go on an Amanda Radley read-a-thon."—*Periwinkle Pens*

"*Under Her Influence* by Amanda Radley is a sweet love story and leaves the reader feeling happy and contented. And that's exactly what I want from a romance these days. Ms Radley keeps angst to a minimum and lets her readers enjoy the blossoming of love between her characters."—*Kitty Kat's Book Review Blog*

Detour to Love

"If you're on the lookout for well-written sapphic romance with stellar characters, wonderful pairings, and outstanding plots, I wholeheartedly recommend any of Amanda's books!!"—*EloiseReads*

Flight SQA016

"I'm so glad I picked this book up because I think I've found my new favourite series!…The love brewing between these two is beautifully written and I was onboard from the beginning. I had some laugh out loud moments because this is British rom-com at its best. The secondary characters really added to the novel and the rollercoaster ride that is this book. The writing is tight and pace is perfect."—*Les Rêveur*

Lost at Sea

"A.E. Radley knows how to write great characters. And it's not just the main characters she puts so much effort into. I loved them, but I was astounded at how well drawn the minor characters were...The writing was beautiful—descriptive, real and very funny at times."
—*Lesbian Review*

"Absolutely amazing, easy to read, perfect romance with mystery and drama story. There were so many wonderful elements that gave twists and turns to this adventure on the sea. I absolutely loved this story and can't rave about it enough."—*LesbiReviewed*

Going Up

"I can always count on this superb author when it comes to creating unforgettable and endearing characters that I can totally relate to and fall in love with. A.E. Radley has given me beautiful descriptions of Parbrook and the quirky individuals who work at Addington's."
—*Lesbian Review*

"It was an A.E. Radley story, so naturally, I loved it! Selina is A.E. Radley's iciest Ice Queen yet! She was so cold and closed off, but as the story progresses and we get a good understanding of her, you realise that just as with any other Ice Queen—she can be thawed. I loved how they interacted, with a wit and banter that only A.E. Radley can really deliver for characters like these."—*LesbiReviewed*

"This story is a refreshing light in the lesfic world. Or should I say in the romance lesfic world? Why do you ask me? Well, while there is a lot of crushy feeling between wlw characters and all, but, honestly that's the sub-plot and I've adored that fact. *Going Up* is a lesson in life."—*Kam's Queerfic Pantry*

"The author takes an improbable twosome and writes such a splendid romance that you actually think it is possible...this is a great romance and a lovely read."—*Best Lesfic Reviews*

Mergers and Acquisitions

"This book is fun, witty, and adorable. I had no idea which way this book was going to take me, and I loved it. Each character is interesting and loveable in their own right. You don't want to miss this one—heck, if you have read any of A.E. Radley's books you know it's quality stuff."—*Romantic Reader Blog*

"Radley writes with a deceptively simple style, meaning the narrative flows naturally and quickly, yet takes readers effortlessly over rocky terrain. The pacing is unrushed and unforced, yet always leaves readers wanting to rush ahead to see what happens next."—*Lesbian Reveur*

The Startling Inaccuracy of the First Impression

"We absolutely loved the way the relationship between the two ladies developed. There is nothing hurried about the relationship that develops perfectly organically. This is a lovely, easy to read romance."—*Best Lesfic Reviews*

Huntress

"The writing style was fun and enjoyable. The story really gathered steam to the point of me shirking responsibilities to finish it. The humor in the story was very well done."—*Lesbian Review*

"A.E. Radley always writes fantastic books. *Huntress* is a little different than most of her books, but just as wonderful. The humor was fantastic, the story was absolutely adorable, and the writing was superb. This is truly one of those books where the characters really stick with you long after the book has ended. I wish I'd read it sooner. 5 Stars."
—*Les Rêveur*

Bring Holly Home

"*Bring Holly Home* is a fantastic novel and probably one of my favourite books by A.E. Radley…Such a brilliant story and one I know I will read time and time again. This book has two ingredients that I love in novels, Ice Queens melting and age-gap romance. It's definitely a slow burn but one I'd gladly enjoy rereading again."—*Les Rêveur*

Keep Holly Close

"It was great to go back into the world of the Remember Me series. The first book in the series, *Bring Holly Home*, is one of my favourite A.E. Radley books. I love Holly and Victoria; they tick all the boxes for me when it comes to my favourite tropes. Plus, Victoria's kids are adorable, especially little Alexia. She melts my heart."—*Les Rêveur*

"So much drama…loved it!!! I already loved Holly and Victoria from the first book in the series, *Bring Holly Home*, so it was brilliant to be back with them. Victoria hasn't changed and I adore her as much as before. She was utterly brilliant at every moment of this follow-up story and she even managed to surprise me from time to time. The Remember Me series is so beautiful and one of my all time favourites. 5 of 5 stars."—*LesbiReviewed*

Climbing the Ladder

"Radley has a talent for giving us memorable characters to love, women you wish you knew, and locations you wish you could experience firsthand."—*Late Night Lesbian Reads*

Second Chances

"This is an absolute delight to read. Likeable characters, well-written, easy flow and sweet romance. Definitely recommended."—*Best Lesfic Reviews*

"I always know when I get a new A.E. Radley book I'm in for a treat. They make me feel so good after reading them that most of the time I'm just plain sad that they have finished…The chemistry between Alice and Hannah is lovely and sweet…All in all, *Second Chances* has landed on my favourites shelf. Honestly, this book is worth every second of your time. 5 Stars."—*Les Rêveur*

The Road Ahead

"I really enjoyed this age-gap, opposites attract road trip romance. This is a romance where the characters actually acknowledge their differences and joy of joy, listen to each other. I love it when a book makes me feel all the feels and root for both women to find their HEA. Hilarious one minute, heart-tugging the next. A pleasure to read." —*Late Night Lesbian Reads*

Fitting In

"Writing convincing love stories with non-typical characters is tricky. Radley more than measures up to the challenge with this truly heart-warming romance."—*Best Lesfic Reviews*

By the Author

Romances

Mergers & Acquisitions

Climbing the Ladder

A Swedish Christmas Fairy Tale

Second Chances

Going Up

Lost at Sea

The Startling Inaccuracy of the First Impression

Fitting In

Detour to Love

Under Her Influence

Protecting the Lady

Humbug

Reading Her

Reclaiming Love

Maybe, Probably

The Flight Series

Flight SQA016

Grounded

Journey's End

The Remember Me Series

Bring Holly Home

Keep Holly Close

The Around the World Series

The Road Ahead

The Big Uneasy

Mystery Novels

Huntress

Death Before Dessert

Visit us at www.boldstrokesbooks.com

MAYBE, PROBABLY

by
Amanda Radley

2023

MAYBE, PROBABLY

ISBN 13: 978-1-63679-284-2

This Trade Paperback Original Is Published By
Bold Strokes Books, Inc.
P.O. Box 249
Valley Falls, NY 12185

First Edition: February 2023

CREDITS
EDITOR: RUTH STERNGLANTZ
PRODUCTION DESIGN: STACIA SEAMAN
COVER DESIGN BY AMANDA RADLEY

For the readers.

Chapter One

G ina Henley paused outside the coffee shop. While she knew that she was late for work, she was also aware of the hangover that niggled at the front of her brain.

It wasn't as bad as it could have been. Gina had long ago decided to keep her heavier partying to non-work nights. But that didn't mean that the occasional weeknight didn't end up lasting a little longer than she had originally planned.

She glanced at her watch. She was already late. Did another five minutes really matter? And her work would obviously be far better if she'd had her morning shot of caffeine to chase away the headache and tiredness that lurked, ready to become full-blown at the first email.

She entered the coffee shop and stood in the short queue. She pulled her phone out of her coat pocket and started to look at the screen full of notifications she had ignored that morning. Her banking app helpfully told her how much she had spent at various pubs and bars around London the night before. She'd been tagged in countless social media posts, no doubt containing photographic evidence of everything that had transpired.

Gina, unlike some of her friends, didn't need reminding. She never allowed herself to drink until she couldn't function or remember. It also helped that she had a very high tolerance to alcohol.

She paused in scrolling through her notifications at the missed call from her mum. Now that she was stopping for a coffee, she had a little time to check in with her. She made sure her phone was connected to the wireless headphones she wore constantly when out—whether she was actively listening to music or not—and called her mum.

It only took a couple of rings before her mum answered. "Hello, Gina love."

"Hi, Mum. How are you?"

"I'm good. Were you out last night?"

The question held the tiniest hint of judgement. Mary Henley always said her daughter was twenty-nine going on nineteen. It was no secret that Gina enjoyed her social life. She hated being cooped up in her apartment and loved to meet new people. But her mum made it quite clear that she thought it was time that Gina stopped heading out into London every night and instead found someone to settle down with, a thought that made Gina shiver.

"I was," Gina said, not wishing to elaborate and give her mum any ammunition. They'd been at this crossroads a few times, and it occasionally led to an argument. And Gina was too hung-over and in need of coffee to have a repeat performance of their last disagreement.

"I was just calling to remind you about Dad's birthday," her mum said, decision apparently made to keep things light that morning.

"That's in May," Gina said.

"Yes, I know."

"It's the start of March." Gina shuffled forward in the queue. She smiled at the barista. "Hold on, Mum. Hey, can I have a cappuccino? Large as they come, thanks!"

"I just want to make sure you're not jetting off to anywhere. Like, oh, I don't know, Peru."

Gina rolled her eyes. "I keep telling you—that was for work." She paid for her drink and stood at the end of the counter.

Her mum made a sound of disbelief. "What kind of work sends you to Peru for a month?"

"Work who want me to be able to draw local architecture and

plants." Gina rolled her eyes again but immediately regretted the move when her head started to throb.

"Backpacking, at your age."

Gina shook her head and took a slow breath in and then out. There was no point in trying to explain anything to her parents. They were absolutely convinced that Gina's career was a temporary gig until she managed to get a real job.

They couldn't understand how being a graphic designer for a video game company was very much a real and highly sought-after job, one that frequently sent designers all around the world to ensure their product was the best it could be. These days, more money was spent on game animation than on most Hollywood blockbusters. And while Gina had tried, on numerous occasions, to explain that, her parents were still absolutely certain that she drew cartoons for a living.

"So, what do you have planned for the old man?" Gina changed the subject back to the apparent reason for the call.

"You know, us and your brother and Claire. Aunt Alison and Uncle John. Probably Julie and Barry, if they're back from France then. All the family, of course."

Gina felt bored already. Her mum's idea of a party differed greatly from her own. She watched the barista racing to make the fast flow of morning orders. It looked like a gruelling task, but she'd gladly hand her phone to him and attempt to make a triple-shot latte with soy milk and caramel drizzle rather than discuss party arrangements with her mother.

Her stomach rumbled at the thought of caramel drizzle. She'd not had time for breakfast that morning, choosing to snooze the alarm a luxurious four times instead. It had felt like the right decision, the only decision, at the time. Now her stomach was regretting it. Thankfully, she knew the kitchen at work would be full of tasty baked treats and fresh fruit. Since starting at The Engine she'd never paid for breakfast or lunch.

Si Carver had hired her on the spot when she turned up for the weirdest interview of her life five years earlier. He'd worn a simple white T-shirt, plain grey hoodie, and black jeans as a tech genius was legally obligated to. While lounging on a beanbag, he'd told Gina of his vision to create the most visually stunning games in the world. His mission was for people to feel like they were in the game, and art was the basis of that. He knew that it would only be a short amount of time before virtual reality took the place of games consoles, and he wanted to be ready with the most breathtakingly accurate art available.

After forty minutes of explaining how he imagined The Engine would change the world of gaming, he'd handed her his iPad Pro and asked her to draw a London Underground station scene for a prototype zombie apocalypse game.

"Dark, ya know?" he'd said. "Gritty. Scary. But familiar. Right? You get it. Come find me when you're done. Nothing fancy. Twenty minutes. See what you can do."

Gina relocated to a table in the break room and drew the scene that immediately came to her mind. Lights from a stalled train illuminating the dark station, an eerie shadow cast against a corridor. It wasn't her best work, but she'd been given a very short amount of time.

He'd hired her on the spot, and she'd been promoted four times since then as The Engine grew from strength to strength. But her parents still told people that she drew for a living in a way that suggested they were hoping she'd get a real job soon.

"I take it that it will just be you?" her mum asked, emphasising the *just* in the way only a worried mother could.

Gina sighed. "Probably, yes."

"Oh, love. You're out all the time—I don't see how you can't have met someone by now."

"I'm picky." Gina stepped forward and took her drink before the barista had time to call her name out.

"Maybe you should lower your standards? You don't want to be single forever."

"Wow, Mum. Really? Lower my standards? How low should I go?" Gina stepped out of the coffee shop and continued her walk to work.

"Don't be like that. I just want you to find someone and settle down. There must be some nice men that you know."

Gina gritted her teeth. Her mum had long been obsessed with her finding a man, but lately it had reached something of a fever pitch. Not a single conversation would go by without a little nudge about how nice it would be to settle down. How pleasant it was to sit in front of the television with your man. How starting a family had a clock attached to it.

As Gina ticked closer to being thirty and single, her mother's anxiety about it being permanent seemed to grow.

"How about Charlie at work?" her mum continued. "You mentioned him a couple of times."

"Sure, I'll propose today. With any luck, you'll have grandchildren before the year is out." Gina sipped her coffee, knowing that the hot beverage now had no chance against the full-blown headache that was raging inside her skull. The hangover had teamed up with maternal guilt and created an unbeatable team.

"Gina, I'm just worried about you. I'm sorry. I don't mean it to come across like that."

Gina swallowed down any further response. She knew her mum was on her case only because she cared so much and wanted her daughter to have what she did.

Gina's parents adored one another. They made other couples roll their eyes at their cutesy behaviour. Even Gina got a bit fed up with the heart eyes across the dining table now and then. The years together had made them stronger, unlike so many other couples who seemed to drift apart.

"I know," Gina said. "I just...We don't all find someone as perfect as you and Dad, you know? But that doesn't mean I want to lower my standards."

"I know. I shouldn't have said that. You'll find someone—I know you will. You know me. I just worry."

"I know."

There wasn't much more that Gina could say. She wasn't going to find someone to settle down with. Her parents wanted her to find a man, and that was never going to happen. Gina had been interested in women since she was a teenager and dating women since she was in her early twenties. She hadn't dared tell her parents. They were traditional sorts, and any time Gina spoke of anything vaguely queer, they clammed up. She had no intention of telling them her truth. Visions of their disappointed looks and the end of their close family relationship haunted her dreams. She couldn't take the risk of rocking the boat. Gina didn't know for sure that they'd disown her if she came out to them, but the fear that they might was enough for her to remain silent.

Despite not being able to be honest with them, Gina did know that they loved her. The endless cycle of comments about her still being single and questions about who she might be seeing and if she'd ever bring a boyfriend home all came from a place of love. Even if it was misplaced.

Gina wasn't a risk taker. She didn't go bungee jumping, not because of a fear of heights but because of the tiny chance that the rope might not be tied correctly. Why take a risk when you didn't have to was Gina's motto.

"I have to go—I'm at work. Call you later?" Gina was thankful to see the office coming into view.

"Okay, have a nice day."

Gina hung up the call. She noticed Julie, one of the junior coders from the development department, exiting the glass revolving door of the office clutching an archive box.

"Moving out?" Gina joked, hoping that Julie hadn't been fired.

"Si is sending everyone home." Julie could hardly contain her glee as she wrestled with the clearly heavy box.

"What? Why?"

Julie shrugged. "He's worried about that COVID-19 thing. Says we need to protect ourselves and the business by working from home. Sweet, huh? Anyway, I have to go—my boyfriend is picking me up. See you!"

Gina watched in confusion as Julie walked away. She'd heard about the illness that had come from China somewhere but didn't know why Si would suddenly change his mind about working from home.

While The Engine was pretty flexible about most things, Si wanted people to work collaboratively and brainstorm ideas in the Idea Lab—a corner of the office filled with whiteboard and beanbags.

Gina had managed to negotiate a flexible working arrangement, but that was only because she'd proved herself to Si over the years. Gina loved her job and routinely worked more hours than her contract demanded. That had led to Si letting her work partly from home, which made her the envy of her colleagues.

She entered the lobby through the revolving doors and saw some people from The Engine standing around reception on their phones. Some of them had archive boxes with them too.

Gina took another sip of coffee. The weird environment was not helping her building headache. She entered the lift and went to her floor, passing someone else with an archive box on the way.

She approached Si's office and watched him packing up his desk into boxes.

"So the money ran out, right?" she joked.

He looked up. His expression was grim. "We need to close the office. I'm going to need your help to make sure people get logged into all the remote working systems. And the project management system. We need everyone on that now, not just for projects. For everything."

"You're seriously closing the office?" Gina couldn't believe her ears. "Isn't it like a cold or something?"

Si paused packing up his desk. "Gina, we don't know what it is. But it's serious. Have you seen the news?"

She hadn't watched the news since she lived at home nearly a decade ago. The news was depressing.

"I lived in Hong Kong when the SARS outbreak happened. People were the same then," Si said. "They thought it was nothing. Couldn't believe that it would be a problem because they didn't want to believe it. And then it got really serious, really fast."

He picked up some more papers from his desk and put them in a box.

"The office closes today, and we'll review every two weeks," he said. "Assume you won't be in the office for a while—pack up as much as you'll need."

Gina slowly sipped her coffee. Si had always been a little highly strung and dramatic. The tiniest problem in a game had him claiming that shareholders would leave in droves. A positive opinion piece in a magazine had him assuming everything he touched would turn to gold.

Gina walked towards the art department. As she did, she watched her colleagues packing up their desks. Some seemed excited, others nervous. Gina personally felt this was another Si overreaction, but she'd enjoy working from home until he came to his senses.

Gina thought about the pastries and fruit in the kitchen. Now *those* she would miss. She detoured away from the art department into the kitchen for one last buffet breakfast on The Engine before she'd have to fend for herself.

She finished off her coffee and placed the cup in the recycling bin. Colin from marketing was already boxing up more pastries than one man should have been capable of eating. He had a doughnut in his mouth and nodded to Gina in greeting.

The television, which usually played a series of promotional messages, was switched on to the twenty-four-hour news channel. The presenter grimly spoke of COVID-19 hospitalisations in Europe and a recently released report which claimed up to a fifth of the UK workforce could be off work sick at the same time.

Gina let out a sigh. Everyone was overreacting.

"Want my advice?" Colin asked. He had swallowed the doughnut and was holding a box of pastries like they were precious jewels. "Get some toilet roll in. Just in case you're stuck at home sick for two weeks."

Colin nodded sagely, obviously convinced that he'd just dispensed a valuable pearl of wisdom. He grabbed a couple of bottles of sparkling water before rushing out of the kitchen.

Gina blew out a breath. "Everyone's losing their mind."

Chapter Two

Eleanor Osborne hurried down the hospital corridor towards the cardiology department. She'd been called to radiology to consult on a couple of cases and was almost running late for the team meeting.

She entered the department and nodded to the receptionist, Sandra.

"Morning, Dr. Osborne. I have some messages for you." Sandra held up a handful of notes.

Eleanor took them. "I was only gone for an hour."

"You're very popular," Sandra said, deadpan.

Eleanor looked at Sandra to see if she could detect any hint of humour, but Sandra returned to typing up letters. Like so many stretched-to-the-limit NHS receptionists, Sandra gave very little away and was all about the work.

That suited Eleanor perfectly.

Eleanor had worked in the cardiology department of the Royal Thames Hospital for ten years, working her way up to deputy head of the department. She'd seen many colleagues come and go. Some went to private practice, some burnt out, some abruptly decided on a completely different career path. Medicine wasn't for everyone.

While the NHS could be incredibly fulfilling, it could also be difficult and emotional. Often, as Sandra proved so deftly, the best way to deal with it was to keep your head down and focus on the task at hand. One foot in front of the other. One day at a time.

That was Eleanor's strategy. She didn't love her job in a way that made her jump out of bed each day and rush to the hospital. But she appreciated that she did a task that saved lives and that she was a required cog in a complicated machine. If she thought too much about the underfunding and far too many layers of management, then she'd probably scream in frustration. And so she didn't think about it and instead focused firmly on her patients. One at a time.

"How's my favourite deputy?" Nigel Hoyle asked.

"I'm your only deputy," Eleanor reminded her boss, who was also her best friend.

They walked together through the corridor towards the staff room that doubled as the meeting room where they held a daily team briefing every day before lunch.

"How's the angel?" he asked.

Eleanor couldn't help but smile at the mention of her daughter.

"She's very well. She's so close to saying her first word," Eleanor said.

She thought back to the evening before when she had enunciated the word *mama* to Sophia at least fifty times in the hope that it would be returned. It wasn't. Sophia had simply stared up at her, wide-eyed and as curious as ever.

"You've been saying that for weeks."

"Well, she is. It's not quite there at the moment. Just noise. Or she's saying something so advanced that I'm not making the connection."

"Enjoy this time," Nigel told her. "Document everything. They suddenly become frightfully irritating teenagers who hate you."

Eleanor chuckled. "You didn't tell me that when you were convincing me to go through IVF."

"I wanted someone to commiserate with. I was hardly likely to tell you the truth about being a parent. Now we're in the same boat just as I'd planned."

"You're a cruel man, Dr. Hoyle."

In truth, Nigel was the kindest man she'd ever known. The moment she'd met him, she'd liked him. Little had she known back then that he'd end up being her best friend, confidant, and ultimately the person who had held her hand through the process that led to her becoming a single mother at the age of forty-six. He'd stated her case to cynical IVF clinics who thought she was too old. He'd been there through the failures and the successes. She wondered if maybe she too might have left the NHS if it hadn't been for him. They were a team, best friends and work colleagues. Both doing what they could. One patient at a time.

They entered the empty staff room. Eleanor glanced at her wristwatch.

"I told everyone to take some time to fill in that new availability timesheet that HR recently sent through," Nigel explained. "Part of the new COVID protocols."

Eleanor stiffened. She'd been watching the news with increasing concern. Things were developing rapidly, and they were still no closer to finding out what was happening and what they could do about the situation. The hospital had a pandemic preparedness plan in the same way she had a fire evacuation plan for her apartment. She sort of knew the event could happen, assumed it wouldn't, and would deal with it when the situation arose. It was the kind of planning that most people did when it came to big, frightening scenarios. The only issue was this particular scenario was currently in the country and becoming more acute with every passing day.

"Forty-seven new cases today," Nigel continued. "Highest daily increase so far."

"It will get far worse," Eleanor said. "I was looking at the Chinese data released a few days ago. The growth rate is extraordinary. I think we'll be seeing tens of thousands of cases a day within a couple of weeks."

Nigel put his hand in his pocket and fished out some coins. He looked at the vending machine and then the coins in his hand.

"You're right," he said. "It's just what those tens of thousands of cases will turn into. And, who knows, maybe we'll have some kind of treatment by then."

Eleanor knew she was considered sceptical and so didn't tell Nigel that she thought his optimism was misplaced. She knew the case numbers would rise beyond anything they could imagine. The

NHS would be put under incredible stress. It was just a matter of when and how much.

"The Trust is developing an emergency plan," Nigel said. "More staff on call, more PPE. But it's hard to prepare for something unknown. We're not far behind the European wave—who knows what will happen?"

"I don't envy them," Eleanor agreed. "I wouldn't want to be drawing up plans for something I didn't understand. What's the plan for now?"

"Carry on as usual. Keep reporting numbers back up the chain. Keep panic to an absolute minimum. People are starting to worry."

"I know how they feel," Eleanor mumbled.

Nigel fed some coins into the vending machine and made his selection. The machine whirred and then made a crunching sound. He placed his hand soothingly on its side. "Hush, now. You can do it, girl. F7. Go on."

"I don't know why you continue to give that thing your money," Eleanor said.

She sat down and leaned back in the plastic chair, listening for the satisfying sound of her spine popping. She really needed to start yoga again. Sophia was nearly a year old, and she didn't want to be the sort of mother who couldn't keep up with her child.

Of course, she'd factored her age and fitness into the equation when she was deciding whether to bring a child into the world. She exercised, ate well, and was generally in good shape. Now she just needed to find the time to continue those good practices.

"It's the thrill of the chase. Like gambling," Nigel said. "Half the time you get nothing. Half the time you get what you asked for. But on a rare sweet occasion, it goes berserk, and you get multiple things. Like a tidal wave of chocolate. Who can resist such a possible bounty?"

"Interesting math skills you have, Nigel."

Any retort was cut off by the rest of the team entering the room. Eleanor heard them murmuring about the COVID plan and could see the concern etched on their faces.

She sat up and smiled, trying to keep morale up. That would be the key to whatever they were about to face. Staying positive and sticking together. She knew that people were pinning their hopes on it maybe not being as bad as some predicted. Sadly, Eleanor knew it would probably be far worse.

❖

Eleanor swiped her key fob on the outer door to the apartment building and then entered the lobby. She unlocked her mailbox and picked up the few items of post. As she flipped through them, she walked towards the first apartment on the ground floor and knocked on the door.

She could hear Sophia's excited cries and imagined that Madeline was building up her excitement that her mother was here to pick her up. Eleanor put the envelopes in her bag and tried to be patient while the very young and very elderly both made their slow but steady way towards the door.

She itched to see Sophia. She'd always known that being a working mother would be hard, and time with her daughter would be precious. But it was at moments like these that she wished she had some alternative, that she could spend far more time with Sophia as she grew into whatever she was going to become.

The door opened, and Madeline stood in the doorway, holding Sophia. Sophia instantly reached out to her, and Eleanor took her from Madeline.

"How's she been?" Eleanor asked.

Sophia played with Eleanor's hair and made some nonsense noises that Eleanor just knew would soon be endless chatter.

"She's been wonderful, as always. No talking. A little standing but those pudgy little legs give out, don't they, precious?" Madeline reached forward and stroked Sophia's plump cheek with the backs of her fingers.

"Thank you so much for taking her again. I am looking for another babysitter, but they are a little fussy with time—"

"Nothing to thank me for—I love having her here. Bring her by tomorrow, and we'll have even more fun than we had today, won't we, Sophia?" Madeline tickled Sophia's side, and Eleanor chuckled as her daughter laughed and squirmed.

"Thank you," Eleanor said. "I feel so guilty taking up your time."

Madeline shrugged. "It's nice to have her here. It gets quiet otherwise."

Eleanor nodded solemnly. Madeline lived alone, had done since her husband had passed away three years before. She'd only ever been the downstairs neighbour to Eleanor up until the day she'd been let down by a babysitter and was frantically making phone calls in the lobby of the building.

Madeline had been returning from shopping, caught the gist of what was happening, and offered to take Sophia for the day. To say that Eleanor had been reluctant to leave her daughter with someone she hardly knew and who was in their eighties was an understatement. But it was the third day in a row that babysitters had let her down, and while Nigel was patient, Eleanor couldn't continue to abandon her duties.

"She reminds me of my granddaughter Felicity—she's nine now. They grow so fast. Especially when you don't see very much of them," Madeline said.

"When are you going to see your daughter next?" Eleanor asked, moving Sophia from one hip to the other.

"Maybe this summer. We're making plans to go to a cottage together. Somewhere by a lake, I hope."

"That sounds lovely." Eleanor's mind flew to the idea of a holiday. Just her and Sophia for a week or two. Somewhere peaceful. She added it to the list of things she needed to do when she got a moment to herself. "I'll let you get back to your evening. Thank you again."

"I'll see you tomorrow. Usual time." Madeline gave one final soft pinch of Sophia's cheek and closed the door.

Eleanor walked over to the elevator and pushed the call button.

"Did you have a nice time?" she asked Sophia.

Sophia continued to play with her hair and said nothing. Eleanor decided to enjoy the silence, knowing that Sophia's verbal skills were developing and before long she'd be making endless noise again.

A young woman appeared beside her. She wore a bright red winter coat, a woolly hat, and had large headphones over her ears. She nodded to Eleanor in greeting before returning to whatever was sucking up her attention on her phone.

Eleanor had seen her a few times. They lived on the same floor, but beyond that she knew nothing about the woman, just that she permanently wore headphones and seemed determined to not make social connections with anyone else in the building.

The elevator arrived, and they both stepped in. Eleanor pressed the button for the fourth floor. She stared straight ahead and enjoyed the peaceful silence, while Sophia leant wildly around to catch a glimpse of the stranger. Eleanor silently prayed that Sophia wouldn't reach for her. She'd recently started to do that with people she thought looked interesting. The woman's bright red coat was definitely going to interest Sophia.

Thankfully, they arrived on the fourth floor without incident. The young woman walked to the right, and Eleanor walked to the left, much to Sophia's irritation. Eleanor adapted her grip as Sophia peered over her shoulder at their retreating neighbour.

"You're so very nosey," Eleanor whispered to her.

She opened the door to the apartment and switched on the lights. She placed Sophia in the playpen in the living room and put her bag on the sofa. She could see the voicemail light blinking and knew that it would be the only person who called the landline. The only reason she had a landline.

She pressed the button, and her sister's voice filled the room, *"Hey Elle, only me. Give me a call when you get a chance—it's been ages. Love to you both."*

Eleanor looked at the two clocks on the wall and calculated the best time to call her back. Her sister's choice to move to Australia five years ago had left Eleanor reeling. They'd never been very close siblings, but the enormous distance in both miles and time zones felt like a heavy weight separating them. Eleanor did what she could to stay in touch, keeping a landline to make the calls cheaper, and having a dedicated clock always showing what time it was in her sister's distant part of the world. But she still struggled with loneliness. Not that she could blame Laura for living her life. She was glad that Laura was happy, even if it was on the other side of the planet.

Sophia giggled, breaking Eleanor from her moody thoughts. She turned to watch Sophia happily throwing a teddy bear around by its ears.

"Time for dinner," Eleanor said. "Will you chop the vegetables, or shall I?"

Sophia looked up and blew a raspberry in response.

CHAPTER THREE

Gina lay in bed and stared at the text message. She sighed and tossed the phone to one side. She'd been looking forward to the trip to the cinema, and now her best friend was bailing on her at the last minute.

She grabbed the phone again. She started to type a reply but paused and instead called Kath. This kind of last-minute cancellation required a conversation.

Kath answered on the second ring. "Hey."

"You're cancelling?" Gina got straight to the point. "Why?"

Kath laughed. "Have you seen the news lately?"

Gina sighed. "Seriously? COVID? It's just some cold or something. Marco said at this point it's probably better to get it and get it over and done with. We'll be having COVID parties before March is over."

"Marco is an idiot," Kath said. "I don't think either of us should be taking advice from someone who took fourteen attempts to get his driver's licence."

"He's not the only one saying it," Gina said defensively. Though, truth be told, it was mainly Marco. And Kath was right that Marco probably wasn't the best person to go to for life advice. It just so happened that Marco was currently saying things she wanted to hear.

"No one knows what it is, but it's not a cold," Kath continued. "People are dying. And before you say it, it's not just old people. Lots of people are dying. And even if COVID doesn't get you, if you need hospital treatment for something else, then you're screwed because they are going to be absolutely full of people with COVID."

"Yeah, okay," Gina said half-heartedly.

"Gina. Seriously," Kath said sharply. "Have you seen the news? This thing is serious. And people don't know what it is. Stay home and stay safe, okay? I have to go. Some of us don't get the luxury of working from home. Yet."

"Okay," Gina said softly, feeling chastised.

She hung up the call and dragged herself out of bed. It was a quarter to nine, and usually she'd be making her way to work. Working from home had its benefits, but Gina always knew that she'd become her laziest self given half a chance.

She'd always wished that she was the sort of person who jumped out of bed with a sense of purpose and drive. Instead, she was the sort of person who rolled out of bed and wondered if she had time for an afternoon nap that day.

In the kitchen, she rubbed her eyes and looked at the selection of breakfast cereals she'd hastily bought the previous day. She opted for the one with the brightest colours on the box. There was a strong chance that it had the most sugar.

It was a mystery to her how getting up later could somehow make her feel more tired. And even though she knew that, she knew without a doubt that she would continue to sleep in.

Overfull bowl of cereal in hand, she turned on the television and scrolled through the channels until she found some news. A grim-faced presenter sat on a bright red sofa that seemed completely at odds with the words they were speaking.

"And, as we were reporting earlier, Italy have now reported over four hundred deaths, with that figure expected to rise significantly. Likely to double in under a week."

Gina paused eating. The spoon hung in the air, droplets of milk splashing back down onto the cereal shaped like stars and crescent moons. She hadn't realised that the death count was so high and expected to grow. She felt guilty for her thoughts turning to people close to home and wondered what that meant for the UK.

She pushed the thought away, both through fear and through the guilt of making this worldwide disaster about herself.

The presenter continued to give a round-up of the situation. Video reports of overflowing hospitals and people crying played on a continuous loop. Gina put her cereal to one side, her appetite now truly gone.

Eventually, the presenter handed over to a weather report, which claimed that it was a beautiful day as if they were completely unaware of the impending doom that had been previously reported.

"So, everyone's going to die, but take an umbrella if you're going out on Saturday?" Gina asked the television. "Make your mind up."

Following the weather, a business presenter took over and explained how millions of pounds were being wiped off the markets with one of the biggest stock market crashes outside of wartime.

Gina had no idea what that even meant. As far as she knew, stock markets were largely made-up money anyway.

"How can people watch this?" she asked herself. She returned to the kitchen and cleared away her uneaten breakfast. The news hadn't informed her of much. All it had done was confuse and frighten her.

She switched off the television and let out a sigh. On one hand she missed the sound of chatter, but on the other she couldn't stand to hear any more ambulance sirens or casualty figures.

She looked around the open-plan living space. It had always seemed perfectly adequate for her, spacious, though not cavernous. Now she felt constricted and like the walls were slowly closing in.

She'd placed her large drafting table in front of the windows to give her as much natural light as possible. The short distance from the table to the living area to the kitchen used to feel convenient, but now it felt constrictive.

Gina loved to roam when she was in the office. Any time her mind refused to focus on something, she got up and walked the floors, not to chat and distract other people from their work, but to stretch her legs and capture some inspiration.

Listening to people on the phone, watching someone take a far-too-big bite of a sandwich and hope no one had seen them, watching the way someone cleaned their glasses and held them up to the light to check for blemishes. It was all input for her.

The truth was that Gina was nosy. Always had been. As a young child she had stolen her dad's birdwatching binoculars to get a glimpse at the neighbours.

She'd taken that nosiness and converted it into a skill she could use. Artists had to be observant. They had to see how facial features minutely changed to represent emotion below the surface. They had to constantly be looking and taking things in.

They had to not be stuck working from home.

Gina looked out of the window down onto the street. It was far quieter than it usually was. The bus stop across the road had no one waiting at it. Even the number of cars on the road seemed far fewer.

Gina hated the quietness. She looked at her watch. Her first meeting of the day wasn't for a couple of hours. And the weather person had said that it would be mild today but would rain later in the week.

It didn't take much convincing for Gina to decide to head outside in search of some life. While she had everything that she needed to make coffee, there was something about having someone else make it for you. Something so nice about being presented with a whole menu of options, and many rotating specials as well. Something about watching the process and knowing that the drink would taste so much better than if you'd done exactly the same process at home. Because laziness tasted divine.

❖

It was only half an hour later when Gina walked through the lobby to head to her favourite local coffee shop. In the lobby, she encountered the posh woman with the baby speaking with the old lady who lived on the ground floor. She knew them to smile and nod at, but beyond that she'd yet to have a conversation with either of them. Which was deliberate.

While Gina loved to socialise, she also liked to keep herself to herself when it came to where she lived. In her previous apartment, she'd received unsolicited comments from people asking if she was off out again or wondering if she'd be cold in her short skirts. People loved to have an opinion. Gina didn't always want to hear it. She had enough of justifying her love of going out to her parents, never mind to strangers she shared elevators with.

So when she'd moved into the new apartment a year ago, she'd made the decision to not speak with anyone. It wasn't unheard of for Londoners not to know their neighbours. And she did always smile, even if she then immediately broke eye contact and focused on her phone instead.

Not speaking with them didn't mean she didn't observe them. The woman with the baby had always fascinated Gina. She walked with confidence and had the look of someone who was pulled together and intelligent. Gina was still trying to figure out how to draw intelligence on a person. It was one of the many artist mysteries she was desperate to crack. But whatever the secret was, the woman had it in spades. Possibly it was the poised and graceful way she held herself, even when clutching a baby.

The baby was a bit of a mystery. She was as cute as a button. But Gina couldn't help but notice the woman seemed a little on the old side to have a baby. Gina wouldn't be surprised if she was approaching fifty. Not that there was anything wrong with that, just that it was unusual. And Gina always noticed unusual.

The other unusual thing was the lack of a spouse. Gina often saw the baby and the woman, but never a partner of any gender. Again, it wasn't important, but it certainly did engage Gina's nosiness.

Outside she took a deep breath of fresh air and realised she was appreciating it in a way she hadn't previously. She chuckled to herself. She was acting like a prisoner who had been locked up for months and granted their freedom. In truth, she'd been working from home for a couple of days and was bored.

A short walk later and she arrived at the coffee shop. It was her lucky day as Maddy, the cute barista she frequently flirted with, was working that morning. Gina took a little longer than usual to decide on her drink order, enjoying being out and around people. Even if the coffee shop was particularly sparsely populated that morning.

In the end, she ordered a caramel flavoured latte and a croissant.

"Quiet in here," Gina commented.

"Yeah, it's been getting quieter," Maddy replied.

"Why?"

Maddy looked at her as if she'd lost the plot. "COVID. People are staying home."

"Oh, right, yeah." Gina felt embarrassed.

Maddy pumped some flavoured syrup into a cup. "I can't get sick. My mum is going through chemo."

"I'm sorry."

"It's okay." Maddy shrugged. "She's doing well. But we don't need this on top of everything else. The branch up at Westminster closed a couple of days ago. I keep asking my manager when we'll close, and she just says she's monitoring the situation. Whatever that means."

Gina felt her eyes widen but tried not to show her shock. The coffee shop was one of Gina's rituals, a luxury that she adored partaking in. With the office closed, spending time at a coffee shop was the next best thing. She'd even planned to work from here one day the following week just to get out of her apartment.

"We're not allowed to wear masks, either. Can you believe that?" Maddy continued complaining.

"Masks?"

"Face masks. We've had a few customers come in wearing them, but my manager says we're not allowed."

Gina slowly nodded. She wanted to indicate that she was following along, but in truth she was surprised. She'd last been in the coffee shop around ten days ago, and everything had seemed normal. Now things were very different. Now the shop had two customers, the staff wanted to close, and it seemed that some people wanted to wear face masks.

"I just think I'm being put at risk, you know?" Maddy said. "My manager said only four people have died. Hasn't she seen

China? Or Italy? It's going to get so much worse. We need to be taking action now."

Maddy's panic was palpable, and it was having a similar effect on Gina. She didn't know if Maddy was overreacting. Maybe she'd been watching too much of the news and had gotten swept up in the doom and gloom narrative. Gina couldn't imagine anyone watching the news and being able to keep a positive outlook on things.

Another customer entered the shop, and Gina saw Maddy flinch. There was nothing threatening about the woman as far as Gina could see. She was in her fifties and smartly dressed. She realised that Maddy was reacting to there being more people in the store, rather than *who* was in the store.

When Maddy handed her the drink—or rather when Maddy placed the takeaway mug on the counter and all but jumped back—Gina departed. The chilly March morning air whipped around her as she walked back to her apartment.

She'd hoped to be out a little longer, maybe hang around the coffee shop and chat to Maddy as she had done in the past. But that was clearly going to make Maddy uncomfortable. Gina started to feel a little guilty for not feeling as concerned as Maddy clearly did.

She wished that COVID would just hurry up and arrive. Wished that it would sweep across the country so everyone could have a cold for a couple of weeks and then get back to normal.

She was struggling with the idea that life could have changed so much and so quickly. Every day seemed to add some extra new challenge. From working from home, to supermarket delivery slots being snatched up, to her coffee shop no longer being a safe haven.

Gina was already fed up with COVID, and it seemed it had yet to even arrive.

CHAPTER FOUR

Eleanor left the ward while jotting down notes on her clipboard. It still irked her that everything in the NHS was paper notes and clipboards. The biggest health service in the world was only part-digitalised, and the hospitals were truly the realm of paper.

At the reception desk, she started to place the various clipboards in the rack where they would be moved onto their next stage in their journey. She had no idea where the clipboards started their lives or where they ended up, just that she was a custodian of them for a short period of time, and Sandra would complain bitterly if her handwriting was unreadable, she missed an important checkbox, or she put the clipboard in the wrong rack.

Eleanor liked that Sandra was on top of things. She had faith that someone was pulling all the various threads together and knew how everything worked. She could stand being berated a couple of times a month if it meant peace of mind that everything was in order.

"You should check the news," Sandra said without looking up from her typing. Her fingers flew across the keyboard while she stared straight ahead at the screen.

Eleanor hesitated a moment. Normally, she would ask for more information. But you simply didn't interrupt Sandra while she was typing.

"Thank you," Eleanor said instead of asking why she needed to see the news. She went to the break room and took a seat on the edge of the sofa.

The news was already on. It was permanently on lately. Gone

were the days of the sound of mindless feel-good programming filtering from the break room. No more chuckling bottom-of-the-pile celebrities talking about recipes, laundry tips, and the latest online scam to avoid. Now it was wall-to-wall news, the same stories on a cycle until a new disaster struck and entered the circulation as breaking news.

The sound of the television was drowned out by someone approaching with a vacuum cleaner. Kate, the primary ward cleaner, entered the break room. Upon seeing Eleanor, she turned off the machine.

"Sorry, Dr. Osborne, I didn't think anyone was in here."

"It's fine," Eleanor said. "You carry on."

Kate looked towards the television. "It's awful, isn't it? The whole hospital is on edge. And every minute there's a new thing. Like the travel."

"What travel?" Eleanor asked. She'd hardly had a chance to listen to the news. They were currently interviewing a scientist from Italy who was explaining exactly what a coronavirus was.

"Travel restrictions," Kate said. She plucked a feather duster from her belt and started to wipe it along the skirting boards. "Spain and the USA. And then there are going to be these daily news briefings. Every day they'll tell us what's been happening. Stop all the fake news spreading around on Facebook."

Eleanor groaned. She hadn't even considered what the internet would be making of all this. She avoided social media. For one, she didn't understand it. Second, she didn't have time. But based on what she gleaned from her friends who did use the various platforms, there seemed to be an awful lot of bad information floating around.

Kate stopped dusting and looked at Eleanor. Fear was clear on her face despite her obvious attempt to hold it back.

"It's coming, isn't it?" Kate asked.

"It is, yes." Eleanor saw no need to sugar-coat the truth. What people needed now was honesty and practical information.

"We've been told to wear masks," Kate said, "all the time. I'm not sure I like the idea of that. I do a lot of physical work."

"Wear the mask," Eleanor said. "We don't know much about

this virus. We do know that it affects older people worse, and I mean even you and I when I say that. Wear the mask. Wash your hands frequently with hot water and soap. Don't touch your eyes, nose, or mouth. Keep a distance from people."

Kate nodded hard. "I will."

"I mean it, Kate," Eleanor said. "Keep yourself safe. This virus is coming, and it's going to get a lot worse. Worse than we can probably imagine."

Eleanor had read through the preparedness report that had landed in her inbox that morning. Nearly all the ventilators had been moved to the accident and emergency department. Huge stocks of personal protective equipment had been ordered. And there was a plan to reallocate ward space to create a zone in the hospital for all COVID patients and treatment staff, so they never encountered the rest of the hospital.

Eleanor knew that was just the tip of the iceberg. They had a handful of COVID patients in the hospital now. They'd even sadly had their first two deaths. But the situation was moving fast, and she suspected it wouldn't be long before things got much worse.

"I heard the surgical wards are closing," Kate said. She was still standing in front of Eleanor, the same worried expression firm on her face.

Eleanor had seen the look a thousand times before. When someone was confronted with the reality that a situation was about to get very bad, they often pleaded for more information, sometimes looking for a grain of hope in an otherwise dark situation, often to fully understand what it all meant and put their mind at ease.

The big problem at the moment was that no one knew what was coming. COVID was a big shadow coming to smother the UK, but no one knew in what way or for how long.

All Eleanor could do was tell Kate what she knew and hope she heeded her warnings.

"Yes. Elective surgery is being cancelled from tomorrow. The surgical bays will be backup intensive care beds."

Kate blew out a breath and shook her head. "It's all getting a bit scary."

Eleanor was about to agree when she heard a line of news that caught her attention. She stood up and moved closer to the television.

"As we have been reporting for the last hour, the health secretary is advising that every UK resident over the age of seventy will be told within the coming weeks to self-isolate for a—and I quote—very long time, to shield themselves from COVID-19." The presenter's professional poise only just managed to cover their surprise at making such a statement.

"What does that mean?" Kate asked. "Self-isolate? See no one? Be locked up indoors?"

"That's exactly what it means." Eleanor now realised why Sandra recommended she watch the news. Madeline would have seen the breaking news alert and was now presumably panicking. "I'm sorry, I have to go."

Eleanor grabbed her coat and her bag from her locker. "Wear the mask, Kate. No matter how uncomfortable you think it is. Keep it on. Wear it as tight as you can."

She paused to make eye contact with Kate to ensure her words sank in. Kate nodded. Eleanor didn't know if she'd really gotten through, but she'd done all she could for now.

She hurried through the corridor and paused briefly at the reception desk.

"Sandra, can you tell—"

"Already did." Sandra didn't look up from her work.

Eleanor didn't need to say anything else. As always, Sandra was on top of everything.

❖

Eleanor knocked on the door to the ground floor apartment. It had been a couple of hours since the news had broken, and she knew Madeline would now be deep in panic mode.

As with so many older people, Madeline's world had become smaller, and so the things within it seemed bigger. Just a few weeks ago, Madeline had become obsessed with the fact the bins were now emptied in the afternoon rather than in the morning. She'd questioned Eleanor on whether she'd noticed, what she thought about it, and started to play a long guessing game of what it could mean and what might come next.

Eleanor really couldn't have cared less. The bins were emptied on the day they were supposed to be emptied. As far as she was concerned that was fine.

But waste bins being emptied and a government directive to self-isolate were quite different, and Eleanor could only imagine what panic was now swirling inside Madeline's apartment.

The door opened a crack. An eye appeared and below it some cloth.

"Do you have it?" Madeline asked her.

"I...don't know," Eleanor said honestly. She took a couple of precautionary steps back. "Probably not."

Madeline opened the door a little more. The cloth around her face was a tea towel from the Beatles Museum.

"They want me to stay in. I heard it on the news. For a long time! What does that even mean?"

"It means they are trying to keep you safe," Eleanor said. "We don't know a lot about this virus. So shielding those most vulnerable is sensible. I can help you with your shopping and—"

"No, no. I can't have you coming near me. You might have it," Madeline said. "I'm sorry, Eleanor. I can't look after Sophia any more. It breaks my heart, but I can't take that kind of risk."

Eleanor held up a calming hand. "Hold on, we can figure something out. I can ensure I decontaminate before I pick her up. We can set up some practices that will mean—"

"No." Madeline shook her head. "No. I'm sorry. You may bring it home with you. You may give it to little Sophia. They say it doesn't affect the wee ones much, but she could give it to me."

Eleanor looked into Madeline's eyes and saw fear. She knew there would be no convincing her. And she couldn't really blame her. Eleanor knew she couldn't guarantee Madeline's safety no matter how many protective practices they put in place. They simply didn't know enough about the virus.

"I understand," Eleanor said. "And I do deeply appreciate all you've done."

Madeline sagged in relief, clearly having braced herself for a long debate. "Thank you, dear. I know it's going to put you in a bind."

"I'll figure it out," Eleanor said.

"I'll go and get her. She's in the playpen." Madeline paused. "Her things?"

"I'll take her upstairs now, and you call me when you've put her things in the hallway, and I'll come down and get them."

Madeline nodded. "I am sorry. I'm sure you don't have it. But I want to be careful."

The door closed as Madeline went to get Sophia. Eleanor rubbed the palm of her hand to her forehead. She had no idea how she was going to find a reliable babysitter. She'd been let down so many times in the past, which was why the current situation was so perfect.

She'd have to redouble her efforts to find someone. And she'd have to do that this evening. There was a creche at the hospital for staff, but Eleanor would never leave Sophia there. She trusted the staff to care for her well-being, but she knew that with so many staff members dropping off their children came a greater risk of sickness being spread. To put Sophia in the hospital creche would be almost guaranteeing she caught COVID. Or worse.

The door opened again. Sophia stood in the doorway clutching the door frame. Madeline took a step back, and Eleanor swooped in and picked up her daughter.

She stepped back. "Madeline?"

"Yes?"

"Go and stay with your family," Eleanor said.

Madeline chuckled. "Oh, I don't want to leave my home."

"This won't be gone in a couple of weeks," Eleanor said. "This will be months, maybe even a year or two. Decide if you want to spend all that time here on your own, or if you want to go and stay with your family. If you don't go now, you might not be able to change your mind later."

The fear returned to Madeline's eyes. Eleanor didn't mind. She wanted Madeline to understand the seriousness of the situation.

"If you stay, I'll help you. I'm sure others in the building will too," Eleanor said. "But I think you'd rather be with your family. Call your daughter."

Madeline didn't need telling twice. She nodded and closed the door.

Eleanor sighed and walked over to the elevator and pushed the button. Sophia let out a sigh, copying her mother.

"Are you mocking me?" Eleanor asked, smiling.

The outer door opened, bringing a blast of fresh air into the lobby. Eleanor turned to see the young woman from her floor. As always, she wore her headphones and had her nose buried in her phone.

The elevator doors opened, and they all entered. Eleanor pressed the button. This time the bright red coat was too much for Sophia to resist, and she reached out towards the young woman.

Eleanor shifted Sophia to her other side. "I'm sorry."

The woman smiled. "It's fine." She looked at Sophia. "Hello, little one. I'm Gina. Don't you have a lovely bow in your hair today?"

"She's Sophia. And I'm Eleanor." Sophia struggled to reach out for Gina again, and Eleanor took another step back. "Enough, Sophia."

Gina had been waving at Sophia and abruptly stopped. She raised her eyebrow, and Eleanor realised she'd been a little too curt.

"I'm sorry," Eleanor said. "I'm just in a panic about childcare. My babysitter just quit."

"The woman on the ground floor?" Gina asked.

"Yes."

"Why did she quit?"

"She's worried about COVID. Worried I'll pass it on to her."

Gina frowned. "How would you manage to do that?"

"I'm a doctor at the hospital."

"Oh. Right. Isn't there some kind of kids' kennel?"

Eleanor laughed. "Kennel?"

Gina grinned wickedly. "Sorry, I mean kids' club."

"There is. But it's not somewhere I would want to put her at the best of times. And certainly not during a pandemic. We don't know what COVID is yet. I can't put her at that kind of risk."

Eleanor started to feel the panic rise within her. Maybe she'd been wrong to bring a child into the world at all. She simply didn't know how to keep her daughter safe. Was that not Motherhood 101?

"Can't your partner take her?"

"I'm single."

The elevator doors opened, and they both stepped out onto their floor.

"I could take her. I'm stuck at home. I used to babysit my brother all the time," Gina suggested.

Eleanor swallowed down her reflexive response. There was no way she was going to hand her daughter over to someone she hardly knew and had only just spoken to in an elevator. The thought was preposterous. She didn't know the first thing about this woman.

"No, thank you. I'll figure something out," Eleanor said.

Gina shrugged. "Okay. I'm at number twenty-six if you change your mind." She waved to Sophia, who chuckled in response. "Bye-bye, little one."

Eleanor watched her walk away, whistling a tune to herself. She seemed young, even for someone who must be in her late twenties. There was a casualness to her that set Eleanor's pulse racing. Eleanor lived on edge—she'd never known herself to be relaxed. She didn't even have a clue how to relax. Meditation was beyond her grasp. She'd love to be as carefree as Gina appeared.

"We'll find someone," she whispered to Sophia before pressing a kiss to her cheek.

CHAPTER FIVE

Gina tossed a peanut in the air and caught it in her mouth. She was lying on the sofa, bored out of her mind. She threw another peanut up, half-heartedly wondering if it was entirely sensible to be throwing nuts down her throat when the hospitals were getting busier and busier.

"You'll be fine." Her mum's voice sounded through the loudspeaker of her mobile phone.

Gina looked despondently at the device. "They've cancelled everything, Mum. Glastonbury, the Radio One Big Weekend. All of it. There's not a single music event or festival happening this summer."

"I know, love."

Gina knew she only had a third of her mum's attention at best. She'd resorted to telling Gina she understood and that everything would be fine, exactly the same as when Gina was a kid and would show her mum something she'd made in school when her mum was busy making dinner.

She didn't mind. She'd only called to complain about everything closing. There wasn't anything anyone could do about it. Gina was so fed up with being stuck in the four walls of her apartment with nothing to do, no one to see, nowhere to go, and no plans to look forward to.

"All the cinemas. Closed. All the theatres. Closed." Gina tossed another peanut in the air. She caught it in her mouth and sat up. "What are we supposed to do?"

"Stay home."

"It's a bad flu. We've never closed the country because of a bad flu." She walked over to the window. The street was deserted. Sitting at her desk over the past few days gave her the perfect vantage point to watch the numbers of people dwindle to a trickle. The buses still passed by now and then, but they were no longer packed with people. Now they were not even a quarter full.

"People are dying, love. It's a lot worse than you think. You have to stay safe. Stay home."

Gina rubbed at her forehead. She knew people were dying. Even while she tried to avoid the news, there was no avoiding COVID news. Every work meeting she was on, every call from her friends, every email cancelling an event mentioned the virus.

"I know. It's just…how long is this going to go on for? Where's the end?" She didn't want to sound callous, but people dying was hardly a new thing. Life was cruel—people were sick, and then they died. It didn't make sense that everything was being so uprooted now.

"No one knows. Maybe it won't end."

Gina spun and stared at the phone in horror. "You can't mean that."

"I don't know, Gi. We have to be prepared for everything."

"But surely things will go back to normal eventually." Gina sat on the edge of the sofa and looked at the phone.

"Why would they? Of course, everyone wants things to go back to normal, but that doesn't mean that they will. It's serious, Gina. Stay in. Get some extra toilet roll."

"What is it with people telling me to get more toilet roll? Are you all eating it? Making beds out of it?"

"If you get COVID, you'll be staying in for a couple of weeks, and you'll be glad to have some extra then."

Gina shook her head. People were losing their minds. She was about to reply when she heard a knock on the door. Which was a surprise because no one had knocked on her door for what felt like a very long time.

"Gotta go, Mum. I'll call you later." Gina hung up the call and hurried over to the door. She opened it and was very surprised to see the woman from the elevator a few days ago, holding little Sophia in her arms.

Eleanor, Gina reminded herself. Posh, attractive, single Eleanor who had piqued Gina's attention.

"Morning," Gina said in greeting.

"Hello." Eleanor shifted from one foot to another. She looked anxious and stressed. "I...need your help."

"Sure, what's up?"

Eleanor wet her lips. She attempted to glance into Gina's apartment in a not-so-subtle way.

"I...you said you might be able to babysit for me?"

Gina felt the smile spread across her face. The prospect of having someone else to spend time with, even a baby, was exciting. Finally, there would be some life in her quiet apartment. Another heartbeat. Sounds other than the ones she made. Someone to talk to, even if the replies would be limited.

"I tried three babysitters. One cancelled at the last minute. Another started to have concerns about my working for the NHS. They were worried I might bring COVID to the other children. The other just stopped replying to my messages. I...I'm out of options. The creche in the hospital has closed—they can't get enough staff." Eleanor paused and took a sharp breath. "Were you serious about watching Sophia for me?"

Gina watched as Eleanor again tried to investigate the apartment behind Gina. Sensing Eleanor's desperation and realising the chance to have a conversation with another person, she opened the door and gestured.

"Absolutely. Come on in."

Eleanor took a step inside and started to look around like the concerned mother she was.

"Open-plan living," Gina explained, feeling a little like she was selling the apartment. "All of the kitchen is childproof anyway. Cupboard doors have those little plastic things so kids can't open them, and neither can I. The oven has protective glass, always cool to the touch. And it's not like I cook much."

Gina closed the front door.

Eleanor held Sophia tight. Her mind hadn't been made up yet, Gina could tell. She was scanning the room, taking everything in. Gina eyed the pack of peanuts on the coffee table and hoped Eleanor didn't see them and pronounce the whole apartment condemned.

"I work from home." Gina pointed to her drafting desk. She stood in the middle of the room. "Which means I can put her playpen here and keep an eye on her."

Eleanor looked at the desk. "You're an artist?"

"Yeah. I draw for video games."

Eleanor looked blank. Definitely not the video game target market, Gina decided.

Gina snatched up the peanuts from the table. "I'd move this table into the bedroom. Sharp corners. Is she walking?"

"It's imminent. She can develop quite some speed holding on to furniture."

Gina looked at Sophia. "Oh, wow. We're going to have you running around in no time."

Sophia giggled and buried her face in her mother's neck.

Eleanor smiled hesitantly. "You babysit often?"

Gina nodded. "I looked after my brother a lot when he was younger. And now some of my friends have kids, so I help out. I love babysitting."

Eleanor looked at the desk. "She'll interrupt your work. I'm not sure this is a good idea."

Gina could feel the opportunity slipping through her fingers. Suddenly, having Sophia in the apartment was the one thing she wanted. She couldn't socialise with anyone else, and the idea of having an actual person close by was exciting.

"I work flexitime," Gina explained. "I always have done. I work at night a lot. Or weekends. I'm an artist. I don't spend a lot of time on calls or doing paperwork. I draw. Having her here would actually be helpful. I'm struggling to feel creative with it being so quiet. I'm used to a noisy office."

Eleanor chuckled. "Well, she can provide noise when she chooses. Wouldn't your manager mind?"

"No. He thinks the world is ending." Gina sighed. Si was spending more time in meetings telling people to get bottled water and toilet roll than he was project-managing the work. Every meeting, someone had to drag him back on topic.

Eleanor walked around the room. Her grip on Sophia had loosened a little as her concerns started to slip away. Gina could tell that she was still unsure. But she also suspected that Eleanor had few options. Eleanor didn't seem like the sort of person who would approach a stranger to look after her baby. Gina must have been the last resort.

"How about a trial?" Gina suggested. "You leave her here for today, and you can FaceTime me whenever you like. No notice. And you can see for yourself how things are going."

"FaceTime?" Eleanor asked.

"Yes, do you have an iPhone?"

Eleanor nodded.

Gina grabbed her phone and showed her the screen. "Great. My phone is always on. You call me on this, any time. When I answer, you can see me—and Sophia."

Gina watched a little more tension leave Eleanor. Her grasp on Sophia was loosening slightly, her tense smile starting to look a little more natural.

"When would you be able to start this trial?" Eleanor asked.

Gina looked around the apartment. "I dunno. Now?"

"Now?" Eleanor looked relieved but uncertain. "Are you sure?"

"Yes. You'll be doing me a favour. I'm climbing the walls with boredom. It will be great to have someone here. A new friend." Gina reached out and softly tickled one of Sophia's feet.

Sophia pulled her foot away and giggled.

"And I wouldn't want to be paid," Gina added. "Consider it a gift to the NHS."

Eleanor shook her head. "No, I must pay you. But I appreciate the gesture. Would you like to hold her?"

Gina eagerly stepped forward and took Sophia out of Eleanor's arms. Sophia sat on Gina's hip, arms loosely wrapped around her neck.

"So, how many words can you say?" Gina asked. "Do you know *ooo*?"

Sophia spoke some gibberish. Gina could tell they were the starts of words, and she smiled. "She's nearly there, isn't she?"

Eleanor smiled. "She is. I thought we had *mummy* a couple of days ago, but it's slipped away again."

"What's her schedule?" Gina asked.

"She gets up at six, when I do. She has some milk. Then breakfast around eight, and after that I leave for work. She has lunch at eleven and then naps at midday through until three. She needs to be woken up, or she'll sleep for too long."

Gina nodded. "A little cuddle and some talking, right?"

"That's right. She's not grumpy when she wakes up, thank goodness."

"A snack after she wakes up?" Gina suggested, hoping to demonstrate her babysitting prowess.

"Yes," Eleanor said. "Dinner with me at six."

"So she'd come here after breakfast. We have some amazing fun times. Eleven she eats lunch. Three-hour nap. Wake her up. Snack. You'll get her after six. Easy."

Eleanor looked at Gina and Sophia thoughtfully. Gina could sense the hesitation building again.

"We'll do a trial for as long as you like. You can call me as many times as you like. Honestly, I don't mind. She's precious—I get that you're concerned."

Eleanor worried her lip before finally nodding. "Okay. Yes, that's very kind of you. I'd like to take you up on that offer."

"Great." Gina beamed. "Do you need some help getting her things? I bet this lady doesn't travel light."

Eleanor laughed. "She certainly doesn't. Thank you, but no. I'll go and get her things. I'll be back in a few moments. I really cannot thank you enough for agreeing to do this."

"I should be thanking you." Gina cuddled Sophia. "I've been so bored. It will be great to have some company."

Eleanor headed out to pick up Sophia's things. Gina walked around the apartment making a mental list of things she needed to babyproof and things she needed to check Eleanor brought back with her. Not that Eleanor seemed like the sort of person who would forget anything.

Not like her friend Dani, who frequently forgot to bring her son's cutlery, or water bottle, or change of clothes. Dani was one of those people who never thought more than two steps ahead. Whenever she dropped Lewis off, she forgot something—it got to be a running joke between the two of them. The positive side effect of that was that Gina had a whole cupboard full of emergency supplies she'd had to pop out and get whenever Dani forgot something.

"So, Sophia, what kind of toys do you like?" Gina asked. "I bet you have some colourful cuddly toys. And I bet there are some stacking blocks. I do love a good stacking block."

Sophia gurgled away as if she was having a conversation with Gina.

"You are the cutest." Gina gave her a little squeeze. "Let me show you around."

Gina walked around the apartment, pointing things out and chatting to Sophia as if she could understand every word she said. One of her favourite things about babies was that they were interested in whatever nonsense you came up with. Not like adults.

Eleanor returned with a pull along wagon overflowing with things, and two rucksacks, one over each shoulder.

"You can put it all there." Gina pointed just inside the doorway. "I can sort it out later."

"Do you want me to go through everything?" Eleanor asked.

"No, it will be fine. We'll figure it out, won't we?" Gina tickled Sophia and was rewarded with a giggle.

"She's being angelic at the moment, but just wait until she's unhappy," Eleanor warned.

"That's humans for you. Fine one minute, screaming the next."

Eleanor unzipped a bag and pulled out a pocket notebook. She opened it up and stood beside Gina.

"This is her routine—times and information on her naps." Eleanor flipped to the next page. "This is about meals. Everything you need is in the bag. She's generally very good with eating. I haven't discovered any allergies yet, but I've listed everything she's eaten, so if it's not on the list, then it's an unknown."

Gina could feel the motherly concern coming from Eleanor in waves. It was obvious that she didn't necessarily trust Gina to read through all the information and so was going to read it to her.

Gina happily allowed it, even leaned in to read portions of the text herself and attempted to make all the right noises. Eleanor was stressed out, and Gina didn't know if that was her usual persona or not. But she did know that Eleanor needed someone reliable to take Sophia, and Gina knew she could be that person.

After a few minutes, Eleanor finished with the contents of the book. Information about bottles, feeding, naps, and toys had all been recited. Even little details such as favourite socks and a fondness for holding hands were included. Not necessary for a babysitter but indicative of Eleanor's love for Sophia and her level of worry at leaving her with strangers.

"Let's exchange phone numbers, and I'll show you how to FaceTime," Gina suggested.

She sat Sophia down on the sofa and took a seat beside her. Sophia was about to try to slip off the sofa to make her escape when Gina handed her a plastic drinks coaster in the shape of a cat's face. Sophia took the coaster and looked at it with fascination, instantly distracted enough to remain seated.

Eleanor got her phone out of her bag. "Oh my, is that the time?"

Gina didn't say anything about the time Eleanor had spent fussing over little details. She got a sense of how difficult this was for her.

Eleanor read her phone number off the screen. Gina bit the inside of her cheek to stop from smiling at Eleanor not knowing her own phone number. Gina's number was as important to her as her birthdate and would be a series of digits forever imprinted onto her brain.

She saved Eleanor's number and then called her on the FaceTime app. Eleanor jumped.

"My camera is on." Eleanor looked adorably confused.

"Yes, but no one can see you unless you answer the call."

Eleanor frowned and looked at her screen. After a moment she swiped a finger along the screen. Gina smiled into the camera and then held the phone in front of Sophia.

She glanced up to see Eleanor nodding.

"Ah. I see."

"So you can call me with FaceTime whenever you like. You'll have to save my number."

Eleanor held her phone out to Gina. "It will take half the time if you do it, I'm sure."

Gina grinned. She took the phone and quickly saved her details. She moved the FaceTime app to the quick menu at the bottom of the screen. She explained that she moved the app and then handed the phone back to Eleanor.

Eleanor nodded and took the phone, but her gaze was firmly on Sophia, who was enjoying bending the soft plastic coaster.

"She'll be fine," Gina promised.

Eleanor woke up from her staring and nodded. "I'm sure that she will. Thank you, I really appreciate this." Eleanor walked over to them and crouched down in front of Sophia. "You be good. I love you very much, and I'll see you soon." She kissed Sophia's forehead before standing up and taking a few steps back, seemingly to take some of the emotional charge out of the goodbye.

There was nothing Gina could do or say. She didn't know the stress Eleanor was going through, couldn't understand the worry of leaving your baby with a sitter. To say she understood would be a lie, and so Gina said nothing.

"I have to go," Eleanor said.

"Okay. I'll speak to you at some point and see you this evening," Gina said, trying to keep things casual.

After a last glance at Sophia, Eleanor nodded, thanked Gina once more, and left the apartment.

Gina watched as Sophia looked towards the front door. Sophia cocked her head to one side, processing how she felt about the disappearance of her mother. Her gaze fell to the coaster she gripped in her hands, and a smile spread across her face.

"You and me are going to be just fine," Gina said.

Chapter Six

Eleanor hurried to the bus stop. The bus had arrived at the moment she stepped out of the apartment building. Thankfully the driver had seen her and nodded to indicate he'd wait.

She stepped onto the bus and placed her card on the reader.

"Thank you," she said to the driver.

He didn't make eye contact, didn't even turn to look at her. Instead, he closed the doors, and the bus started moving again, a big difference to the usual jolly bus drivers who manned the busy route, who often had a big smile and a greeting to give. But this time, there had barely been a flutter of acknowledgement.

He's scared, Eleanor realised.

She took a seat, one of the single ones at the front of the bus to ensure that no one would sit next to or near her. She wasn't all that surprised that he was frightened, but the realisation would take some getting used to.

Of course, anyone forced to work in a role that involved face-to-face interaction with countless people every day felt the same kind of fear. Supermarket workers, bus drivers, delivery services—they were all in the same boat of not having the luxury of working from home.

She closed her eyes and leaned back against the chair. COVID had arrived, but it hadn't even begun to show the full power of its strength yet. More would come but no one knew how much or for how long.

Each day, more people arrived at the hospital with COVID. Over the last couple of days, she had been summoned twice to the accident and emergency department to assist as the staff there became overwhelmed with numbers and some became sick themselves and had to self-isolate.

On top of the stress from work came the worry about Sophia's new babysitter. Gina seemed to know what she was talking about and had given Eleanor no reason to doubt her abilities. But Eleanor couldn't help but worry.

She'd been let down by a few professional babysitter services recently, often at the last minute. Eleanor needed someone reliable, and she had no idea if Gina was that person. She also had no choice but to try in order to find out.

She heard a cough. She opened her eyes and looked down the bus. A man at the very back of the bus coughed again. The other passengers all immediately tensed. The atmosphere in the vehicle became suddenly charged, fear tangible in the air.

Eleanor pulled out her phone and started searching for bikes. It had been a long time since she'd cycled to work, and she didn't relish the idea of doing so in March as the weather was still so changeable. But she knew it was the right decision. If she was going to be of any help to her colleagues, she needed to try to stay healthy.

While she walked around work covered in sheets and sheets of protective plastic, that helped no one if she caught the virus simply by using public transport. Worse still, she could easily transfer those germs to colleagues and have no idea.

She paused her search, staring ahead into nothing.

There was still so little known about the virus. Testing was starting to filter through, but it was hard to get hold of a test. Even once you had the result you still didn't know if it was completely accurate. So much about the virus and everything related to it was unknown. She hated the not knowing.

She shook her head and returned to her search for a bike. Using the shopping filters, she found one that was a reasonable price with good reviews and could be delivered the next day. She added a helmet and some reflective bands to her basket before checking out.

Just as her order confirmation message came through, her phone rang and Nigel's name flashed up on her screen.

She answered the call. "I know, I know. I'm on my way."

"I'm just checking that you're okay," he said good-naturedly. "Find someone to take Sophia?"

Eleanor sighed and leaned her head back against the headrest.

"I did. I'm so sorry about this. I thought I would be able to juggle work and being a single mother, but it seems I'm making a mess of it."

Nigel chuckled. "Everyone thinks that they'll be able to juggle it, but no amount of preparation prepares you for it. And this is a very weird situation. It's not like you can plan for finding childcare in a pandemic."

"I was struggling before that. There is a lack of childcare in the city," Eleanor said.

She'd always wanted a child. From when she was as young as she could remember, having a child was a goal for her. When it became obvious that she wasn't going to find the perfect match in a relationship, she wondered about going it alone. Some research turned into an obsession. Deep down, a niggling concern grew. Wanting a child had slowly consumed her every waking moment over the years. At first, she thought having a baby was simply a nice idea. Later she would find herself holding baby socks in clothing stores and wondering how long she had zoned out of reality for.

The IVF had been a long, expensive, and emotional experience but Sophia had been the result, and Eleanor hadn't regretted a second.

Until now. Now a tiny seed of doubt was beginning to take root. Had bringing a child into this world been the ultimate act of selfishness? Had she made the right decision?

She realised Nigel had been talking, but she hadn't heard a word. She *hmm*ed to indicate she was still listening and hoped to catch up.

"So you'll see the new route when you get here, but just avoid the main entrance," he said. "It's for the best. Cross-contamination is our biggest worry now."

Eleanor looked around the bus. "Yes, it is."

"Between you and me," Nigel said, his voice dipping, "there's a rumour about a lack of PPE."

"We don't listen to rumours," Eleanor reminded him.

Rumours and the NHS went together like a hand in a glove. With such a sprawling network of people, trusts, hospitals, and administrators, it was impossible for there not to be a rumour mill powering every break room.

"This one we do," he said. "We've missed two deliveries. There are promises that nothing is wrong and it's all just a logistics problem. But I think the logistics problem is that every hospital in the country, and most of the world, now needs ten times more PPE every day than it used to. We must be running out."

"It sounds possible," Eleanor conceded.

The man at the back of the bus coughed loudly again. It was a chilly day, and all the windows were closed. She could almost see the invisible virus working its way from the back of the bus towards her.

"Nigel, I'm going to walk the rest of the way." Eleanor stood up and pressed the stop button with her elbow. "I'll be there in twenty minutes."

Chapter Seven

Gina placed Sophia on her knee and pointed to her laptop screen. Her work colleagues instantly reacted with delight. Being stuck at home, a surprise toddler was probably the most exciting thing to happen to them all day. It certainly was for Gina.

"Oh, wow, she's adorable." Caitlin sighed. "Now I want a baby."

"I read that we're going to have another baby boom," Mark said. "Everyone at home with nothing else to do."

"I have plenty to do, thank you very much," Gina replied. "And just who in their right mind is thinking about bringing a new life into this world now? I can't imagine doing that."

"We're all different. Some people will want the companionship," Jose pointed out.

"Let's get back on track, shall we?" Chris said. "Let's all welcome our newest team member. Hi, Sophia."

The design team all waved and said hello. Sophia giggled and fell into Gina. Gina pulled her into a cuddle and listened as Chris started the team briefing.

They were meeting less frequently now than they had been. The first couple of days of home working, the meetings were endless. Gina was never off video conferencing as people complained about how difficult it was to focus, talked about where to set up a temporary workspace, and debated if the world was ending.

Eventually, the others seemed to acclimatise to the idea of working from home. And that was when Gina realised that they all had family. She'd been sort of aware of that fact, but now it was very apparent.

While her colleagues spoke about schools closing, home-schooling, and who would have the dining table to use as a makeshift office, Gina looked around her empty apartment and wondered if she was lucky or not.

She didn't have to worry about her kids going to school. She didn't have to share her workspace with anyone. But only because she was alone.

She held Sophia a little tighter. Or she had been alone. It had only been a few hours and already Sophia had brought an explosion of life to Gina's quiet world. Toys were scattered everywhere, a playpen was set up next to the sofa, and blankets lined one of the armchairs. Sophia was everywhere. And Gina loved it.

Sophia happily sat on Gina's knee for the duration of the fifteen-minute check-in meeting and then waved goodbye to everyone at the end. Gina suspected this was a one-off. While everything was new and exciting, Sophia was probably going to do what she was told. But once the novelty wore off, Gina was prepared to have a battle of wills with the cutest baby she'd ever laid eyes on.

"What now?" Gina asked.

Sophia looked up at her. Her brows knit together as she tried to process what was happening around her. Gina loved this age. Children at this point were on the cusp of something great. They were soon to speak and walk. They were soon to show their personality in bigger ways than ever before.

"Shall we put you in your prison for a while?" Gina asked.

She was about to put Sophia in the playpen when her phone rang. She'd assigned Eleanor's number a loud tone to make sure she didn't miss a call. Sophia looked around in shock at the sudden noise.

"It's Mummy," Gina said, injecting as much excitement as she could into her voice.

She angled the phone so that both she and Sophia were in frame. Eleanor appeared on the screen and Sophia started to bounce with excitement at seeing her mother.

Gina adjusted her grip to make sure she had a good hold on the excitable child.

"Hey, how are you?" Gina said.

Eleanor looked exhausted and stressed. Her hair was hidden away behind a headscarf, and Gina could see the blue edge of the scrubs she was wearing. Behind her was a plain wall that must have been a hospital corridor.

"Good," Eleanor said in a way that indicated it was a pleasantry and certainly not the truth. "How are you two doing?"

"We're good. We played. Ate lunch. Napped. Woke up and had a snack. Now we're thinking either play for a while or head out to the park. I assume you're okay if I do that?"

Eleanor had delivered a buggy and outdoor clothing, but Gina thought it best to be certain.

"She loves the park," Eleanor said. "If it's not too much trouble to take her, I know she'll enjoy it."

"I like the park, too," Gina said.

It was partly true. The park was one of the few places open where she was guaranteed to see people. And so, with no other options, Gina was suddenly interested in the park.

Gina could hear typical hospital noises around Eleanor. Beeps, people talking, the trundling sound of gurneys. Eleanor's gaze flicked from the screen to whatever was happening in front of her.

"You doing okay?" Gina asked.

Eleanor returned her full attention to the call. "Yes. I'm sorry. It's very hectic here."

"I bet." Gina didn't really know what the hospital was currently like. Or ever like. She'd been there once to accompany a friend for a scan. Aside from that, she'd been lucky and had never needed hospital treatment in her life.

She had a vague idea of what it was like, mainly from watching television. But the idea of working there was alien to her. And the idea of working there right now was not something she wanted to put much thought into. She respected those who worked in the NHS. It wasn't something she thought she could ever do.

"She seems well," Eleanor said.

"She's having a great time." Gina looked at Sophia. "She'd give me five stars if she knew how."

Eleanor smiled. "Well, I'll let you get on. I'll be back before six, but I'll head to my apartment to get changed and should be with you by ten past."

"No problem. See you then. Say goodbye, Sophia."

Sophia's attention had turned to the ceiling light, but Eleanor said goodbye anyway. Gina pocketed the phone and looked at Sophia's wide but tired eyes. It had been a busy day of new experiences, and she imagined that Sophia was becoming tired. New input was exhausting for children, and eventually that would lead to tears and tantrums.

"How about a nice quiet walk around the park?" Gina suggested. "Who can be upset when you're feeding ducks?

❖

Eleanor hung up the call and put her phone back in her locker. Nigel walked into the break room.

"Everything okay?" he asked.

Eleanor nodded.

"And how are things really?"

She flopped into the tatty armchair that she hated so much. It was old and worn, and she'd never understood why anyone would want to sit in such a thing. Her standards were lower now. She felt bone-achingly tired, and the quality of the furnishings was the least of her concerns.

"This is the tip of the iceberg, and already I'm struggling," she acknowledged aloud for the first time.

Nigel perched himself on the edge of the coffee table and looked at her.

"You're not alone. But we're stronger together. I know that's not your thing, but Eleanor, we have to pull together for this. We will work side by side and we will grieve side by side. It's the only way that we're all going to come through this together."

Nigel knew her well. Eleanor was a strong proponent of teamwork, but she equally appreciated her alone time. When she had a hard day, she never showed it. Instead, she waited until she was alone to cry or scream. She'd built up a reputation as unflappable. It wasn't as if she cherished the title. But it was usual and expected of her to be the strong one. Nigel was the only person who saw her through it all.

"How's Sophia?" Nigel pivoted to a subject that always snapped Eleanor out of any dark mood.

"With a stranger." Eleanor barked a laugh. "I hardly know this woman. But she has my child."

"I left Camille on a train once. She met a nice old lady who took her to an equally nice stationmaster, and they waited for me to get the next train to meet her." Nigel put his hand on her knee. "As parents, we're expected to be superhuman at all times. But that's just not possible. You do your best. And sometimes you look back and wish that you'd done things differently, but that's just being a parent."

Eleanor put her hand over his. "I know. I just don't like losing control like this. I always thought that I'd find a reliable babysitter and we'd slip into a convenient pattern. But instead, I've spent days coming into work late and leaving work early because I can't seem to find someone to do the simplest thing. Now, my daughter is with someone I met in the lobby of my building."

"Well, you know where she lives. That's the main thing." Nigel squeezed her knee and removed his hand. "You wouldn't have left Sophia with someone you didn't trust. There must be something about this woman that made you feel she was a good person."

He got up and walked over to the vending machine.

"She seems very good with children. Knowledgeable. She says she's looked after children before. Her home is clean and looks safe." Eleanor stopped when she realised that she was convincing herself as much as explaining to Nigel. "I suppose I just didn't think being a mother would look like this. Odd, I suppose. I thought I'd done all my research."

Nigel fed some coins into the vending machine. "You can research all you like, but you can't account for everything. Life is wibbly-wobbly."

"It is. And very precarious. I thought I knew that, but I'm having my understanding of it tested."

Nigel pressed some buttons. The vending machine whirred and clunked. He leaned closer to the glass, watching to see if the mechanism was going to prove successful this time.

Eleanor stood and walked over to him. They both watched the mechanical arm behind the glass move up and down haphazardly. A claw reached out hopelessly to thin air and delivered precisely nothing to the drawer at the bottom of the machine.

"You win some, you lose some," Nigel said.

Eleanor looked at him. "To think I ever took any advice from you."

Chapter Eight

"Clap, clap, clap." Gina clapped her hands slowly in time with the words.

Sophia looked confused for a moment before clapping her hands together haphazardly.

"That's wonderful," Gina said enthusiastically. "Look at you go. Let's do it again. Clap, clap, clap."

This time Sophia clapped harder, giggling as she did.

"You're super clever," Gina told her.

Sophia clapped again but this time so heartily that she fell onto her side, cushioned by the blanket and soft mattress of her playpen. The fall distracted her from the clapping exercise and instead she crawled towards a cuddly toy.

There was a knock on the front door. Gina looked at her watch and was surprised how quickly the day had raced by. It was ten past six on the dot. Exactly when Eleanor said she'd be by to collect Sophia. And Eleanor seemed like the sort of person who would be precisely on time.

She answered the door and gestured for Eleanor to come in.

"Thank you," Eleanor said, her tone soft with relief.

She quickly approached the playpen and lifted Sophia into a hug. Gina closed the door and stayed back, allowing Eleanor some time to hold her daughter in peace.

She busied herself in the kitchen, wiping down an already clean worktop surface while looking at Eleanor and trying to work her out. There was a story in Eleanor, and Gina had yet to figure it out.

Gina knew many people from all different walks of life. Many of them lived outside the normal conventions. But that didn't stop her from being curious about Eleanor. After all, it wasn't every day that Gina came across a single mother in her forties.

Working in computer games meant being enveloped in storytelling at all times. When creating a character, it wasn't enough to show simply what they look liked. You needed to go deeper. Does the adventurer wear her hair up so she can fight without strands of hair whipping into her eyes? Does the hitman not take out the elderly man who saw him commit a crime because he reminds him of his elderly father? Those details needed to be brought forward and presented in the game without fear and without doubt. Players needed to see what Gina wanted them to see. Those details had to shine through.

Which meant that Gina was always looking for the story. Working people out and figuring out how much they were showing through their facial expressions and movements were second nature to her.

Now and then she came across a mystery. Like Eleanor. Gina had already compiled a list of potential storylines that could fit her. There was a possibility that she was a widow. But Gina didn't think so. She'd said she was single, not widowed. Nor did she say that Sophia's dad had passed away, something many people would do to prevent further questions.

"Is everything okay?" Eleanor asked.

Gina realised that she had been staring. She finished wiping the counter and put the cloth away.

"Yes, sorry, daydreaming about what I'm having for dinner," Gina lied. "What time do you want to drop her off tomorrow?"

Hesitation briefly crossed Eleanor's face. "Is eight o'clock okay?"

"Absolutely."

Eleanor looked around the apartment. Sophia's belongings had quickly taken over—bags, blankets, a stack of clothes, cuddly toys, books, and more.

"I'm sorry that we've taken over your home," Eleanor said.

"Babies don't travel light," Gina said. "It's fine. I really don't mind."

"Are you sure I'm not imposing on you?" Eleanor asked.

"Absolutely not. I really enjoyed having her here. Honestly, it's been really quiet, so it was nice to have some company. You can only have so many conversations with yourself."

Eleanor sighed. "I long for quiet," she said softly.

Gina was about to reply, but Eleanor quickly smiled and snapped out of wherever she'd been in her mind.

"I should leave you to your evening. Thank you, again. I can't tell you how much I appreciate this."

Gina walked towards the front door. "I appreciate you trusting me. And getting the chance to spend time with this little one."

Gina made a face that had Sophia in a fit of giggles. Eleanor smiled, a genuine one this time. Gina filed away the knowledge of what a real smile looked like on Eleanor. She opened the door.

"See you tomorrow morning," Gina said. "Night, Sophia."

Sophia waved her hand a little. And Gina started to think about how she'd introduce some more development training into their play over the next few days. Sophia was like a piece of clay ready to be moulded.

"See you in the morning," Eleanor said.

Gina closed the door. She stopped for a moment to think about the day. It had looked like it was going to be any other quiet workday until Eleanor had knocked on the door and turned her life upside down. Gina looked at Sophia's toys and accessories scattered throughout the apartment and couldn't help but smile.

❖

Gina had eaten dinner, watched a true crime documentary, and double-checked the deadbolt on her front door before settling down to call her mum that evening. Before COVID had arrived, they spoke around once a week. Since then, it had increased to three or four times per week.

Gina didn't mind. It wasn't as if she had anything else to do.

They lived ten miles apart, a distance that Gina had always considered relatively small. She could get to her parents' home in thirty minutes if her dad drove her, fifty minutes if she took public transport. The other day, she found herself looking at how long it would take her to walk. Just in case the buses ever stopped running. The app told her it would take three hours, but Gina imagined it would take her longer. She'd never been one for long walks.

They started the call the way they always did. They each asked how the other was, and each lied about being fine before going into detail to explain everything that was wrong.

It was her mum's turn to start. Her work colleagues were struggling to adapt to videoconferencing. Some people in particular seemed to not understand when to mute and unmute themselves, and this relatively small issue had become big news for her mum.

"It's on the screen," she complained. "It's red. You can see it. Red means people can't hear you. Although, I have to say, sometimes it's a blessing. Ralph talked for a few minutes yesterday, and none of us could hear a word he said. But we all nodded along anyway."

Gina chuckled. She was happy to let her mum talk. She didn't feel much like talking. For a brief moment, she'd considered telling her mum that she was babysitting but then she saw all too clearly just where that conversation would lead. In a short couple of steps, she'd be told that time was running out to get married and have kids of her own.

It was a conversation that came up often with most of her family. Cousins, aunts, distant relations multiply removed would all gather around to ask when she was settling down, as if she had psychic insight into that kind of thing.

It was obvious that they considered her immature and assumed that family life would snap her into adulthood. Everyone was keen for Gina to be in the same situation they were. As if to be married with a child was some success story to be achieved at any cost, and Gina was failing in some manner.

If Gina was to marry and have a child, it would be because she'd met the right person and they felt the time was right. Not because people told her that her biological clock was ticking. Or that she spent too much time enjoying her life. Which was apparently a bad thing.

"Have you been watching the news?"

Gina chuckled. "Yeah. Once. Then I turned it off again. It's so depressing."

"Life's depressing, Gina."

"Have you been freelancing writing greetings cards again, Mum?"

"I'm being serious. I'm thinking of cancelling Dad's birthday party."

Gina perked up at that. "Oh, really?" She tried to sound glum, but in truth her heart was soaring. Avoiding family and family friends would be a dream come true.

If there was ever going to be a place where she'd have to explain her job, life choices, and politics multiple times over and over, it would be a family birthday party, surrounded by family members who were settled in their lives, as her parents thought she should be. Hours would be spent with her mother covertly pointing to a cousin who had quit a career to have her third child as if that was a goal Gina should aim toward.

"Yes, this COVID thing is going to get bad. I think we will all be locked down soon. Like they did in Italy."

Gina stood up from the sofa and stretched her back out. She walked over to her desk and sat on the stool to look out of the window. It was dark, and no one was in the streets. It felt as though they had already been locked down.

"Just because Italy did it doesn't mean we will," Gina said.

"Oh, we will." The certainty in her mother's voice concerned Gina.

"They can't just lock us up," Gina said.

"For our own good, they can. To stop the health service from being overwhelmed, they can. Italy have been locked down for two weeks and there's no sign that they will be let out again any time soon. Things are getting worse and worse. People say we're not far behind."

"Well, don't believe everything that people say." Gina picked up a pencil and started doodling on some scrap paper.

"You can't ignore everything, either. Gina, I know you don't think this is as big as people say but—"

"I get what's happening, Mum," Gina said with a sigh. "I just think that maybe some people are overreacting. Maybe what happened in Italy isn't about to happen to us. I think people are getting drawn in to the news and panicking."

"People are only panicking because there is something to panic about."

"Can we talk about something else?" Gina asked. "Did Dad get that new lawnmower he was talking about?"

Her mum launched into a story about the lawnmower of all lawnmowers. The lawnmower that had been researched for a whole year. Gina tuned out. She'd heard it before. Every five years, her dad decided it was time to buy a new lawnmower, the perfect lawnmower, never realising that he did the same thing every half decade, like clockwork. He researched the topic to death for months before finally making a purchase and being deliriously happy for a few weeks. Then he found the little quirks of the machine that prevented it from truly being perfect.

The make and model changed, but the story didn't. Gina listened to her mum's tone, enjoying the fluctuations as she swung from fondness to exasperation.

It was comforting to hear the familiar story at a time when so much was changing. Gina had to wonder if her mum was right. Were things about to get so much worse? Everyone seemed to think so, but Gina couldn't imagine it.

The idea of being told to stay in her home felt like something that happened in faraway countries where the military had control, and not in their country, with its democratically elected government.

Then again, Gina knew that government had been elected to tend to the best interests of its citizens. To keep them safe from harm. Harm was coming—Gina knew that much. But she was having difficulty grasping the potential scale of that harm.

Luckily, she knew someone on the inside now, someone who was seeing things as they unfolded. She decided to ask Eleanor for her opinion the next morning. Eleanor seemed calm and level-headed. Surely she'd present a more likely scenario than her mum's doom and gloom.

CHAPTER NINE

Eleanor held the spoon and waited for Sophia's attention to return to the task at hand. Her daughter was usually well behaved at mealtimes, but lately, and especially when Eleanor was in a hurry, Sophia's gaze would start to wander.

It seemed that this would be one of those mornings.

"Darling…"

Sophia continued to look around the dining area.

Eleanor softly snapped her fingers to get Sophia's attention. Sophia looked at her as if seeing her for the first time.

"Welcome back," Eleanor said. "Let's finish up breakfast, or we'll be late."

As she spoon-fed Sophia, she realised she was already out of time. She placed her phone on the table and tapped out a short text message to Gina, one-handed, apologising that Sophia's breakfast was taking longer than it usually did.

Gina replied in a flash. As suspected, she was unconcerned by the change of plans and looked forward to seeing them when they arrived. Eleanor smiled. Gina seemed to be the sort of person who took life as it came. Eleanor wished she was a little more like that.

Another text arrived. Gina offered to feed Sophia breakfast. Eleanor pushed the phone to one side. She didn't like that idea, even if she knew in the back of her mind that it was probably a good solution.

"What's the point in me if you never see me?" she asked her daughter.

Sophia looked at her with wide and clueless eyes.

"I love you with all my heart, but what have I done, bringing you into a world like this?"

Sophia tried to speak, instead rejecting the most recent spoonful of food. Eleanor caught the food and sent it right back to where it had come from. She fed her daughter only three of her six meals per day, a fact that gnawed at her. While she'd always known that being a single mother would be tricky, and would involve childcare, she was now struggling with the reality of that.

Others saw more of Sophia than she did. The majority of the time Eleanor spent with her daughter was when they were both asleep. And things were about to get worse. She knew that many hours of overtime would be coming her way shortly.

The uptick in COVID cases was gradual but the pattern was undeniable. They would soon reach incredible daily figures. Eleanor knew she'd be stationed in A & E and the newly created COVID wards before long. Staff numbers were dropping, and they needed everyone they could get.

Dropping Sophia off with Gina earlier and not having to worry about breakfast would help her, and therefore her team. It was another bitter pill that Eleanor was just going to have to swallow.

So far motherhood seemed to encompass an enormous amount of guilt. She hoped that would change soon, but right now she couldn't see an end to it.

❖

Sophia didn't want to be carried. Usually, Eleanor would delight in holding her daughter's hand as she tottered along, so close to being able to walk. But right now, Eleanor was running fifteen minutes late, and the relatively small distance from her apartment to Gina's seemed like an odyssey.

When they finally arrived at Gina's door, Sophia slapped both her hands on it. Eleanor knocked a little louder to be sure that Gina would hear. Sophia shot her a look of irritation that she had gotten involved.

Gina opened the door and swept Sophia into a hug. "Munchkin!"

"She's not in the best mood today," Eleanor warned.

"Not surprising. Yesterday was a lot. I bet she's been busy processing everything she saw." Gina lifted Sophia high in the air. "And now you can fly."

Eleanor couldn't help but smile. Gina's enthusiasm really was heart-warming to see.

"Did you mean what you said in your text?"

"About breakfast? Sure." Gina lowered Sophia into the playpen and handed her a couple of colourful bricks to keep her entertained. "I have to eat, she has to eat, might as well eat together."

"It would help me out—I just don't want to impose more than I already am," Eleanor confessed.

"You're not imposing." Gina batted the statement away with a casual swipe of her hand. "Coffee? Or are you in a hurry?"

Eleanor looked at her watch. She knew she was running late, but the thought of going into work, considering just what that entailed these days, caused her to want to hang around a little longer. Gina's bright smile would win over the dismal scenes at work any day.

"I have a few minutes," Eleanor said.

Gina asked how she preferred her coffee and started pushing buttons on a fancy-looking machine.

"Is that new?" Eleanor asked.

"Yes, it came a few days ago, but I hadn't had time to set it up." Gina laughed. "Okay, I've had time. Just not the energy. The instruction manual is like a paperback."

"And here's me struggling by with a kettle," Eleanor kidded. She looked at the machine. "What does all of that do?"

"I have no idea," Gina confessed. "So far, I've got the basics down. Which is about half the buttons. I'm a half-the-buttons kind of person."

Eleanor suspected that meant that she was a quarter-of-the-buttons person but said nothing.

"Can I ask you a question?" Gina asked.

"Of course." Eleanor braced herself. She wasn't entirely keen on questions out of the blue, but it seemed that Gina was the chatty type.

"Do you think this virus is going to be serious? I mean, I know it's serious. But really serious?"

"Yes. It's going to be very serious. A lot of people are going to get sick, and a great number will die."

Gina handed a mug of coffee to Eleanor. Her eyes were wide and her face had paled. Eleanor realised that her famously terrible way of delivering bad news had shocked the young woman. She'd worked hard on a bedside manner over the years and had managed to soften the blows in that setting. But outside of a patient consultation, Eleanor was blunt and honest. Sometimes she realised what she said was hard for others to hear. In this case, it was important that Gina understood the gravity of the situation, and she felt no shame in spelling out how bad things were about to get.

"Isn't that all a guess, though?" Gina asked.

"Not really. We're seeing the start of it. It's impossible that it will all just go away. We have evidence from many other countries now of what to expect. With our population, what we have already observed, and what we can see happening, it's only a matter of time. Things will get a lot, lot worse."

Gina visibly swallowed. She picked up an espresso and thoughtfully sipped at it. After a few moments, Gina put down her cup.

"Well, I'll keep a positive mindset. Hopefully things won't get that bad. I know we have to prepare for it. But we can also hope for better, right?"

Eleanor sipped at her coffee. She wanted to explain to Gina just how unlikely that scenario was. Hope was a lovely sentiment but powerless in the face of a virus that was already causing havoc. But it wasn't Eleanor's place to lecture Gina. Gina was young, younger than she looked in many ways, and seemed naive. She had her head in the sand about what was coming, and Eleanor couldn't help but think how nice that must feel. If she could turn off the ever-present sense of doom in her mind, then she would.

The problem was that naivety went hand in hand with bad decisions. Eleanor looked over to where her daughter played.

"You don't have people coming over here at the moment, do you?" Eleanor asked.

Gina chuckled. "No. No one wants to. They're all afraid."

Eleanor rolled her eyes. Gina was isolating herself, but that was apparently not by choice.

"They are right to be." Eleanor finished her coffee and placed the cup down on the counter. "If you're going to look after Sophia, I must insist that you do not have anyone else come into contact with her. If that's going to be a problem, you should let me know."

"It's fine," Gina said. "As I said, no one wants to come over anyway."

It wasn't the answer Eleanor wanted. She wanted Gina to understand the risks of transmission associated with inviting people over. But then she didn't want to reprimand her babysitter of just one day.

It was a conversation for later, she decided. Hopefully, Gina would realise the dangers for herself. There was little Eleanor could do now.

She looked at her watch and grimaced. "I really have to go."

"Okay. Call whenever you like," Gina said. "Have a good day."

Eleanor blinked for a moment. It was certain that she would not have a good day. Her days were likely to get increasingly worse, too. She envied Gina the little bubble she lived in.

"Thank you," she finally said. "You, too."

Chapter Ten

Gina pulled off her headphones and placed her pencil back on the desk. She glanced over to where Sophia slept to check on her. It had been hours since Eleanor had left that morning, and still Gina couldn't shake the feeling that she had been reprimanded.

She didn't like the way Eleanor had spoken to her or rolled her eyes at her. It wasn't as if Gina was planning to throw a party. She'd never be that irresponsible during a health crisis. But if she wanted to have a close friend visit her in her own apartment, then surely that was her decision and not something for Eleanor to sneer at.

Her phone rang, and she grabbed it before the noise could wake Sophia.

"Hey, have you heard?" her friend Kerry asked.

"Heard what?"

"The news," Kerry said.

Gina scoffed. "You know I don't watch the news."

"You might want to start. All cafes, pubs, and restaurants are being asked to close from this evening."

Gina frowned. "What do you mean? Close early?"

"No. Close."

"I don't—"

"Shut down. Close up shop. Stop trading. Today is the last day that they will be open. If you want a posh coffee, then today is your last day."

Gina stood up. "What? Until when?"

"They don't say."

"But they can't do that. They'll…I mean…businesses need to be open to make money. How will they pay rent? Wages?"

"It's wild, Gi. The government is going to pay people's wages. They get to stay home and get paid. Rents are frozen or something. I don't know. They are literally hitting the pause button on the economy. Isn't this so weird? It's like something out of a movie."

Gina paced in front of the window. She'd seen people on social media talking about the lockdown in Italy, but she never thought it would honestly happen in Britain. She couldn't grasp that shops were being asked to close. The very thought of it was rejected by her brain.

She couldn't understand what it meant. Would she be able to buy food? What about clothes? Were the high streets going to be deserted? Would there be a rise in crime?

"And don't get me started about toilet roll. Everyone has lost their minds. I swear some people must be eating it," Kerry continued in her ear.

"What about supermarkets? Are they closing?" Gina asked.

"Nah. They are essential shops. We have essential shops and non-essential shops these days, Gi. Keep up. You might want to turn the news on, so this weird new world can be explained to you."

"So I can get food?"

"Well, the supermarkets are open, but whether or not you can get food is an interesting question. People are panic-buying. If you want pasta or anything in a can, then you're probably out of luck."

"People are losing their minds," Gina whispered.

"They are. Honestly, you see people on social media with shopping trollies piled high. I didn't panic-buy—I just got what I needed. Well, and a little bit more just because things were running low."

The phone beeped discreetly. Gina looked at the screen.

"Kerry, I have to go. My mum's on the other line."

"Okay, speak later."

Gina answered her mum's call. "Hey, Mum."

"It's happening. We're locking down. Did you go out and get supplies like I suggested?"

Gina hadn't. She'd assumed that people were exaggerating, and now she wondered if maybe she should have listened.

"I got some things," she lied.

"People are stocking up. Oh, you should have seen this woman at the supermarket last week. Trolley stacked to the ceiling. You'd think she was planning to stay home for a year with a family of twelve. Stripped the whole store of pasta. She'll be backed up for a month if that's all she's eating. Wouldn't have killed her to have grabbed a bag of frozen veg to give her intestines a chance."

Gina tuned out her mum's rantings. She walked into the kitchen and started opening the cupboards to check what she had in. In usual times, Gina rarely ate at home. The staff room at work kept her going most of the day, and often she was out in the evening, so her main grocery shop consisted of snacks and toiletries.

Thankfully, she always kept a few things in stock just in case. The real question would be if any of it was still in date.

As she started to look at the contents of the cupboard, she heard Sophia make a noise. She abandoned the cupboard and rushed to the playpen and hoped that Sophia was simply turning over and not about to wake up.

Sophia stood in her playpen looking at Gina with a mischievous smile. Gina held out her hand pointlessly. It wasn't as if Sophia had any control over the sounds she made.

She gurgled, then laughed, and then started to clap her hands as she had been doing before her nap.

"What's that?" her mum asked, abruptly ending her tale of the poor panic-buyers incoming bowel issues. "Is that a baby?"

Gina slumped. "Yes. I'm babysitting for someone."

"Oh! How old?" Her tone perked up. "Boy or girl?"

"She's thirteen months, Sophia."

"Sophia, that's a lovely name."

"She's really cute," Gina admitted.

"You're babysitting?"

Gina bit her lip. She'd had no intention of telling her mum about Eleanor and Sophia because she knew what would happen.

"Yeah. There's someone in the building who was having trouble with finding someone. I offered. Which is cool because it was pretty quiet here and now I have some company."

"That was kind of you. It will make you want your own, I bet," her mum said gleefully. "And they're so cute at that age. And they smell so good. One day you'll have your own little one running around. Maybe more than one."

"Maybe."

"Probably," her mum insisted. "Probably two or three. I think three is a good number. Get them all out quickly, and then you are done."

Gina didn't ask why she only had one sibling if her mum was convinced that three was the better number, or why there was a ten-year gap between them. Or mention that having three children under the age of six to look after sounded like a nightmare to her.

"One step at a time, right?" Gina said.

"Yes, of course. You'll find someone. You might want to get your skates on, though. You're not getting any younger. Have you tried online dating? Or that app?"

"I'm really not looking for anything serious at the moment, Mum," Gina explained as she had done so many times before.

"You have to grow up eventually, Gina."

Gina bit the inside of her cheek. First Eleanor talking down to her and now her mum on her case. On top of that, the world seemed to be closing down.

"I have to go. I have a work call," Gina lied. "I'll call you later."

She hung up the phone and tossed it onto the sofa.

A cuddly bunny rabbit hit her foot. She looked at Sophia, who was laughing heartily that her projectile had hit its target.

"Oh, you think that's funny, do you?" Gina laughed.

She scooped up the rabbit and handed it back to Sophia.

"Why is everyone on my case today?" She lifted Sophia up and held her. "Your mum thinks I'm having parties, my mum wants me to get married and start popping out kids. And from this evening I won't be able to go out and get a coffee or eat in a restaurant. What's happening?"

Sophia took hold of Gina's glasses, thought for a moment, and then let them go again.

Gina looked out of the window at the sunny spring day. She couldn't believe this was the last day of normality. Shops and cafes would actually close their doors tomorrow. And no one knew how long for.

"Maybe we should go out," Gina mused. "Maybe we should go and get a coffee. One last time. Who knows, the store may go under. I might not get the chance again."

Sophia put her hand on Gina's cheek.

"They probably need the money, to be honest," Gina continued.

In her heart, she knew that was an excuse. She was feeling cooped up and claustrophobic, more so now that she knew things were actually closing down in just a few hours. The need to go out and see people, to be a part of society one last time, was strong, and she itched to get out of the apartment. A little afternoon snack felt like a good idea, a couple of hours out before the next step in the pandemic that was drastically changing her life.

"Let's head out," Gina said. "One last hurrah. Well, we'll hope it's not. But as it might be, it would be silly to waste the opportunity. Live for the now and all that."

Sophia looked passively at her, not understanding a word Gina said. Truth be told, Gina didn't really understand it either. She just had to get out. The walls felt as if they were closing in. The pull to go out and see the world, possibly one last time, was more than she could stand.

❖

Just a few hours later, Gina was full of regrets. She paced the apartment with Sophia in her arms. She couldn't believe she had taken such a ludicrous risk. All for coffee and cake.

"Fool." Gina reprimanded herself. "What the hell is wrong with you? All you had to do was stay home, and you can't even do that."

Sophia coughed. Gina stopped and looked at her.

The cough had started half an hour after they got home. At first, Gina hadn't really noticed. But once she did, the repetitive cough haunted her. Sophia hadn't been coughing at all that morning, but now, since they'd been out, she was coughing every few minutes.

Gina held her hand to Sophia's forehead and then her cheek. She didn't feel fevered, but then it was very early on in whatever Sophia had. She knew what she thought it was. COVID. Everyone was talking about the COVID cough.

Gina held Sophia closer to her and continued to pace. She felt sick with worry. What would she do if she had taken Sophia somewhere and exposed her to COVID? She'd never forgive herself. That's if Eleanor didn't kill her.

Gina sat on the edge of the sofa, her knee bouncing with nervous energy. Eleanor had explicitly said to ensure no one else came into contact with Sophia. She'd been talking about anyone coming to Gina's apartment but obviously that extended beyond that. It certainly extended to superfluous trips to coffee shops.

Sophia coughed again. Gina wrapped her arms around her and held her tight to her chest.

They'd only been in the coffee shop for an hour. They'd warmed a bottle for Sophia, and Gina had ordered a cup of coffee and a slice of walnut cake. It hadn't even been that good. And now there was a very real possibility that Sophia had a deadly virus that everyone was doing their best to avoid. Everyone except Gina because she was an absolute fool.

She didn't understand what had come over her. The very thought of her privileged life being altered in any way had sent her into a spiral. She hated herself for putting Sophia at risk. Couldn't recognise herself and her selfish behaviour.

Sophia coughed again and this time started to cry.

Gina got to her feet and held Sophia close, and she softly bounced her.

"It's okay, don't worry," she whispered.

As much as she hated the idea, she knew she had to call Eleanor. She pulled her phone out of her pocket and made the call. She held the phone to her ear with one hand while the other held Sophia.

The crying was beginning to dissipate, which Gina was very grateful for. Eleanor's voicemail service kicked in, and Gina left a short message asking Eleanor to call her when she got a chance. She knew that it was likely to panic Eleanor. It wasn't a great start to day two of her new babysitting gig, but she knew she couldn't wait the two hours until Eleanor got home.

She put the phone on the kitchen worktop and clutched at Sophia. She tried to soothe the squirming child with softly spoken words and some songs.

While her tone was calm, her mind was whirring with chastisement. Forefront of it all was the acknowledgment that she was exactly as self-centred and childish as her family considered her to be.

She didn't know how much time had passed when she heard the phone ringing. She adjusted her grip on Sophia and grabbed the phone up from the counter. Eleanor was ringing back on FaceTime.

Gina answered the call and was taken aback by Eleanor's appearance. The tops of her cheeks and the bridge of her nose were marked dark red, almost bruised. Her hair was swept back, and Gina could see the top of a plastic apron that was tied around her neck. She looked exhausted and terrified all at once.

In a flash, Gina knew that now was not the time for hesitation. Eleanor was busy and she was frightened. All thoughts of softly introducing the fact that Sophia was coughing floated out of her mind.

"Sophia has a cough, I wanted you to know," Gina said.

She opened her mouth to explain about the coffee shop but found she couldn't find the words. Seeing Eleanor's daily reality for herself made her feel even worse about the risk she had taken. A few hours ago she could easily explain her decision. Half an hour ago she realised she had been stupid. Now, seeing Eleanor, she realised she had been more than just stupid. She deserved Eleanor's wrath. But she was too scared to admit to her failings.

"Does she have a fever? Any other symptoms?" Eleanor's tone was all business. Gina stiffened.

She turned the phone so that Sophia was on camera.

"No. Nothing I can see. I thought I'd let you know. Because of, you know."

She couldn't even bring herself to say the word. The guilt gnawed at her, but she couldn't find the strength to admit what she had done. Not when Eleanor was on the screen looking like she was in the middle of a war zone.

"Keep an eye on her. Keep her hydrated. If there are any sudden changes, call an ambulance," Eleanor instructed. "I'll bring a COVID test home with me. I'll leave now."

"It's fine. You don't need to do that. I just wanted to let you know. But I've got this. I'll keep a close eye on her. Don't worry." Gina hated that her moment of selfishness was now causing ripples in Eleanor's working day.

"I can't stay if I may be infected," Eleanor explained. "If there's a chance that I have given Sophia COVID, then I have to leave now in case I'm infectious."

Realisation dawned on Gina. Guilt ate at her for potentially bringing Eleanor home early for nothing. Although she couldn't be sure that Sophia had COVID, and if she did that she had caught it at the coffee shop. There was a slim possibility that Eleanor had brought it home at some point. Gina didn't know if it was even possible for Sophia to have contracted COVID at the coffee shop and be showing symptoms so soon.

"Okay. I'll see you soon," Gina said, deciding there was little she could say with absolute certainty.

Eleanor hung up and Gina let out a long breath. She'd have to let Eleanor know the truth, but she didn't know how she was going to manage to do that.

Sophia coughed again, and Gina placed a soft kiss on her cheek.

"Don't worry, I've got you."

A pudgy hand rested against Gina's clavicle. And Sophia let out a tired sigh as she leaned against her.

"Promise me that you don't have COVID, and I promise you that I'm going to grow up. I swear."

Gina softly rubbed at Sophia's back. She sat on the sofa and stared straight ahead, lost in thoughts as to why she had done something so risky. Everyone had told her to stay home and stay safe. But she'd ignored them all when she became frustrated with feeling locked up, and her mother and Eleanor treating her like she was immature.

She shook her head. She'd proved them right. She was immature.

"Time to grow up, Gi," she whispered to herself. "It's getting real now. You need to grow up."

Chapter Eleven

Eleanor threw her PPE apron into the clinical waste bin and made her way through the clean ward. It was still eerie to think that just a couple of weeks before, the ward had been filled with beds and patients. Now it was empty, a no-man's-land in between the COVID wards and the rest of the hospital. A strange space where no one was allowed to loiter or talk to one another.

Staff had run through PPE drills in the same way she imagined soldiers prepared for war, a training series explaining exactly which elements of PPE to remove in which order, where, and how. Hastily printed signs hung as reminders as to what someone could and could not do in each area.

Everyone took it seriously because they all knew that allowing the virus into the rest of the hospital would be disastrous. Some vulnerable patients had been moved to the very far end of the building, and a series of systems put in place to ensure that they never came into contact with anyone who had even walked through the main hospital corridors.

Her own cardiology ward had been cleared. Half of the team were reassigned to helping in the accident and emergency ward, while the other half maintained a new cardiology ward set up in another building of the sprawling hospital estate.

To avoid mixing, the staff rooms were still open despite the wards being empty. There was no point in everyone socially distancing and taking every safety precaution if they all then gathered around the same kettle to make a cup of tea during a break. That meant that Eleanor continued to use the cardiology department break room, a small amount of normality in an otherwise unrecognisable workplace.

But despite all that, there was a possibility that she had somehow taken the virus home to her daughter. There had always been a possibility that it might happen, no matter how tightly Eleanor fastened her mask, no matter how many layers of PPE she wore. No matter how much tape the staff nurses used to effectively seal her in a bubble of sheets of plastic, there was always a chance that she might catch and transmit COVID.

Thankfully, she felt fine. But that didn't mean she wouldn't be taking the matter extremely seriously. She had removed her FFP3 face mask but had quickly replaced it with a standard surgical mask. She'd also exchanged her gloves for a fresh pair.

She paused at the entrance to the cardiology ward. A corridor led down to the front reception desk where Sandra worked. She hadn't seen Eleanor, and Eleanor knew she couldn't simply walk into the ward if there was any chance that she was infected. She pulled out her phone and called Sandra.

Sandra looked up at her. Then looked at the phone ringing. She answered the call.

"Do you think you're infected?" Sandra asked, already understanding why Eleanor was telephoning her from just fifteen metres away while they were in each other's line of vision.

"I'm not sure. Sophia has a cough. It could be nothing. Is anyone in the staff room?"

"Nigel is in there. I'll have him bring your things to you."

"Can he also bring me three lateral flow tests and three PCRs?"

"I'll let him know."

Sandra hung up the phone. She got up from the desk and walked down the corridor and out of sight. Eleanor was grateful for the unflappable receptionist's professionalism. She didn't feel strong enough to cope with an emotional reaction right now. If someone showed her even a modicum of concern or pity, there was a chance that she'd lose her composure.

She waited in the corridor, looking around to check no one was coming, although it would be extremely unlikely considering the hospital was like a ghost town lately. Gone were the background sounds of constant conversation and beds and wheelchairs being rolled from one part of the building to another.

"Eleanor?" Nigel's voice caused her to turn.

She took a step back, but he was already holding a hand up to indicate he wouldn't come any closer.

"Were you exposed?"

"I don't think so. Sophia has a cough. I feel fine, but I need to check."

He held up her rucksack with her cycle helmet clipped to the handle. "I put the tests in here. Do you need anything else?"

"No. Thank you."

He placed the bag in the middle of the floor and then took a few steps back so she could retrieve it. Once he was clear, she walked over and picked up the bag.

"I don't know how I could have caught it," she said. "I've been so careful. More so than most. After I've decontaminated outside the wards, I go home and shower and change clothes again. I've been meticulous."

"We know so little about the virus," Nigel said. "It's certainly highly transmissible, but how that happens..."

Eleanor picked up the rucksack and checked the contents.

"Just remember that no children have been admitted yet," Nigel added. "It's the elderly who are taking the brunt of this. I'm sure that if Sophia does have it, she'll be fine."

Eleanor scoffed. "Well, I'm at risk there then."

"Forty-six isn't elderly," Nigel said.

"Isn't it?" Eleanor asked. "I'm not so sure. And I'm not sure why a forty-six-year-old thought it was such a good idea to have a child."

She turned and left before Nigel had a chance to reply. She couldn't stand around and have a conversation any longer. Nor could she believe how selfish she had been to bring a child into a world with no support system in place. She had been so assured of her abilities that she didn't think she needed anyone else. Now she was starting to understand just how wrong she had been.

❖

Decontaminating quickly was a difficult task. Eleanor stood beneath the hot stream of water and scrubbed the soap on every millimetre of her skin. She wanted to hurry so she could see Sophia all the quicker. But a fast shower could well be a pointless one.

There was every possibility that Sophia had a simple cough and Eleanor could give her something far worse in her eagerness to see her. She had to make sure that she obeyed every rule of the decontamination process that she had painstakingly created for herself.

It focused on categorising things as either clean or dirty and figuring out a way to make the dirty clean in an order that meant minimal cross-contamination. There was also an order to things, making sure that a process was followed to move things from dirty to clean in the most sensible way.

When she entered the apartment, the first thing she did was remove her clothes and load them into the washing machine. Then she wiped down the washing machine with a cleaning wipe. Then she showered, systematically cleaning herself and washing her hair with products that didn't have the nicest of scents but would kill almost any virus they came into contact with.

It couldn't be rushed. But she wished it could. The need to see Sophia and hold her in her arms was stronger than it had ever been before. She fluctuated between feeling guilty for having brought Sophia into the world and then guiltier still that she'd thought that.

She finished showering and dried off with a towel. In the bedroom, she grabbed some fresh clothes to throw on. Usually, she ran the hairdryer over her hair, but today she simply did the best she could with a towel to save time. A few minutes later, she had the COVID tests in her hand and was walking up the corridor to Gina's apartment.

Gina answered the door in record quick time. Sophia was in her arms and looked happy to see her mother, which Eleanor took as a good sign.

"There's been no change," Gina said. "She's still coughing but it's not getting any worse."

Eleanor closed the front door behind her. She looked closely at Sophia's face, checking for clarity of vision and any other danger signs.

"I have tests for us all," Eleanor explained. "I'll need your help to get a swab sample from Sophia. She's not going to like it."

"Whatever you need."

Eleanor put the test boxes down on the kitchen counter. She looked around for some disposable kitchen paper and some washing-up liquid. After quickly cleaning down and drying the area, she opened the lateral flow test boxes and laid out the items.

"What do we need to do?" Gina asked.

Eleanor pulled a cotton swab from its protective packaging. "We need to swab up her nose and her throat. She's really not going to appreciate this. Can you hold her still?"

Gina turned so Sophia faced her mother. Eleanor stepped closer with the swab. Sophia turned away, knowing that something unpleasant was about to happen.

"I'm sorry, but you're really going to have to hold her still," Eleanor explained.

Gina nodded. She sat on the edge of the sofa and placed Sophia on her lap, holding her still with her arms and holding her head in her hands. Eleanor knelt in front of them and cupped her hand under Sophia's chin.

Sophia looked curiously at her. Eleanor opened her mouth poked her tongue out. Sophia giggled and opened her mouth in reply. Once she did, Eleanor held her jaw open with her thumb and fingers and with efficient strokes swabbed the inside of Sophia's mouth.

Sophia squirmed and gagged.

"It's okay, darling," Eleanor whispered. "Just a moment."

Gina clutched Sophia a little firmer, and between them they

managed to hold her still for the first part to be over. Eleanor let Sophia go and leaned back to let out a sigh.

"That wasn't fun, was it?" Gina said to Sophia. "But it's all over now."

"Nearly," Eleanor said. "We have to swab her nose."

Gina looked from the swab to Sophia. "Her nose is tiny—is that going to fit?"

"Yes. We're remarkably flexible. As you'll find out when we do it on you shortly."

Gina grimaced at the thought but resumed her position to hold Sophia still.

Eleanor took a deep breath and leaned forward again. Sophia recoiled from her, and Eleanor felt her heart break. She wished she could explain, but right then and there all Sophia knew was that her mother had caused her pain.

Eleanor buried the guilt and got on with the task at hand. She held Sophia steady and inserted the swab into her nose. Sophia squirmed more this time, but Eleanor wanted to make sure that it wasn't in vain and swabbed correctly.

When she was finished, she returned to the kitchen to finish up the test. Sophia started crying and Gina comforted her. Eleanor gritted her teeth as wave upon wave of guilt flooded over her.

She finished up the test and bagged up the waste to prevent cross-contamination, then let out a small sigh. It was done. All she could do now was wait. Since she'd first learned of Sophia's cough via the video call, she'd been desperate to get to this point, to be with her daughter, simply waiting for chemicals to react and tell her whether she'd brought COVID home despite her meticulous processes.

She turned back to face Gina. She felt weak now that the adrenaline had passed and the task of the first test had been completed. Sophia was quickly transferred between them. With no more than a look, Gina knew that Eleanor needed to hold Sophia now, seemed to understand that Dr. Osborne was gone, and a frightened mother had replaced her. Eleanor held Sophia tight and whispered soothingly in her ear. Apologies and promises that everything would be okay flowed from her. Gina busied herself in another room, giving them some much needed privacy.

After a while, Sophia calmed down. Thankfully, she was still young enough to not be able to focus on being upset for too long. Eleanor placed a kiss on her cheek and put her in the playpen, where Sophia immediately started to play with some toys, drama forgotten.

If only it was that easy for me, Eleanor thought.

Gina returned. "Everything okay?"

"She's settling down." Eleanor looked at her watch. They still had a while before the results would be in. "We should test ourselves."

Gina grimaced. "Do we have to? I feel fine."

"So do I, but that doesn't mean we're not currently incubating."

Eleanor opened a swab and held it out to Gina. "You'll need to swab the back of your throat."

Gina looked like a deer in headlights. "Where? For how long?"

Eleanor snapped back into work mode. This test had to be done properly or there was no point at all in doing it. She approached Gina. "Open your mouth."

Gina promptly did as she was told.

Eleanor hid a smile. She'd always known her work tone brokered no discussion.

She swabbed Gina's throat and then, without warning, her nose. She suspected that Gina was the sort of person who would recoil at the idea of what was about to happen. So it seemed reasonable to simply do it instead.

After, when she was dropping the solution into the cassette, Gina leaned on the counter and looked at her thoughtfully.

"How long does it take to get it?" Gina asked.

"The results? Half an hour for these. We'll also run PCR tests, which will take a day or two."

"No, I mean if you were exposed to it?"

Eleanor opened another swab. "I've no idea. It's not something we're certain of yet." She put the swab into her mouth and took a sample. The first couple of times, she had needed a mirror to see what she was doing. Now, it had become second nature to her.

"We must have some idea. Is it an hour or a day?" Gina asked.

Eleanor shrugged.

"Like, could it happen in an hour?" Gina pressed.

Eleanor removed the swab from her mouth and paused. Gina seemed adamant to get an answer to this question. A little too adamant.

"Why?" Eleanor asked.

Gina stood up straight. "No reason." She attempted to appear casual, but Eleanor could see right through it.

Eleanor narrowed her eyes.

Gina looked from Sophia to Eleanor. "Um. I…look, I know I shouldn't have done it, I get that. But we kind of went to a local coffee shop this afternoon."

"What?" Eleanor demanded. "You…Why? Of all the stupid… we discussed this. This morning, in this very spot. You took my daughter to a coffee shop during a pandemic? Why? I mean…why?"

Gina bit her lip and ducked her head. "I know. I'm sorry. I just, I felt so claustrophobic, and then I heard that they are all closing. I wanted to go one last time. I know it sounds silly."

"Why would you take such a risk? Do you have any idea how dangerous that was? For you? For Sophia? For me!" Eleanor jabbed the swab up her nose to take the rest of the sample. As furious as she was, she wasn't about to waste a precious test.

"I know!" Gina raised her voice. "I get it. I didn't think, okay? There's no point in shouting at me now."

Eleanor completed the swab of her nose and then yanked out the swab. "Oh, I'm sorry. Let me know when it's appropriate to shout at you for potentially infecting my daughter with a virus that is sweeping across the country and about to cause hundreds of thousands of people to die. I'll keep to your schedule next time."

"If you took a minute to listen to me, then maybe you'd understand," Gina said.

"Listen to you? I don't need to listen to you." Eleanor angrily mixed the liquid and pressed it into the test cassette. She'd be stuck there for another half an hour now to wait for the results. She wished this argument had come earlier. At least then she could leave with Sophia.

"I don't go out any more," Gina said. "I'm stuck in here. In these four walls."

"Good!" Eleanor shouted. "That's what you should be doing. You should feel blessed that you have the option to do so. Do you have any idea how lucky you are? I work with people who would love nothing more than to stay home and protect themselves from this virus. But they can't. They have to work. So they can be there for people like you."

"Okay, timeout. I'm doing you a favour here. You don't get to talk to me like that. You don't know me or my life. You have got no idea what it's like for me." Gina folded her arms.

"I'm sure it's agony to know the coffee shops are closing. My deepest sympathies for your loss."

Gina opened her mouth to retaliate but stopped as Sophia started to cry. Eleanor hurried past her and picked Sophia up.

"Shh, it's okay, sweetheart. I'm sorry, were we being too loud?" Eleanor held Sophia close and soothingly rubbed her back.

Gina came over and took one of Sophia's hands in hers. "It's okay. We're fine. No more shouting." She looked at Eleanor. "No more shouting, right? We can talk about this like adults. Even if… even if I haven't exactly acted like one."

Eleanor felt her eyebrow rise at the acknowledgement. She was pleased that Gina could see that she had acted recklessly. At least that meant there was some potential for a reconciliation between them.

She felt a duty of care to try to get through to Gina how reckless she had been and why she should stay home. Gina was clearly completely unaware of the reality of the situation.

She slowly nodded her agreement. "Let's keep our tempers in check and talk about this."

❖

Gina sat on the edge of the coffee table and looked down at her feet. She was ashamed of herself. Deep down, she had known before, during, and after her trip to the coffee shop that it was the wrong thing to do.

And yet she did it anyway.

She'd convinced herself that it was no big deal. Or even the right thing to do in order to support some local business. But the truth was that she'd gone because she felt sad that something was being taken away from her.

She knew the reason wasn't good enough, but it was all she had. She couldn't explain her actions to Eleanor because she couldn't really explain them to herself.

"I shouldn't have gone," Gina said, looking up. "In fact, I have no idea why I did. I started to panic, and then I decided to go out and have one last visit to a coffee shop. And I know that was stupid, and I know I can't justify why I did it."

Eleanor sat back on the sofa as she held Sophia in a hug. She looked over her daughter's head at Gina. Confusion, anger, and exhaustion marked her features. The red marks and bruises on Eleanor's face that Gina had noticed on the call earlier were still slightly visible.

"I convinced myself that it was okay," Gina continued. "I think I'm still in shock that all of this is happening. That's no excuse, but I think that's what happened. And I want to assure you that it won't happen again. Whether you trust me to look after Sophia again or not. I'll stay in. I'll stay safe. Whatever the guidance is, I'll do it."

Eleanor let out a sigh and kissed the top of Sophia's head. Panic was obviously giving way to exhaustion. Gina couldn't blame her. She couldn't imagine the shock and stress of wondering if your child might be ill. Especially now.

Eleanor frowned. "Why are you looking at me like that?"

"The marks on your face, are they from wearing masks?"

A blush touched Eleanor's cheeks. "Ah. Yes, I must look awful. I think we're all beginning to bruise at this point."

"You don't look awful," Gina said. "Just like you've been through the wars."

"I have," Eleanor said simply. "I am. Every day."

Gina nodded. She felt small again. She was living in a different world to Eleanor, one where having her summer plans cancelled caused a massive inconvenience worthy of hours of complaining. Seeing Eleanor in front of her right now was starting to put that into perspective.

"How does it work? With the masks? They must be on really tight to bruise you like that." Gina was hoping to get Eleanor to open up. Hoping to get their relationship back on track. She didn't want to ruin what they were building. Having a friend in the building would be nice. Helping Eleanor with Sophia was fun. Now she needed to prove that she was worthy of continuing to do it. To prove that she wasn't as foolish as she must seem and that she had learnt her lesson.

"We wear semi-rigid masks over our mouth and nose. Then goggles and a face shield. And then multiple aprons and gloves. We've started using tape to keep the gloves and the sleeves of the apron sealed."

Gina tried to picture what all of that would look like, what it would feel like. She wanted to see it. Weirdly, she wanted to draw it. Long ago, she'd realised that she used art as a way of processing her thoughts on something. Staring at a sheet of paper or a graphic on a screen for hours at a time as it came to life was a great way to analyse feelings on a subject.

"Are there many patients with COVID?" Gina asked.

"Around one hundred and twenty. But we get an extra twenty every day."

"Every day?"

"Yes. Last week that figure was five. Five patients a day last week. That's shot up to twenty. Predictions say we'll have an extra fifty every day by next week."

Gina tried to picture what that must look like. Fifty extra people coming in every single day. It wasn't something she could comprehend. On top of a hundred people already in the hospital. Or, by that point, more like three hundred.

She wanted to ask if they had space for that many people. Staff to care for them. But she knew to question Eleanor now would just load more stress on top of her. Eleanor didn't have all the answers. She was doing the best that she could, taking each day as it came and hoping that things would be okay.

Gina was getting a small insight into the things that probably kept Eleanor up at night. She now realised why Eleanor had lectured her that morning. And why Eleanor would have every right to lecture her again right now.

But Eleanor didn't lecture her. She was too exhausted—Gina could see that easily.

"Do you have anyone to talk to?" Gina asked.

Eleanor chuckled. "No. And I don't need to. I'm fine."

"I don't see how anyone can be fine right now," Gina said. She stood up and walked into the kitchen. The three plastic tests sat on the worktop performing whatever science they were tasked with.

"Do we need to do anything with these?" Gina asked.

Eleanor's head snapped up as if she'd forgotten about them. Gina realised just how exhausted she must be.

"Just read the results. How many lines are on them?"

"One on each."

"Are you sure?" Eleanor made a move to get up.

Gina held up her hand. "It's okay, I'm capable of looking for lines." She bent over and scrutinised each test. "Definitely one line on each."

Eleanor nodded and leaned back.

"I take it that's good?" Gina asked.

"It is. It means it's negative. Two lines is a positive result."

"So we don't have it?"

"Well…" Eleanor chuckled. "It means at the time of the test we did not have active virus particles. We might be asymptomatic or presymptomatic. For now, we don't have it."

"It's really complicated, isn't it," Gina mused. "Can I get you a hot drink? Coffee? Or tea? I have almost every flavour of tea you can imagine."

Eleanor looked at her thoughtfully for a moment. Gina knew she was weighing up how angry she was with how much she needed

Gina's help. And Gina couldn't blame her. She would be doing exactly the same.

If Gina wanted any chance of redemption, and she did, she needed to earn it. She needed to prove that she was sorry and that she knew what she did was wrong.

"Do you have vanilla tea?" Eleanor finally asked.

"Do I have vanilla tea?" Gina scoffed. "I have three kinds. I have vanilla chai, spiced camomile and vanilla, and vanilla caramel."

"Vanilla caramel?" Eleanor looked intrigued.

"It's good," Gina promised.

"Okay," Eleanor said.

Gina made two cups of tea, watching as Sophia became bored with sitting still and started rocking on her mother's lap. Eleanor played a game with her, holding her hands and tilting her backwards a little before rescuing her from falling. The sound of Sophia's happy giggles filled the room, and Gina couldn't help but smile.

She placed the cups on the table, away from where Sophia might be able to reach.

"You're so good with her," Gina commented.

"Thank you." Eleanor blushed. "I wish I could spend more time with her."

Gina's curiosity kicked in. It was the perfect chance to ask about Eleanor's situation, but she didn't know if Eleanor wanted to talk. Gina couldn't contain herself and decided to tread carefully.

"Did you always want kids?"

"Oh yes, since I was very little," Eleanor explained. "My parents were nice people, but they were very distant. So I was naturally distant with them. But I had this feeling that I wanted to have a connection, a strong bond. I had it to a degree with my sister, but I always felt something was missing."

Eleanor lowered Sophia to the floor and encouraged her to stand and hold on to her hands. Sophia stood and wobbled a little.

"Then my sister had children, and I saw how much joy that brought to her. And to me, obviously. But it's different from having your own. I'd always thought I wanted children, but once I had my nieces and nephews in my life, the idea really cemented itself."

Eleanor chuckled. "Of course, there was the small issue that I was single and hadn't managed to find the right man to settle down with. Time was hardly on my side, as I'm sure you've noticed."

Gina took a sip of tea. It wasn't a statement she was going to comment on. If she said no, she'd be lying. If she said yes, Eleanor could be offended. Sometimes saying nothing was the right thing to say.

"Nigel, my boss—who is also my dearest friend—tried to help me find someone. So I suffered through a couple of years of some of the most awful blind dates and double dates ever conceived of. Then one night, Nigel and I were sitting with a couple of glasses of wine and dissecting the most recent dating disaster when he suggested I go it alone. If I wanted a child so desperately, why not do it myself?"

Sophia collapsed into a sitting position, giving up on the idea of taking any more hesitant steps for a while. Eleanor handed her a cuddly toy and kept a close eye on her.

"I was beyond the cut-off date for IVF treatment. Age-wise." Eleanor tucked a strand of hair behind her ear, ducking her head and blushing at the admission. "But Nigel knew someone in the industry, and we managed to convince them that I was a good candidate. I'm in good condition."

"You make yourself sound like a car," Gina said.

Eleanor smirked. "There are similarities. You must be a certain age. Must pass certain tests. It costs a lot of money."

Sophia started to crawl away. Eleanor lifted her and put her back where she'd started. Sophia crawled away again. Eleanor picked her up and put her in the playpen this time, attracting her attention with some toys. Sophia soon settled and started to play.

"And so it's just the two of us. But I have to wonder if I did the right thing."

Gina put her mug of tea down on the table. "Of course you did. Look at her, she's perfect."

"She may be. But I'm not. I brought her into the world, but look at the state of it." Eleanor turned away from the playpen and faced Gina. Gina watched Eleanor rapidly blinking, trying to hold back tears. "Why did I think it was a good idea to bring a baby into the world now? On my own? What happens if something happens to me? What happens to her then? I didn't consider any of that. I just wanted what I wanted, and I did it. I was selfish. So selfish."

As the tears finally fell, Gina jumped up. She pulled Eleanor into a big hug. She suspected Eleanor wasn't the hugging type but didn't let that stop her. Sometimes people needed to be held and the way Eleanor leaned into the embrace made Gina know that she'd read the situation correctly.

"You're not selfish," she said.

"I am. She didn't ask to be born." Eleanor leaned her head on Gina's shoulder.

Gina laughed. "Well, technically, no one asks to be born. We're all pretty much left out of that decision."

"What if I die?" Eleanor asked.

"Then I'll ring your sister. And I'll probably ask if I can have that tweed coat you wore over the winter because it looks amazing."

"You noticed my coat?" Eleanor took a step back and wiped at her eyes with the tips of her fingers.

Gina grabbed the box of tissues and held it towards Eleanor. "Yeah. I see people. I just don't talk to them."

"Everyone thinks you're very unsociable." She took a tissue and dried her eyes.

Gina barked out a laugh. "I'm probably the most sociable person you know, and that goes for the whole building. Just not here."

"Why not here?" Eleanor asked.

Gina shrugged. "I like my me time. I go out when I want to socialise. Well, I did."

"Sorry for that outburst. I'm not usually this emotional."

Gina couldn't help but grin. Eleanor's *emotional* was nothing compared to some of her friends who would literally fall to the floor and cry if things didn't go their way. Gina wondered if she was more like them than she was Eleanor. Perhaps she had been a few years ago, but she had changed. Maybe she was slightly more mature than she gave herself credit for.

"Nothing to apologise for." Gina lifted Eleanor's cup of tea and held it out to her. "Have you been keeping that locked up?"

Eleanor took the mug. "Yes. It's not exactly a nice thought to have rolling around my head. I thought I had everything figured out. But somehow I've managed to bring a child into this world without thinking of the very real consequences. I'm alone. I'm in a dangerous job. And I brought her into the unknown."

Gina picked up her own mug and took a sip. "Yeah, I'm sure you considered a global pandemic when you made your pros and cons list about having a child."

Eleanor rolled her eyes. "Well, no, of course, I couldn't consider every angle. Obviously. But here we are. This is the reality of the world. I should have…I don't know. I should have…"

"Eleanor," Gina said seriously, "this is a really weird situation. No one predicted this. Okay, maybe that Microsoft guy, but other than him I don't think anyone was thinking this would ever happen. This has thrown off loads of people. You can't beat yourself up about this. Sophia is loved—that's the most important thing."

Eleanor looked down at Sophia in the playpen. The way Eleanor's expression turned from distress to fondness fascinated Gina. There was no question that Sophia was Eleanor's world.

"You regret having her, but then you feel guilty for thinking that," Gina surmised.

Eleanor looked horrified. "Don't say that."

"Because it's true?"

"I don't regret having her," Eleanor said.

"But you do regret bringing her into the world now, while things are so…whatever it is we're living through." Gina sipped her tea. "It's okay, you know. You can say it. You're allowed."

"It's a terrible thought to have."

"What? To wish your child didn't have to grow up in a pandemic? I think that's a really nice thought to have. I think, if we had the ability to see into the future, parents would plan to have their children at the perfect times. No pandemic, war, extraordinary natural events." Gina sat in the armchair and crossed her legs. "You're not wishing she was never born—you're wishing that she didn't have to live through this. There's a difference, and you're allowed to have those feelings."

Gina watched as Eleanor focused her gaze on Sophia and seemed to consider what Gina had said.

"I feel selfish," Eleanor finally said. "I really do. I wanted a child, and I went ahead and had one. And now I'm a forty-six-year-old single mother working a job that could possibly bring illness to my daughter or leave me incapacitated or dead."

"You're allowed to feel selfish," Gina said. "I don't think you're selfish. I think you brought Sophia into the world because you wanted to shower love on someone. People have children for worse reasons. And as you went through IVF, I'm guessing you spent a lot of time thinking about whether it was the right decision or not."

A trace of pain crossed Eleanor's face. Gina knew little about IVF, but she did know that it was often a long and arduous process. And Eleanor had gone through it alone, save for one friend. Gina didn't know Eleanor very well, but she imagined that Eleanor wasn't the sort of person to show her emotions easily.

"You can only do your best," Gina said. "And I think you're trying to do your best."

"I am," Eleanor agreed.

"There you go." Gina put her mug on the coffee table. "I'm sorry that I didn't do my best today. Really sorry."

Eleanor turned to face her. "Why did you do it? Especially after I asked you not to."

Gina bit her lip. Her first reaction was defence, but she knew she had to explain. Eleanor wasn't her. Nor was Eleanor experiencing the pandemic in the same way she was.

"I spend more time out there than I do in here," Gina said. She pointed to the window. "I'm either at work, at a friend's house, or out. I'm rarely home. Having to work entirely from home was a really big change for me. I've worked from home before, but it was always my choice. My office is closed, and that feels so weird to me. All of my co-workers are working from home. That's just...I can't process that."

Eleanor sat on the sofa and sipped at her tea. She looked at Gina thoughtfully. Gina knew it was make or break time. Whatever she said now would decide whether or not they would see one another ever again. Gina wanted to keep both Eleanor and Sophia in her life. Not just because it was painfully quiet without them, but because she was finding she really liked them.

"When I heard that everything is closing tonight, I felt panic. I know that sounds weird. But that's honestly how I felt. Restaurants are closing. That's bizarre to me. Ignore the fact that they should, just think about it."

Just thinking about it made Gina jump to her feet. She paced a little before standing in front of the window and calming upon seeing a couple of people out for a walk.

"I felt claustrophobic, I think. And like everything is out of control. And I wonder if anything will ever be the way it was before. And that scares me so much I can't even think about it for too long without struggling to breathe. I know you have to go and work in horrible conditions," Gina said. "I get that. I thank you for doing it, I really do. But I'm feeling trapped. I'm feeling like I'm not allowed out. Like society is closing down. Like everything I ever knew is somehow coming to an end, and there is nothing I can do about it. I know to some it's just a coffee shop closing, but it's bigger than that. It's the whole damn world changing. And will anything ever be the same again? Where will this end? Will it end?"

Gina felt a hand on her shoulder. She took a shuddering breath. She closed her eyes and breathed in slowly through her nose and out through her mouth.

"You're right," Eleanor said, her voice soft and calm. "I can't understand what this must be like for you. Much like you can't understand what it is like for me. But I think it's clear that we're both suffering in different ways through this nightmare situation."

Eleanor removed her hand and Gina missed the sensation immediately. The connection was nice. It was more than nice—it felt necessary. Gina couldn't remember the last time she touched someone other than Sophia. But holding a baby was different to a real physical connection with another adult.

She turned around and took another deep breath to clear her mind.

"Do you forgive me?" Gina asked.

Eleanor's expression remained unchanged. Gina tried not to read anything into the lack of an immediate reply.

"I do," Eleanor said finally. "I don't necessarily understand your thought process, but I do feel that it was a one-off and won't happen again. Am I right?"

"Absolutely. I'm over it. This has shaken me up so much that I don't know if I'll ever want to go out again."

Eleanor looked at her for a few silent seconds before speaking again. "It takes seconds for a virus to transmit to another. And we don't know enough about this particular virus to know how and when that happens. But letting your guard down for a moment could be dangerous," Eleanor said. "And you're not alone any more. You'll come into frequent contact with Sophia. And, by extension, me."

Gina nodded quickly. Another time, this might have felt like a lecture. But now Gina considered it an olive branch. She needed to prove she could listen and take in this important information, so Eleanor might be able to trust her again.

"I can't allow Sophia to be exposed to risks. I'm taking enough risks myself. And I have to make sure I'm not putting my colleagues at more risk than they already are." Eleanor's expression hardened. "But, as you know, I have little choice in the matter. I need your help."

Gina swallowed. "I know. But that doesn't mean you need another thing to stress about. I've received this message loud and clear. I'll make sure we don't go anywhere other than the park, and when we do that, I promise we'll stay away from people."

Eleanor gave the smallest nod of agreement. It seemed that Gina had dodged a bullet, one she didn't entirely think she deserved to dodge. She promised herself that she would do better.

"We need to prepare the PCR tests."

"More swabs?" Gina asked. She grimaced at the thought. The swab had been uncomfortable and invasive, even if administered by Eleanor's skilled hands.

"I'm afraid so," Eleanor said. "I'll take them with me into the lab tomorrow, and we'll have an answer within a day."

Gina had many questions. What would they do if a test came back positive? How many tests were the hospital running a day? What was the capacity in light of the hundreds of people who were about to arrive at A & E? But she knew Eleanor needed separation from work.

It was then that Gina really understood what Eleanor needed. She needed a safe space where she could be herself, relax, and not have to think about work. Somewhere to cry or laugh or whatever else she needed to do.

She'd had an insight into *Dr. Osborne*, and she knew she differed from *Eleanor*. Gina needed to help her become Eleanor after a hard day at the hospital. To give her permission to let go of all the stresses. It was a little thing, but she imagined it would have a huge impact.

Gina smiled. "Okay, me first. I'm ready." She opened her mouth wide, stuck her tongue out, and said, "Ahh."

Eleanor laughed at the unexpected move.

Chapter Twelve

"Y ou don't have COVID," Nigel said.

Eleanor looked up from her sandwich and frowned. "Excuse me?"

Nigel sat on the sofa opposite her. "I just got your test results back. Three negatives."

Eleanor chuckled. "Good grief. I'd forgotten all about them."

Nigel kicked off his shoes and massaged his feet through his socks. Usually, Eleanor would have said something about feet being so near her food, but life had become weird lately. Things that used to feel so important now had no significance at all.

"It's been a long two days," Nigel acknowledged. He looked up at her, then looked at his watch. "Late lunch?"

"Yes. It's been back-to-back new arrivals this morning."

"I know. I was out the front directing ambulances at one point. The overflow is full already." Nigel slipped his shoes back on and leaned back. He looked as exhausted as she felt. She wondered what on earth she must look like. She'd stopped bothering to look in mirrors. Everyone looked the same, absolutely drained and near the breaking point. But no one wanted to break, and so everyone simply ignored how they felt and carried on.

It was only the beginning. They all knew that.

Eleanor returned to eating her sandwich. Swabbing for the test felt like at least a week ago, not two days. Since that heart-wrenching and stressful evening, Gina had been the perfect babysitter. In fact, she was turning into a lifesaver.

Eleanor had started dropping Sophia off in the morning for breakfast with Gina. Eleanor tried to call a couple of times throughout the day but had so far only managed once.

Seeing Sophia's face was the energy boost she needed. Knowing that Sophia was waiting at home for her was enough to get her motivated to finish her shift and hurry home, no matter how bone-achingly tired she felt.

Like now. She was eating only because she knew if she didn't, she'd regret it. As a doctor, she knew the body needed sleep and fuel. Sleep wouldn't come for many hours yet, and so she needed the fuel. Even if it was the last thing she wanted to do.

"How's Sophia?" Nigel asked.

He was slumped on the sofa, head back, eyes closed.

"She's good. Nearly took a step the other day but ultimately was distracted by a piece of thread on her sleeve. Which I cut off and a fifteen-minute crying fit ensued."

"You monster," Nigel whispered.

"That's me. It's okay, though, she probably won't recognise me soon. She's spending more time with Gina than she is me." Eleanor bit into her sandwich.

"That's good. Gina can deal with the tantrums. That's why people have a nanny. Hand them off when they get irritating."

Eleanor chuckled. She didn't want to hand Sophia off, even when she was crying. She enjoyed all her time with Sophia, even when things weren't going smoothly.

She finished up her sandwich.

"Try to eat something," she told Nigel. "Something from the cafeteria. Don't rely on that vending machine."

"One day I'll win its riches," he insisted.

Eleanor sighed. He was an impossible man. She finished her sandwich and cleared her things away.

"I better get back to it," she said.

He grunted a farewell. She didn't mind. If he hadn't walked in when he did, there was a very real chance that she might have fallen asleep on her sandwich.

It was only a couple of hours later when she was cycling home, but it felt like so many more. Being rushed off your feet meant time started to travel in a different way.

Sometimes being busy meant looking at the clock and wondering where the hours had gone, happily signing off with a spring in her step. But sometimes she felt every single one of the minutes that had passed. She might have been busy, and time might have rushed by, but the things she'd seen, heard, and done during the time were etched into her body and soul.

It was times like those when Eleanor knew what exhaustion was.

The streets were nearly empty. It was surreal to be one of the very few people out. She'd never seen the roads so clear. One bus in the distance was the only sign of life. The route was usually packed with all kinds of vehicles vying for space, the pavements full of pedestrians.

But today it was Eleanor and the one lone bus. That was until another bus came out of nowhere and nearly hit her. She squeezed the brakes hard and closed her eyes as she braced for impact. Thankfully, she stopped in time. She felt the air brush along her face as the bus moved just in front of her. It had been close. Far too close.

It wasn't the bus driver's fault. It was all Eleanor. Too swept up in her own thoughts, too tired to safely cycle on a completely empty street. She stepped off her bike and wheeled it to the pavement. She lowered it to the ground before sitting on the kerb.

She took a few deep breaths to calm herself. If she was going to get through the next few weeks, she needed to find a way to process what was happening. Walking around in a zombielike state wasn't going to help her or anyone else.

She'd laughed the previous day when Gina asked if she had anyone to talk to. She was surrounded by people all day, but none of them were people she could talk to. Each of them was suffering the same way that she was. To start the conversation could start a chain reaction. People were holding on by a thread, and if Eleanor started to tug on it, she feared what might happen.

But stumbling from one point to another wasn't working. If she carried on, then COVID would be the least of her worries, and an unfortunate encounter with a bus or even tripping on the stairs would be what took her out.

When her heart rate returned to normal, she stood up. She lifted the bike and walked with it, not feeling confident enough to cycle. It would take her a little longer to get home, but it was worth it if she arrived in one piece.

❖

Eleanor was just out of the shower when she heard the insistent knocking on the front door. She wrapped the towel around her and looked through the peephole.

A panicked Gina stood on the other side of the door, Sophia in her arms. Eleanor opened the door without hesitation despite a puddle of water pooling at her feet.

"What's wrong?" she demanded.

Gina walked in and closed the door behind her, not answering the question, waiting to be invited in, or seemingly even seeing Eleanor.

"We have to stay home," Gina said. She paced the living room. "He said it, the prime minister, so it's like an order. The police will enforce it. You have to stay home. This is it. We're locked down."

Eleanor adjusted her towel to ensure it was staying put. Her worry faded as she realised this was simply a matter of Gina's worry rather than an actual emergency.

In fact, Eleanor thought it was about time. The health service had been calling for a while for a way to stop people from mingling and spreading the virus. Working from home was a start, but they needed to go further. They needed to do what other countries had done and prevent people from coming together at all. A tall order, but one that would ultimately save lives and hasten the end of the wave of the virus.

"It will be reviewed in April. So we're not allowed out for about a month. Just shopping and an hour of exercise. But we can't meet people when we exercise. It's weird. We're a bubble."

"A bubble?" Eleanor tried to cover a smile. Gina's panic wasn't amusing, but there was something endearing about seeing her come to terms with what Eleanor had known would be coming for a while.

"A support bubble. We're allowed to see each other. Because we support each other. But we can't bring other people into our bubble. And our bubble is limited in size. I'll need to read the details again."

"I see. Do you mind if I go and get dressed?"

Gina stopped her pacing and looked at Eleanor, shock clear on her face.

"Oh! I'm sorry! I didn't know! Sure, sure. I didn't mean to…I was just, lockdown. You know?"

"I'll be back in a moment. Make yourself at home."

Eleanor went to her bedroom and closed the door. She quickly dried herself off and put on a T-shirt and some loose-fitting trousers. Her focus had shifted away from work and over to figuring out how to comfort Gina and explain to her that this strange situation was actually for the best.

It had become obvious that Gina was the kind of person who lived life to the full. Just that morning she had spoken of a time where she had gone on a trip to Marrakesh on a whim because a friend had a spare ticket. Eleanor didn't know anyone who would suddenly offer her a ticket to Marrakesh, leaving in a few hours. But if she did know anyone, she categorically knew that her answer would be no. Thank you, but no. Even before Sophia came along.

Gina was different to Eleanor in almost every way imaginable. And Eleanor found that she enjoyed that a great deal. She believed in sharing space with different people to better yourself.

She dried her hair as best she could before returning to Gina and Sophia.

"You were saying?" Eleanor asked. She took Sophia out of Gina's arms and hugged her.

Sophia looked pleased to see her and leaned in for a big hug. Eleanor felt her emotional batteries recharging with the contact.

"We're a bubble," Gina said. "So we can't see anyone else. Just the three of us. And everyone is locked down. It's going to be so weird. They've closed the country down."

Eleanor kissed Sophia's cheek. "I see."

"Doesn't that bother you?" Gina asked, seemingly surprised at how Eleanor was taking this momentous news in stride.

She looked at Gina. "Gina, what do I do for a living?"

Gina looked at her as if she had lost her mind for asking. "You're a doctor."

"And do you think this news will change my daily life in the slightest?"

Gina thought for a second before saying, "Oh."

"You'll be more affected by this than I will, I'm sorry to say," Eleanor said. "Do you want to stay for dinner?"

Gina looked as if she was still trying to catch up with the fact that this earth-shattering news meant nothing at all to Eleanor.

"So, are you in a work bubble?" Gina asked.

"I really have no idea. I'll be carrying on as I always have. Dinner?"

Gina nodded. "Yes, please. Sorry. I must sound a little pathetic to you. But this has really shaken me up."

"I imagine it has." Eleanor walked into the kitchen, gently bouncing Sophia as she did. "It's a big change. And I'm sorry that it will obviously be a struggle for you to not see anyone or be able to go anywhere."

"Yeah. Stuck inside for a month." Gina followed her. She leaned back on the kitchen counter and folded her arms.

Eleanor bit her lip. "Um. I'm sorry to say that I think it will be much longer than that."

Gina looked at her with wide eyes. "What do you mean?"

"You have to think about the lifecycle of the virus." Eleanor handed Sophia over to Gina. She opened up some cupboards as she thought about what to cook. "Someone is infected on day one, they become ill on day three or four. It may take another seven days before they are hospitalised. They may be in hospital for a week, or even three. We don't know yet. Sadly, some will die, some will need further treatment. But what we do know is that some of the people who are infected today will need hospital treatment in a week or two."

"This is sounding more and more like a maths puzzle," Gina complained.

"Pasta?" Eleanor asked.

"Sounds great."

"It is a bit of a maths puzzle. While we're trying to save lives, we're also trying to stop the hospitals from being overrun. Life doesn't stop because we hit the pause button. Babies will still be born. People will still have heart attacks. Life goes on in many ways." Eleanor placed a saucepan of water on the hob. She turned towards Gina. "To you, it will seem as if all life has stopped. For me, it will look largely the same. A lot of this is about perspective. The world isn't ending, Gina."

"When do you think we'll be allowed out again?"

"June?" Eleanor guessed.

"June?" Gina screeched in panic. "It's March."

Sophia became upset with Gina's outburst. Gina looked immediately apologetic and hugged her close. "I'm sorry. Everything's okay. It's just that your mummy thinks I'm going to be locked up for around three months," Gina said sweetly.

Eleanor laughed. "Well, maybe I'm wrong."

Gina narrowed her eyes and glared playfully at Eleanor. "I bet you're not. I bet you're right. Annoyingly."

Eleanor smiled and shrugged.

Gina tickled Sophia's stomach. "I think you're going to have to grow up with a clever mummy."

Sophia giggled.

"Seriously, we're expected to stay at home for weeks and weeks on end?" Gina asked.

"Yes. And you're extremely privileged to be able to do that," Eleanor pointed out. "You may not like the rules, or the situation, but at least you'll be safe. If you were in charge and you saw a powerful virus about to sweep through the country, then I dare say you'd be making the same decisions."

Gina let out a small sigh. "Yeah. You're probably right. I just feel so...trapped."

"Are you claustrophobic?" Eleanor asked.

"A little." Gina looked uncomfortable and walked away, playing with Sophia as she did.

Realising she'd touched a nerve, Eleanor let her have some privacy. Eleanor could understand Gina's upset at being told to stay home. Much in the same way a child railed against being grounded, Gina hated the very thought of not being allowed to do something. Hated the idea that her world was fundamentally changing.

She could hear Gina playing with Sophia in the other room. Unlike Gina's apartment, Eleanor's was not open plan. She was old-fashioned in that way. She enjoyed having a separate dining area, living area, and kitchen. She knew it wasn't as light and airy as some of the apartments in the building, but she loved being able to close the doors and create cosy spaces.

She prepared dinner, enjoying the sound of Sophia's laughter floating from the other room. Usually when she cooked, Sophia was in the kitchen with her, and Eleanor had to race around to entertain her while not allowing anything to burn.

Half an hour later, Eleanor was plating up some pasta in sauce with garlic bread for the adults and a bowl of chicken casserole for Sophia. Not that it could be identified as a chicken casserole. It was gloopy and had come out of a pouch. Though it was full of nutrients and Sophia enjoyed eating it, Eleanor hated the look of it.

"Dinner!" she called out.

She carried Sophia's bowl into the dining room and was surprised to see Sophia and Gina already in there. The table had been set, and Sophia was in her highchair, bib firmly attached and spoon in her hand.

Gina's chair was angled towards Sophia, and she had a second spoon in her hand. Without a word, she took the bowl from Eleanor.

"Wow, Sophia. Look at this delicious looking glue."

Eleanor laughed and returned to the kitchen to get their plates. When she returned, Gina was feeding Sophia.

"I can do that. Don't let your food go cold," Eleanor said.

Gina shook her head. "It's fine. I'm happy to do it. We have a pattern now."

Eleanor sat down and started to eat her food. She watched as

Gina attracted Sophia's attention with a finger flying around in front of her face and then slowly drew Sophia's gaze to the next spoon of food. She was right—they did have a system, and it seemed to be very successful.

"So you think this stay-at-home thing is a good idea?" Gina asked.

"I do."

Gina nodded and carried on feeding Sophia. Eleanor felt as though she could hear the cogs turning in Gina's mind, as she came to terms with the new reality.

"Are things bad at work?" Gina asked.

"Manageable," Eleanor said. She sipped some water. "But yes, I've never seen anything like it. And it will get worse."

"Because of the lag between people becoming infected and people showing up at hospital," Gina said.

"Yes." Eleanor watched Gina carefully. She'd had similar conversations with patients and family members throughout her working life. There was something in some people's brains that just prevented them from taking in bad news. Sometimes it took a while for the information to sink in and be processed. She was seeing that exact situation happen with Gina. From disbelief to anger to understanding. A shortcut through the stages of grief.

It reminded Eleanor of how youthful Gina was and how different they were from one another. Gina piqued her curiosity in many ways because of those differences. She never knew what Gina would say or do next, but never in a bad way. Being unpredictable wasn't something Eleanor normally liked in a person, but Gina's unpredictability came in the shape of helpfulness and witty jokes.

"So, with us in this bubble," Eleanor began, "will there be a special someone you can't see?"

Gina chuckled. "Nope. I'm single. Perma-single. I can't seem to find the right woman."

Eleanor detected a trace of bravado as Gina delivered the sentence, an overconfidence that maybe Gina didn't quite feel. Not surprising as she had just come out to Eleanor and obviously had no idea what Eleanor's reaction would be.

She wondered if Gina was always on edge and wondering if someone would take the news of her sexuality badly. She suspected that was the case, judging by the brave delivery that didn't quite seem heartfelt. She hated that there were people in the world who made a big deal out of who someone chose to love. Eleanor wasn't one of those people and decided to do her best to make Gina feel safe and comfortable.

"Perma-single," Eleanor mused. "Yes, I think that label applies to me, too."

Gina grinned. "Never been able to find the right woman?"

Eleanor chuckled. "No, but then I've focused my search on men."

"You should try women," Gina said. "They're a lot easier to figure out." Gina paused. Her eyes widened as she looked at Eleanor. "I'm not coming on to you—I'm just making a comment."

Eleanor smiled. Gina's embarrassment was adorable. She almost wanted to tease her, but she didn't feel that their relationship was in the right place yet for that. And she didn't want to give Gina the wrong idea. She knew she was straight. Always had been, always would be.

"It's fine. You're probably right. Men are a mystery to me," Eleanor said.

Gina looked at Eleanor in confusion for a moment before looking away and continuing to feed Sophia.

"What?" Eleanor asked.

"Nothing. Just being nosy. I'm chronically nosy."

"What are you being nosy about?" Eleanor asked, her own curiosity flaring up.

Gina remained silent for a while longer, obviously weighing up whether or not she wanted to admit to her inquisitive thoughts.

"I'm not sure why you're still single," Gina said. "You have a good job, you're attractive, you seem normal enough. You can cook."

Eleanor burst out laughing. "I seem normal enough?"

Gina's mouth curled into a grin, indicating the comment had

been left deliberately for Eleanor to react to. Sophia rejected a spoon of food, and Gina gave up and started to eat her own dinner.

"Yeah. I've not seen anything too suspicious in here," Gina continued. "I'll obviously continue my investigations. But yeah, normal enough."

Eleanor laughed. "Well, maybe I'm just boring."

"That's a possibility," Gina said, a grin on her face. She took a bite of food. Eleanor reached for Sophia's bowl and attempted to get her to finish her meal. She imagined it was pointless but worth trying just in case.

"But seriously, I'm surprised you're single," Gina continued.

"You're not the only one," Eleanor confessed. She held out a spoon to Sophia, who just looked at it and turned her head away in boredom. "Maybe I'm too fussy."

"What does your ideal man look like?" Gina asked.

Eleanor smiled at the question. She tilted her head to the side and thought for a moment. "He's kind and thoughtful. Funny, but not a practical joker. Likes to talk but also knows how to listen." Eleanor chuckled. "I don't think I'm asking for much, am I?"

Gina grinned. "Is that literally all you're looking for in a man? What about looks?"

Eleanor shrugged. "I'm not fussy about looks."

"Okay. What about job? Does he have to be a brain surgeon or something?"

"Not at all. As long as he's happy in his career and it's not something all-consuming that he brings home with him."

"And you've found no one?" Gina sounded as confused as Eleanor felt.

"No. As I say, maybe I'm fussy. I just don't seem to click with anyone. I can't explain it. I just don't...feel anything for any of them. And some of them were perfectly nice. Just not someone I felt I wanted to spend the rest of my life with."

Eleanor gave up attempting to get Sophia to eat and focused on her own food.

"Maybe you *are* interested in women," Gina mused.

Eleanor chuckled. "I don't think so."

"You've never connected with a man? Could be a sign," Gina said in sing-song.

"I think I'd know if I was gay," Eleanor pointed out. "Especially after this many years."

"I knew a woman who came out in her forties. She'd been married to a man for twenty years." Gina picked up Sophia's spoon and attempted to get Sophia to finish her dinner.

"That must have been a tricky situation," Eleanor said. She couldn't imagine waking up one day after twenty years of marriage and realising she wasn't straight after all.

"It wasn't great," Gina confessed. "But she realised she'd gotten into a comfortable relationship, and she wasn't really in love. Well, she loved him, but it was more affection. Does that make sense?"

"It does. What happened?" Eleanor was surprised how intrigued she felt by the story of a woman she didn't even know.

"She had a chat with him. He said he'd suspected as much. They agreed to sleep in separate beds, and then after a while she started dating. She's getting married in the spri—" Gina paused. "Well, maybe she won't be now."

"To a woman?" Eleanor clarified.

"Yes. I was going to her hen weekend in Spain. I suppose that's off, too," Gina said.

Eleanor couldn't wrap her head around the fact that someone could wake up one morning and realise that their life needed to profoundly change. It seemed bizarre, not to mention frightening, that someone with an obviously settled life could change everything. Reinvent themselves in their forties. Start over completely.

Eleanor had always thought that life was a series of milestones and that you built on them as time went by. For some that meant marriage and children. For others it might be career progression or developing a craft. The idea of resetting everything and starting over sent a small shiver up her spine.

She was sure Gina's friend was happy and doing the right thing. But the fact that someone could be so unaware of themselves worried Eleanor. She wasn't one for internal reflection. Could she be in the wrong career? Heading down the wrong path in her life? She already had doubts about her biggest decision to date—Sophia—as much as she hated to admit it.

She pushed a piece of pasta around her plate. She was fairly sure that she wasn't gay. She'd never looked twice at another woman. Not in that way. Then again, she'd dated a number of very nice men and had felt nothing for any of them.

She'd read an article on asexuality, but that didn't seem to fit her situation either. There'd been a time when she almost hoped she was asexual. At least that would allow her to close the door on the question of why she was nearly fifty and still single. But Eleanor knew she was interested in sex, and she found some men sexually attractive.

"When did you know you were gay, if you're comfortable answering that? No pressure, of course."

Having encouraged Sophia to eat one spoonful of food, which she then spat out again, Gina also gave up and moved the bowl away.

"I was in my teens when I thought I might be. I was twenty-one when I first dated a woman, and then I knew I was a lesbian. Up until then, I'd thought I might be bisexual."

"How did you know?"

"I just did. I'd dated a few men and didn't feel anything like what I felt for this woman. Everything clicked into place. I realised what I wanted versus what society had taught me I wanted."

Societal pressure was something Eleanor understood well. She lived her life by it. Traditions, expectations, the natural ebb and flow of individuals in the community, it all influenced Eleanor's life in some way. She'd always been vaguely aware of it but never enough to really think about whether she'd have made the same decisions in the absence of those things.

Sophia let out a big sigh and started to rock backwards and forwards, indicating that she was done with the boring task of dinner. Gina stood and picked Sophia up.

Eleanor stood as well. "I'll take her—you finish your dinner."

Gina hesitated a moment, looking longingly at her half-eaten plate. Eventually, food won and she handed Sophia to Eleanor.

"Sorry for barging in earlier," Gina said.

"That's okay. I'm glad you came over." Eleanor removed Sophia's bib. "It looks like we're in this together."

"Yep. In our support bubble."

Eleanor laughed. She didn't really understand what a support bubble was, but she guessed it was some government language to explain to the public just who they could see and who they couldn't see.

She wasn't about to waste her time understanding the rules because many wouldn't apply to her. She wouldn't be staying home, nor would she be able to restrict how many other bubbles she came into contact with.

Gina's and Eleanor's experiences of the pandemic were about to take another turn, each of them suffering in precisely the opposite way to the other. But Eleanor felt grateful that she had Gina by her side for whatever might be coming next.

CHAPTER THIRTEEN

Gina lay on the floor, bum to the skirting board and her legs in the air. It was the only way she had found that helped soothe her back when she'd had a long day of carrying Sophia and then hunching over her desk in the evening.

But lying on the floor wasn't very entertaining, and so she'd called Kath. It had been three weeks since they'd seen each other in person, and Gina was pretty sure that was some kind of record.

Back in the normal days, which is what Gina had started to call anything before March 2020, they'd see each other at least once a week and often more. Dinners, drinks, cinema trips, music festivals. That had all ended, and now Gina only ever spoke to her best friend via the phone.

The weird thing was that Gina had learnt more about Kath over the past three weeks than she had over the past ten years. With no distractions, they talked and ended up going down a hundred different rabbit holes of conversation.

Before, when they socialised, they were doing things and dropping fragments of conversations between drinks and activities. Now they just talked, and conversation flowed in a way it had never had the chance to. Gina didn't like to admit that she quite liked the change.

"She's gay," Gina said. "I just know it."

"You have the worst gaydar I have ever seen in a person," Kath said. "Remember that woman in Hillingdon? I had to tell you that she was checking you out."

"It was dark! I couldn't see her properly."

"She was staring at you like you were the last turkey in the shop on Christmas Eve."

Gina laughed. "First, eww. Second, that's not what we're talking about here. I'm talking about Eleanor."

"Why do you think she's gay?"

Gina shifted a little, allowing her spine and neck to release a few small pops. "She's nearly fifty and she's single. She's a doctor, a really good-looking doctor. She's intelligent, funny, so kind and loving. You should see her with Sophia."

"That doesn't explain why you think she's gay," Kath pointed out.

"She says she can't find the right man. Like, there's something wrong with all of them. She's been on blind dates, set up with friends of friends, online dating and nothing. She says she never felt anything for them. Any of them. Weird, right?"

Gina pushed her shoulders down away from her ears. Since the lockdown started, she'd been reminding herself constantly to lower her shoulders and relax. Not an easy task.

"Maybe she's just not found the right man," Kath suggested.

Gina scoffed. "Oh, come on. She's been on, like, a million dates. She's not connected with any of them. Not at all."

"Maybe she's fussy."

"She said that. I don't buy it, though. She seems pretty easy-going. No, I think she's blissfully unaware that she would be far happier with a woman. Happens to people, we know that."

"Gi..." Kath's tone took a serious turn. "Are you interested in her?"

Gina laughed. "No. Of course not." She paused. "Well, I mean, she's good-looking—"

"Yeah, you mentioned that."

"But she's not my type. I just think it would be nice if she could find someone, you know? Everyone deserves love. She'll never find it if she's looking for a man and she's gay. I think I'm going to help her see that."

"Do you think it's a good idea?"

"Is what a good idea?"

"I don't know, whatever you're planning on doing. I mean, I don't want to be rude, Gi, but you're sort of not the best person to guide someone on coming out. You're not even out to your parents."

Gina felt her shoulders rising back up. "But you *know* why that is."

"I know that you have your reasons," Kath said. "I'm not saying anything about that. Just pointing out that maybe you're not the best person to guide someone else out of the closet if you're not exactly out fully yourself."

"They don't get me," Gina continued. This was a conversation she frequently had with her friends. No one seemed to be able to understand why Gina didn't tell her parents that she was gay, no matter how many times she explained it. Her shoulders tightened up at the realisation that even her best friend wasn't convinced about her reasoning. Very reasonable reasoning, as far as Gina was concerned.

"I know, Gi. But like I always tell you, you'll have to tell them eventually."

Gina didn't reply. All her friends said that. As if the inevitability of it meant she'd suddenly change her mind and would leap out of the closet to her parents. In reality, nothing was going to change her mind. She'd managed ten years without telling them. Aside from batting back questions from her mother about settling down with a man and having kids, she was doing just fine without them knowing. Who knew what might happen if she told them the truth? And if she didn't know, then Kath and others certainly didn't.

Her friends struggled to understand the issue because Gina's parents were basically very nice people. No one could understand Gina's reluctance. No one had the insight Gina did. Or rather, the insight she didn't have.

Because she had no idea how her parents would take the news. None whatsoever. And that was what was so very frightening. She had a great relationship with her parents and wanted to keep it that way.

She'd read horror stories of families being torn apart, kids thrown out of homes, people never seeing each other again. She couldn't stand the thought of that. She loved her parents too much. Even if they were incredibly frustrating at times.

"They still think I draw cartoons for a living," Gina said. "Dad emailed me the other day about a job as a trainee accountant."

"He's clearly never seen you try to split a restaurant bill three ways," Kath quipped.

"Or he has and is so embarrassed he thinks I should redeem myself by joining one of the most boring professions in the world."

Kath laughed. "Hey, if you become an accountant, you'd be a bean counter."

"Is that a lesbian joke?" Gina held back a laugh. Laughing while lying on the floor took twice the usual amount of effort.

"Could be." Kath snorted, indicating that it was. "I'm sorry your parents are still on your case about work, though. Have you tried explaining it to them?"

"Once a week for the last few years. They just hear *drawing* and then a load of white noise. Truth is, they want me to get married and be a full-time mum. And if that's not going to happen, then they want me to be an accountant so I can make good money, as they see it. Especially my mum. She was so happy to find Dad, settle down, and start having kids. She thinks it will make me as happy."

"I'm sorry, Gi."

Gina let out a sigh. She hadn't considered her complicated relationship with her parents when she'd thought about helping Eleanor to see the way forward.

"You know, you're right. I should leave Eleanor to figure things out for herself. I don't need to upend her world. Not right now. I'll just carry on helping her out with Sophia. That's probably the best thing I can do right now."

"How are you getting on with her? Is she still adorable, or has that worn off yet?"

Gina chuckled. Kath didn't have a maternal bone in her body. She hated kids, and when Gina had told her about Sophia, she'd been horrified. Peace and quiet was a new concept which Kath was enjoying. Not going to work and being alone for long periods suited Kath more than either of them had expected.

A couple of days after being told to work from home, Kath had taken up yoga and painting and planned to landscape her entire garden. Her reaction to being locked down had been the complete opposite to Gina's.

"She's still adorable. Not that you care," Gina joked.

"Nope. I can't imagine all the noise and mess."

"She's actually pretty quiet."

"Wait a sec. Gi, I'm going to hold my phone out. Listen."

Gina listened. She couldn't hear a thing. She closed her eyes and focused, but still nothing.

"Did you hear it?" Kath asked.

"No?"

"Exactly."

Gina rolled her eyes at being caught out by one of the oldest tricks in the book.

"Absolute silence. Honestly, it's so nice and peaceful. I had no idea how much noise there was in my life until it wasn't there any more. It's so calming."

"I'm climbing the walls," Gina confessed. "I'm realising how much I need company and people in my life. It's like I don't know how to be alone."

She swung her legs to the side and sat with her back against the wall, looking at her empty apartment. She'd turned a lamp on a while ago, but the sun had now completely set, and rather than looking cosy, it looked bleak.

"It's an adjustment," Kath said.

"Maybe." Gina stood up and hit the light switch. "I'm glad I have Sophia here, though. She's been a lifesaver. I couldn't imagine being on my own here all day, every day."

"It has worked out well," Kath said. "I was a bit worried about you at the start of lockdown, but it sounds like you're getting on well now."

"It is. I started cooking again."

"You found the kitchen?" Kath gasped.

"I did. And I remembered that I actually like cooking. But who can be bothered cooking for one?"

"You're not feeding a one-year-old your curry, are you?"

"She's fine. She just goes a little red in the cheeks," Gina joked. "No, Eleanor comes over here for dinner now. We've been doing it for a couple of days. It's working out really well. I get to cook, and she doesn't have to hurry home."

"You're so domesticated!" Kath teased.

They talked a while longer about Kath's plans for her garden. She'd moved into a brand-new house two years ago and had done nothing with the plain slab of grass at the back of the house. Now she had the time and the desire to do big things.

Gina envied her friend's enthusiasm for the opportunities the pandemic was bringing. She wished she could feel the same, but the looming sense of loneliness and grieving her old life were always present. Gina longed to spend an evening at a concert or planning a weekend away in Europe.

The days were getting easier with Sophia's, and now Eleanor's, presence. It helped to have people who needed her, relied on her. Gina was realising that she liked to be needed, and she enjoyed being helpful.

She mused that maybe she wasn't so different from Kath. Maybe she was finding out about herself, albeit in different ways.

❖

Eleanor locked up her bike in the bike shed outside the apartment building. She removed her helmet and shook her hair out. She looked at the bike shed door and frowned. For a moment, she simply couldn't remember if she'd locked it. She was sure she had, but she had no recollection of it. She tried the handle and was surprised when it opened. She put her hand in her pocket and frowned further when she couldn't find her keys.

She put her bag and helmet on the floor and patted both her

pockets but still couldn't find her keys. As a last resort, she stepped into the shed and saw her keys still attached to her bike lock.

She shook her head at herself. Her lapses were increasing as her tiredness grew. She felt exhausted and wanted nothing more than to go to sleep. Although she knew from experience that if she went to bed early, she would simply lie awake and repeat the day over and over in her mind. Questions about every decision she made would be brought up, and sleep would never come.

Tiredness battled her overactive mind throughout the day and night lately. She felt ready to sleep while standing up, and yet her brain would simply not stop providing questions and what-if scenarios.

How much longer would the pandemic go on for? How much worse would it get? When would some kind of treatment come, so she didn't feel so useless in the face of a disease that no one currently understood?

She shook the thoughts away and grabbed her keys. She checked the bike lock just to be certain. She locked the bike shed and double-checked that she'd done it right before picking up her things and heading inside.

Her evening routine had become so ingrained by now that she hardly thought about it as she methodically and meticulously washed everything she had touched, placing her clothes into the washing machine and herself into the shower. The strong chemical smell of the soap no longer bothered her. All she cared about was ensuring that she killed any lingering fragments of virus that might linger on her body following another arduous shift in A & E.

As bad as things were, she didn't dare complain. The people she treated and their families were having as bad a time as she was, and often far worse. She had her health. She used to laugh when her grandmother would say such things, but she now realised that being healthy really was a blessing.

When she finished her shower, she entered the bedroom to get dressed. For a moment, she looked at her bed longingly. The desire to slide into bed and sleep for at least an entire day was strong. But she knew the physical exhaustion was only that. Her brain would continue to race and prevent her from getting much actual rest. She needed to decompress.

Eleanor had never had much of an evening routine before. She'd often worked or read in bed before turning the light off and going to sleep without a problem. Nowadays she needed time to process what her day had brought her. It wasn't necessarily that she wanted to talk about it, but she needed the time to come to terms with it.

She pictured someone at the back of her mind slowly filing away the things that had happened, so she could deal with them another day, out of her immediate thoughts to allow her to rest.

Pushing the thoughts of an early night out of her mind, she got dressed and made her way to Gina's. She was excited to see and hold Sophia and hear about what had happened while she'd been gone.

So far, she'd not missed any large milestones. But she knew it was only a matter of time before Sophia started walking and talking. Each day she half hoped that Sophia would progress, and half hope that she hadn't missed anything.

Gina opened the door wearing a chef's hat. Sophia was in her arms, wearing a much smaller chef's hat with an elasticated strap under her chin.

"Bonjour," Gina said. "Welcome to Chez Sophia. We're making a delicious meal for you tonight."

Eleanor took Sophia from Gina and gave her daughter a kiss on the cheek.

"Why, thank you. What a lovely restaurant you have here."

Gina closed the front door. "I'll leave you with our head chef. I'm just the minion who does the chopping anyway."

Eleanor took a seat at the breakfast bar and placed Sophia on her knee. Sophia immediately started to make sounds that almost sounded like conversation. Eleanor imagined that Sophia was telling her about her day, and so she nodded along.

Gina flitted around the kitchen like a professional. A few days before she had managed to snag a highly coveted slot for grocery delivery, and since then she had been cooking dinners for the two of them. Eleanor had to admit that she'd been surprised that Gina could cook.

In fact, Gina seemed to constantly surprise her. From their shaky start and the questionable decision to go out to the coffee shop to now, Gina was different these days. At the beginning of the lockdown, Gina constantly felt she wanted to go out, only to realise that going out would be pointless as everything was closed. After a few days, she had acclimatised to that fact and was instead making the best of the situation.

Cooking seemed to be an outlet for her frustrations.

"What delight is on the menu?" Eleanor asked.

"Sea bass. I've never cooked it before, so if it's gross, then the recipe I found online is at fault and not me."

Eleanor had no doubt that it would be delicious, just like everything else Gina had made so far.

"I'm sure it will be lovely. How was today?"

"It was good. Sophia hated me for about twenty minutes because I didn't let her bang her head on the floor. Then she refused to put the shapes in her box and decided to throw them. But when she got her chef's hat on, she became an angel."

Eleanor laughed. "She has always liked a good hat. Sorry if she was troublesome today."

"Not troublesome, just your average baby," Gina said with a shrug and a smile.

Eleanor smiled. Gina was very understanding of Sophia's typical baby mood swings, seemingly taking them all in her stride. Nothing that Sophia did seemed to faze Gina. In fact, as a whole, Gina was extremely laid-back and relaxing to be around.

Eleanor often felt herself feeding off Gina's calm. The apartment had become a sanctuary of sorts, a place for jokes, good food, and even better company. Once the door closed, COVID remained outside. All the stresses of the workday ebbed away. If Eleanor wanted to talk about things, she did. If she didn't, then Gina gladly filled the silence.

The exhaustion that Eleanor carried with her throughout the

day like a lead balloon seemed to lift when she arrived at Gina's. The pleasant atmosphere, smell of a homecooked meal, feel of her daughter in her arms, and the knowledge that things were okay in her corner of the world lifted her spirits.

She watched Gina flitting around the kitchen, talking about Sophia's latest obsession with hiding the TV remote control in between the sofa cushions. A question niggled at the back of her head: What would her evenings be like if she hadn't met Gina? How close to the breaking point might she be without this wonderful woman in her life? She pushed the thought away and simply enjoyed the moment.

Chapter Fourteen

Gina groaned at the sound of her phone ringing. She squinted in the darkness to try to orientate herself. A brief fight with the bedsheet and she was free and reaching for her phone that was charging on her bedside table.

"Hello?"

She sat up and rubbed at her eye with the palm of her hand. She had no idea what time it was other than it was the middle of the night.

"It's me," her mother said.

"What's happened?" Gina suddenly felt more awake. She jumped out of bed and stood uselessly in the middle of the room. Panic coursed through her, but she didn't know why. Yet.

"It's Dad. He, um, he's in the hospital."

Gina sat on the edge of the bed. "What? What's happened?"

Her mum let out a shaky sigh. "He got a cough the other day. It got really bad, and then today he stayed in bed most of the day. We thought it might be the COVID but didn't think much of it. Tonight, though, he was struggling to breathe. In the end, I had to call an ambulance."

"Why didn't you call me earlier? I didn't know he was sick." Gina's hands shook, and she suddenly felt icy cold.

"We didn't think anything like this would happen. It was just like a bad cold, and then it suddenly got worse. The paramedics were good with him. They did what they could and then said they had to take him in. But I can't go and see him, so I have no idea what's going on."

"How are you feeling?" Gina asked.

"Fine. I had a scratchy throat yesterday but nothing else."

Gina knew little about COVID, even now. She had friends who'd had it and had been fine and some who had been bedridden for days. There didn't seem to be a pattern.

"I want to come over," Gina whispered. "I know I can't. But I want to."

"I know, love. But it's pointless. There's not a lot you can do, and I might make you sick. Maybe I made your father sick. Who knows? We've been so careful."

Gina swallowed. "I'm sure it wasn't you. And I'm sure he'll be fine. They'll have him in for the night, and then they'll be sick of his bad jokes, and they'll send him back home."

Her mum chuckled. "We can hope. I'm sorry to wake you up. I thought you ought to know."

"It's okay. I'm glad I know. I just wish there was something I could do. Where did they take him?"

"Royal Thames."

Gina stood up again. The Royal Thames was where Eleanor worked. She hurried over to the chair where she kept her clothes that weren't ready to be washed but also couldn't go back into the wardrobe. She tossed some leggings and a sweater onto the bed.

"What was he like when they took him away?"

"Not good." Her mum's voice wavered a little. "He was really struggling to breathe. They brought some oxygen in to help him. But he couldn't say a lot. It took him over really quick, Gi. I know I've said it before, but stay safe. This virus isn't messing about."

"I know. I'm being safe," Gina promised.

"I better go. I need to call your brother."

"Okay. Let me know as soon as you hear anything."

"I will. I love you, Gi."

"I love you, too, Mum."

Gina hung up the call and hurried to get dressed. Her heart was slamming against her ribcage. She hadn't seen her father for months, and now he was suddenly in hospital. She regretted not calling him more, not replying to each of the silly little jokes he sent via WhatsApp, and secretly planning a way out of attending his birthday party, when it had still been happening.

He had COVID and she didn't know what that meant. The death toll was climbing, and even though Gina avoided listening to the news when they started announcing how many people had died each day, it was impossible to avoid hearing the numbers.

Work meetings had become sombre affairs where those gathered would talk in hushed tones while they spoke of how many deaths and hospitalisations happened every day. Eventually, they'd change topic back to work, but the facts and figures would stay rattling in Gina's brain.

She grabbed her keys and headed out of the apartment and along the corridor. She needed to know more. Everything she had been trying to avoid, she now wished to know—likely survival rates, what the illness did to the body, where her father would be, and if anyone would be with him.

She pressed the doorbell to Eleanor's apartment and waited. Her mind overflowed with questions that she desperately needed to ask. Was her mum going to be the next one to suffer the same fate? She wished she'd taken more time to see them when she could. Going out and travelling the world had always seemed more important.

Now she regretted every decision that had taken her away from them.

"Gina?" Eleanor pulled a robe tightly around herself and blinked at the bright hallway light. "What is it? Are you okay?"

Tears streamed down Gina's face. She threw herself into Eleanor.

Eleanor held her and closed the front door with her free hand.

"Gina? What is it? Are you hurt?"

"It's my dad," Gina mumbled into Eleanor's shoulder.

"What's happened?"

"He has COVID. He's in hospital. They took him in this evening," Gina said. "He's going to die. He's going to die, and he hardly knows me. Like, we're almost strangers these days. I could have changed that, but I didn't. And now he's sick, and I can't even see him."

Gina held tightly onto Eleanor—the one adult in her so-called social bubble. The only person she was legally allowed to see and be in contact with. The world didn't make sense any more.

Her father was in hospital, and she was supposed to do nothing. Any other time, she would have raced to see him, even if it meant pacing a hospital corridor throughout the night. Now, she couldn't even do that. She'd never felt so useless.

"I'm sorry," Eleanor said. She adjusted her grip and placed a hand on the back of Gina's head and soothingly stroked her hair. "I'm so very sorry."

Gina closed her eyes and breathed in Eleanor's scent. In the mornings, Eleanor smelt of freshly applied perfume. In the evenings, an almost bleach-like smell lingered on her hair and skin. Not unpleasant, but a chemical reminder of where Eleanor worked. Now, she smelt different. Gina couldn't identify the smell other than the fact that she enjoyed it. In fact, she found herself melting into the comforting hold.

That realisation caused Gina to take a step backwards. She couldn't feel that way about Eleanor. It wasn't right in a moment of comfort. She wiped at her tears and tried to get her thoughts in order.

"Will he die?" she blurted out. "I can take it. I just want to know the truth."

Eleanor looked uncertain. "I couldn't say."

Gina could tell Eleanor was deliberately holding back, which made Gina worry all the more.

"So he will die?" Gina asked.

"I have no idea. It depends on so many factors. And even then, it's very hard to predict what COVID will do to an individual."

Gina nodded. Of course Eleanor couldn't know what would happen. They'd spoken about how difficult to predict COVID could be. If she'd stopped panicking and just thought for a second, she would have realised that herself. Instead, she'd stressed herself beyond belief and even dragged Eleanor into things.

"I'm sorry, I shouldn't have come here." Gina looked at her wrist only to realise she hadn't put her watch on. She tapped her pocket. Or brought her phone with her.

"Five o'clock," Eleanor supplied.

Gina winced. "I'm sorry. I didn't think."

She wanted to kick herself. Eleanor needed rest. Every evening she came to Gina's looking like someone who had been in a war zone. And slowly, over dinner and the course of the evening, Gina took her mind off whatever was happening at work. Eleanor always arrived looking tense and exhausted and left looking less so. Gina considered it her efforts towards the pandemic, a small contribution but one that she was proud of.

And now she had barged in on Eleanor at five in the morning.

"It's okay. Do you want a hot drink?" Eleanor put her hand on Gina's back and guided her towards the kitchen. "I might as well stay up. I could go into work and grab an extra shift. If you don't mind watching Sophia?"

"I don't mind. But I feel so guilty for waking you," Gina admitted.

In the kitchen, Eleanor got two mugs out and started to fill the kettle.

"It's okay. I was in and out of sleep anyway."

Gina leaned against the worktop and watched Eleanor making two cups of tea. She'd spoken in the past about how difficult she was finding it to get to sleep, despite feeling exhausted. Gina had guessed that Eleanor was suffering something akin to PTSD.

While Eleanor never spoke about how work was, Gina could tell by the tired look in Eleanor's eyes that she was working through something beyond anything she'd seen before. Eleanor was a collected sort of person who seemed able to deal with anything. The fact that she was struggling gave Gina a good idea how bad things had gotten.

"But you could still get another hour of sleep," Gina argued.

Eleanor smiled sadly. "I doubt I'd be able to sleep. Thank you, though."

Eleanor made tea, and they sat in the living room in

companionable silence. Gina felt calmed by Eleanor's presence, something that she didn't think was possible considering how out of her mind with worry she had felt upon arrival.

"Which hospital did they take him to?" Eleanor asked.

"Yours." Gina had been so turned around that she hadn't thought to provide that essential piece of information.

"Oh, what's his name? I can see if I can find anything out," Eleanor offered.

"Patrick Henley," Gina said. "Thanks."

"No problem. I can't guarantee I'll be able to find anything out, though. It's very busy on the wards at the moment."

Gina thanked her again. A few moments later, Eleanor excused herself to go and get ready for work. She invited Gina to stay, somehow aware Gina didn't want to go back to her lonely apartment.

Gina sipped her tea and stared at the carpet beneath her bare feet. If the world had felt odd before, now it felt unrecognisable. Shops closing were nothing in comparison to the sudden realisation that she might lose her father. She couldn't believe she had spent so much time worrying about coffee shops, music festivals, cinemas, and anything else that now seemed so utterly pointless.

She felt sick for only now coming to this conclusion. This was the reality that other people had been facing every day for weeks. And she was one of many who were feeling this way right now. But until she was in the situation, she had been unable to understand it. Did that make her selfish? Immature? And what would come now?

Gina didn't know how much time had passed when Eleanor reappeared in the living room dressed and ready for work. Somehow Gina had allowed her tea to go cold while staring into the mug and wondering what would happen next.

"Will you be okay?" Eleanor asked.

She sat on the sofa next to Gina and placed a hand on her back.

Gina nodded. "I will. I'm sorry. This is all a bit new to me."

"You and many others. That doesn't mean your feelings aren't valid, though. It's a lot to process."

Gina couldn't believe that Eleanor was about to return to the war zone that was her hospital but was still taking time to check that Gina was okay. She knew for a fact that she would not be as thoughtful and composed if their positions were reversed.

"I'm just sorry that you're heading into work early," Gina said.

Eleanor hadn't moved her hand. It still rested lightly on Gina's back, and Gina enjoyed the sensation. As with the earlier hug, she was finding that she wanted to be physically near Eleanor.

She wondered if she was starved of the human touch. Or if this was specific to Eleanor. Unfortunately for Gina, she thought it was the latter, which seemed completely inappropriate, but Gina was not in the position to be able to control her thoughts and feelings right then.

"It's every hand to the pump," Eleanor said. "You're doing me a favour. Besides, if I fall back asleep now, so close to my alarm going off, I'll fall into a deep sleep and will wake up feeling rotten."

"If it's okay with you, I'll stay here and let Sophia sleep."

Eleanor stood and Gina instantly missed her touch.

"I think that would be for the best, if you don't mind. She'll be a beast if she doesn't get her sleep. She was already up and down most of the night."

"I don't mind." Gina nodded to the television. "As long as I can watch something."

"Of course." Eleanor picked up her rucksack from a closet and started to pack her things. "Sophia's in my bed. She was restless so I brought her in with me."

Gina realised that she was about to be left alone in Eleanor's apartment—ordinarily not a problem, except for the fact that Gina was incredibly curious about Eleanor's life. Now the opportunity had presented itself for her to explore the apartment, a welcome distraction as she planned to have a look around and check out the bookshelves and the like.

She didn't feel bad about it as she had already caught Eleanor twice doing the same thing in her apartment. Gina hadn't commented on the behaviour, knowing that she would do the same given half a chance. Now that chance had presented itself, and she fully intended to take advantage of it.

Eleanor picked up her cycling helmet and rucksack and looked around the apartment one last time before saying goodbye to Gina and promising that she would call soon.

Gina watched the door close and counted to ten before she stood up and started to look around the apartment. It wasn't the first time she'd been in Eleanor's apartment, but it was the only time she'd been there alone. Aside from the sleeping Sophia in the other room, of course.

She made a beeline to the bookshelf and ran her finger along the spines of the books. Everything seemed to be non-fiction, somehow not a surprise. A lot of the titles were complicated medical terms that Gina had no idea about.

It seemed, somewhat unsurprisingly, that Eleanor took her work home with her. At the bottom of the bookshelf lay a couple of crime novels, which seemed to be the extent of her collection of fiction.

Gina strolled around the living room, looking at photographs of who she presumed were friends and family and the odd trinket that was displayed on a shelf.

Everything looked very elegant and in its rightful place. But she didn't feel as if she was getting to know Eleanor. There were very few personal effects.

Gina wandered around the dining room and even the kitchen. While the rooms were not sterile, they were clean and unfussy. Gina couldn't help but wonder if Sophia would change that. She imagined that as Sophia grew, her own influence would be stamped upon the apartment. If, of course, Eleanor decided to stay there.

A shiver ran up Gina's spine at the thought of Eleanor and Sophia not living in the same building.

Gina decided to check on Sophia and walked into Eleanor's bedroom. After assuring herself that Sophia was safe and asleep, she walked around the room. There was a little more personality in the bedroom, where the cream walls of the rest of the apartment gave way to a light dusky pink.

A few items of clothing were casually draped over a chair in the corner of the room. Gina smiled to herself—it seemed she wasn't the only one who had the chair-drobe approach to clothing.

On the bedside cabinet lay a stack of books—more non-fiction, and even more complicated titles that Gina could not even begin to pronounce. Bottles of perfume were neatly lined up next to a make-up mirror on top of the desk. Gina glanced at the labels, recognising some as expensive brands.

Her gaze travelled to the bed. In the middle of the king-size bed lay Sophia. A pillow on one side prevented her from rolling away. On the other side were creased sheets and a duvet, which had been kicked back, presumably when Eleanor rose to let Gina into the apartment less than an hour ago.

Seeing the soft inhale and exhale from Sophia reminded Gina just how tired she was. The shock of being abruptly awoken was wearing off and being replaced with tiredness.

Gina climbed into the bed and positioned herself beside Sophia. She watched Sophia's face, noting the way her eyes lazily moved around beneath closed eyelids. She wondered what Sophia was thinking. And she also wondered what Sophia would think when she woke up to see her mother was gone.

She hoped that she would be able to fend off any tears before they arrived by distracting Sophia. In order to do that, she decided to lie in the bed and wait for Sophia to wake up.

She happily inhaled the scent of Eleanor from the pillow. She lay still and watched Sophia sleep, feeling content in a way she hadn't felt possible just a few minutes ago. The calmness from Sophia and the comfort of Eleanor's familiar scent relaxed her. She let out a long breath, forced her shoulders down away from her ears where they had gradually risen, and allowed herself to rest.

Chapter Fifteen

The nurse looked at Eleanor curiously. Eleanor couldn't decide if it was because she was in far earlier than usual, or because the PPE she was wearing made it impossible to identify her.

She'd noticed more and more doctors and nurses were writing their names on sheets of paper, which they taped to the backs of their PPE aprons so they could be easily identified by colleagues and patients alike. She wondered if she should do the same.

"Oh, hi, Dr. Osborne," the nurse finally said.

Eleanor didn't know her name. She felt guilty, but the volume of new staff pouring in to A & E from all over the hospital was enormous. As deputy head of a department, Eleanor supposed she was more identifiable than most.

"Good morning," she replied.

"Getting an early start?" The nurse flipped through some paperwork to assign cases to Eleanor.

"Yes. I couldn't sleep. Also, a friend's father has been admitted, Patrick Henley?"

The nurse paused looking through the papers and turned around to look at the large whiteboard that contained all the bed and patient information. On her back was a piece of paper with her name—Marissa—and a smiley face.

"Henley, Henley...I know I saw that name," Marissa said.

The board, usually neat and legible, had become a mess of names and information. The clean lines that used to separate the bays had all been split into three lines, allowing for more data to be stored on the one whiteboard. But it still wasn't enough. Pieces of paper taped to the wall listed more vital information that couldn't fit on the board.

"Bay twelve," Marissa said. "Ward three."

Eleanor nodded. "Thank you. I'll check in with him, and then I'll be back."

The A & E department used to be one ward, but now it was sprawling its way along the hospital, slowly sucking up wards that had been emptied to create a buffer zone between COVID patients and the rest of the hospital.

But as more people were admitted, the A & E swelled to take them in, and no one seemed to know when it would stop. Temporary tents had been set up in the car park as an emergency overflow for the A & E patients who were COVID-negative because hospital business as usual had to continue. Somehow.

As Eleanor walked through the wards, she noticed that nothing had changed since her last shift. She'd learnt over the years that hospitals ebbed and flowed with patients. Sometimes it was quiet, sometimes busy. Nowadays it was always busy, no matter the time of day. Patients were brought in. Some were moved to the ventilation wards. Some were given emergency assistance. It seemed never-ending.

She focused on her task of finding Gina's father.

She'd been awake when Gina had knocked on the door that morning, staring at the ceiling with questions tossing over and over in her mind. Seeing Gina had been a relief for a split second, until she realised how distressed Gina was.

She hadn't thought twice and had pulled Gina into a hug. Gina had clutched at her in tears, and in that moment Eleanor would have done anything to help her. Except there was little that she could do.

Information was about all she could offer.

She approached bay twelve. The man in the bed was holding an oxygen mask to his face. He looked tired, and his breath rattled as he breathed.

"Mr. Henley?" Eleanor asked.

He looked at her and nodded.

"I'm Eleanor Osborne, I'm a...friend of your daughter."

His eyes lit up. "Gina?" His voice was rough.

"Yes. We live in the same building." Eleanor glanced at the whiteboard above Patrick's bed to check his status. He was in the early stages of the illness, a time where it could go either way. Some fought their way through, and others ended up being intubated. It was impossible to know who would go which way. She'd seen people in their early thirties on ventilators, and she'd seen people in their sixties stabilise and start to recover.

"She isn't worrying about me, is she? I'll be fine." He tried to take a breath but seemed unable to catch it. He slowed down his breathing and took in a shallow gulp of air. "I have to be fine. People need me."

"You need to focus on you," she told him.

"I have a wife and two kids who need me. I have to be okay."

Eleanor had heard that line of argument before. Many patients became so stressed with ensuring they were well enough to look after family members, that they took longer to recover.

"If they were here, they'd tell you to look after yourself, I'm certain," Eleanor said.

A ghost of a smile curled at his lip. "Yes. They probably would. But I can't help but worry about them."

Eleanor grinned. She knew without a shadow of a doubt that she would feel the same way. If anything was to ever happen to her, the first thought in her mind would be Sophia, whether Sophia was one or forty-one.

"Being a parent does come with a lot of worry," Eleanor agreed, "but sometimes we have to focus on ourselves. Especially when we're sick."

"This thing took me down fast," he said. "I felt fine. A cough. Then I was breathy. Then I couldn't breathe at all."

"I know. We're doing what we can. Try to take slow and even breaths. I know it's difficult."

He took a few breaths, clearly attempting to take a deep breath but never quite managing.

"Tell Gina I'll be fine," he said.

"When we speak next," Eleanor said. She had no intention of telling Gina that he would be fine. She had no idea which direction his condition might take, and she wouldn't give Gina any false hope.

"She's a good kid," he whispered.

"She is," Eleanor agreed. For some reason, the term *kid* irked her. At first, she too had considered Gina to be on the young side. Maybe even immature. But Eleanor's perception was changing fast.

"Bit lost, though," he added.

"Is she?"

"Yes. She doesn't want to settle down."

"Maybe she hasn't met the right person yet."

"That's what she says. And then there's her job. She needs to get out of there."

"Why's that?"

"Well, it's not a real job. She gets paid good money, but it's one of those modern places with glass windows and beanbags everywhere. They have a kitchen with breakfast for everyone. How long can that kind of thing really last? No, she needs a real job before it all goes up in smoke."

Eleanor chuckled. "It looks real enough to me. She's forever drawing something new. She's very talented."

He tried to laugh but didn't have enough breath for it. He coughed a couple of times to clear his throat.

"Oh yes, she's talented. But it's just…drawing. It won't last. It's not a real job. Sounds like a house of cards ready to fall over."

"I think it is a real job. The video game industry isn't exactly my domain, but I know it's enormous. Bigger than the movie industry." Eleanor hadn't known that until Gina had told her. She hadn't believed it until she'd looked it up one evening before bed. She'd been shocked to discover just how big the games market was. Gina had explained that part of it was because of smartphones. People had a gaming console in their pocket at all times.

Eleanor knew she underutilised her phone and was fully expecting Sophia to teach her all the features in a couple of years.

Patrick looked uncertain. "She was planning to be an accountant when she was little. I remember her walking around with a calculator and a pencil behind her ear. She was only eight, but dead set on being an accountant."

"Pencil behind the ear sounds more like a builder to me," she said.

"True. I suppose they can be pretty creative with their accounting, too."

Eleanor smiled. She could see Gina in the man before her. The tone of his voice, the hint of humour, the shade of eye colour—there was no doubt the two were related.

"She's always been rudderless," he continued. "Her mum and me have been trying to get her to settle down. But she won't. She's always off seeing the world or going out with her friends. Well, used to be. She's probably climbing the walls now."

Eleanor smirked inwardly. "She was, a little. She's settled down a bit now."

"Are you the one she's babysitting for?"

"That's me."

"She loves your little girl. What's her name again?"

"Sophia."

"That's it. When we talk to her, it's *Sophia did this, Sophia did that* all the time. It's really helping her."

"She's really helping me," Eleanor said. "Good childcare is hard to come by. Especially now."

"I bet."

"She handles a lot. She's working a full-time job, looking after Sophia, and even looking after me sometimes," she admitted.

"Well, it's just drawing, so I suppose she has some time," Patrick said. "But I'm working on her. I'll get her into a real job soon. Which is why I have to survive this damn thing. Be honest with me, what are my chances?"

Eleanor knew better than to answer such a question, especially these days when life felt like a lottery.

"Gina is doing just fine," Eleanor said. "She's an independent and capable woman. I wouldn't trust just anyone with my daughter. Concentrate on getting yourself well, and then maybe she can explain to you what she does."

Patrick opened his mouth to reply, but Eleanor shook her head. "That's enough of your energy expended on this. Please rest, Mr. Henley."

He nodded. Eleanor returned the nod and then left. She hoped that he would make it. It was increasingly difficult to know who was going to be able to fight off the virus and who would be pulled under by it.

There was nothing she could do other than hope, a position she didn't relish or feel comfortable in. Eleanor's medical career had revolved around preventative action, surgery, medication. Now she had little more than hope and the most basic of medical triage.

She wondered if she should contact Gina immediately or wait until she was on a break. If she left the COVID wards now, it would mean a change of PPE. The protective equipment stocks were said to be running low. The reporters on the news certainly believed that the national stocks had been raided and that there was little left.

Common sense said to wait until she was on a break. But the feel of Gina wrapped around her that morning, sobbing on her shoulder, was still fresh in her mind.

She approached an unused reception and picked up the phone. She called the cardiology ward and crossed her fingers that Nigel had arrived. After what seemed like an eternity, Nigel answered.

"Cardiology, what's left of it, how can I help?"

"Very sarcastic, Dr. Hoyle," she said.

"Oh, hello. Where are you?"

"One of the COVID wards. I need you to do me a favour."

"Sure."

Eleanor always appreciated Nigel's no-nonsense manner. He instinctively knew when it was time to drop the jokes and do what she was asking him to do. For years, he'd been the only person she felt she could trust. Nowadays she felt blessed to have two people like that in her life. And she was about to ask one to contact the other.

"Gina's father got brought in this morning. I've just checked on him, and he's doing okay. I need you to text Gina for me. My phone in in my bag—you know the code."

"No problem. What's the message?"

"Let her know that I've spoken to him, introduced myself, and I'll keep an eye on him for her."

"Okay. I'll go and send that now."

"Thanks, Nigel."

"Good luck today," he said, his tone turning serious.

"You, too."

She hung up the phone. She took a breath as deep as she could from the confines of her mask before starting her day.

Chapter Sixteen

Gina paced in front of the playpen. Once Sophia had woken up, Gina had brought her back to her own apartment. Being in Eleanor's place was nice, but Gina felt as if she was intruding. Her initial curiosity had quickly given way to guilt when she woke up confused and disorientated—and in Eleanor's bed of all places.

Her emotions had been running high, and she'd felt the need for comfort. But when she'd woken up and had managed to process events, she decided that it was time to leave.

Sophia was happy to be in her playpen and attempting to master the stacking cups that were far beyond her skills. Thankfully, unlike some other children, she didn't get frustrated and seemed content to try again and again.

Gina called her mum. It was only eight o'clock in the morning, but she felt as though days had passed since they'd last spoken. In reality, it was less than four hours. She knew part of that was the fact that she hadn't seen her mum in person for a while. It felt like a very long while, but she knew it was no longer than any other period of time that they hadn't seen each other.

Choosing not to do something and not being allowed to do that same thing seemed to make time pass at different speeds.

"Hello?"

"It's Gina."

"Oh, hello. I don't have any more news, I'm afraid."

"I do. Remember the woman I babysit for? She went into work, and she's spoken to Dad. I don't have much information, but I know they had a conversation. So that's good news. He's talking."

"Oh, thank goodness. I had dreams of him being put on a ventilator. That's what they're doing to people, you know. You see it on the news all the time."

Gina shivered. She knew it was necessary, but the thought of a tube in her throat made her uncomfortable.

"Well, they've not done that. So maybe he is responding to some treatment."

"I hope so. You know, we've not been apart for thirty-two years. Not even a single night. He slept in the hospital when you were born. I was in and out on the same day when your brother was born."

Gina sat on the edge of the sofa and smiled. Her parents were the ultimate example of two people who were supposed to be together. They finished each other's sentences, found the same jokes funny, spent every moment together. If two people were ever crafted in order to be together, it was them.

"I miss him. I don't want to lose him."

"You won't," Gina said. She had no idea if it was true or not, but she knew she had to say the words.

"What's your doctor friend's name?"

"Eleanor."

"Eleanor. She seems nice, going in and finding your father."

"She is very nice."

"Shame she isn't a man," her mum added.

Gina slumped. Even now, her mother was going to guilt her about being alone.

"A doctor would be quite a catch. And you live local, would make dating easy. Oh well."

Gina itched to respond honestly, to come out to her mother, but she had no idea what the reaction to that would be. Especially now at such an emotional time.

So despite wanting to say something, she said nothing. As always. And the embarrassment and guilt burned at her.

"I have to go. I'll call you if I find out anything else," Gina said.

"Okay, love. Thanks for letting me know. Speak soon."

Gina hung up and threw her phone onto the sofa. She rubbed the palms of her hands into her eyes and let out a low growl.

Every time she got close to coming out to her parents, they said something that reminded her she was better off staying in the closet. The little microaggressions and heteronormative comments that they left in their wake were enough to discourage her from sharing her true self with them.

She stood up and grabbed a cardigan from the back of the sofa and pulled it on. She suddenly felt chilly and knew it was nothing to do with the temperature in the apartment.

She hated not being honest with her parents. Her parents had never been outright homophobic, but her dad told jokes that left a bad taste in her mouth, and even when Gina was a teenager going through a phase of short hair, rainbow T-shirts, and Doc Martens, nothing had been said.

It was as if they both studiously ignored every hint that Gina had dropped. Until Gina had felt so uncomfortable that she had started to lie to them. When she spoke of a boyfriend, light shone in her mother's eyes as she asked about every single detail.

All that had done was split Gina in two. To her parents, she was one person, to the rest of the world she was another. She dated women but never introduced them to her parents, and never allowed it to get too serious. What would be the point?

At home and with her family, she was simply someone who had yet to find love. Someone who needed to be pushed to settle down on a weekly basis. Someone who maybe had high standards. Someone Gina didn't recognise but whom her parents seemed to love.

She folded her arms and looked out of the window. Her dad had no idea who she was. He didn't understand her job, had no idea of her sexuality, didn't really know her at all. It was Gina's fault. Every time he asked a question, she deflected. She'd been so used to creating a wall between them that it was second nature these days.

Eventually, he'd stopped asking and came to his own conclusions. She was too fussy to date. Her job was temporary. His daughter was a mess, but he loved her anyway.

And all of that was Gina's doing. She could see that, had known that for a while, but had never really cared. It kept the status quo, and that was the most important thing to her.

Now there was a very real chance that he might die. And if he did, he'd do so with no idea who Gina really was. Strangely, despite never having any intention of telling her father the truth, she now burned at the knowledge that he would never really know her.

For a brief second, she wondered if she should have told him more. Maybe the wall she'd put up between them hadn't been the best idea, even if it had protected them from any potential arguments about her sexuality.

She shook her head. It had been the right decision to keep that information to herself. She'd sucked up the odd ding about her being permanently single, and in return she'd had a relationship with her family. They'd shared family dinners, parties, birthdays, holidays.

Feeling the need for comfort, she picked Sophia up out of her playpen and cuddled her. Sophia put her short arms around Gina's neck and held on, smiling at her.

"You have a very supportive mother," Gina said. "You'll be just fine. She loves you to the moon and back. And she will, no matter what you choose—I'm certain of that."

Sophia giggled and patted Gina's cheek with the open palm of her hand.

Gina laughed and leaned in to the almost affectionate touch. Sophia's motor skills weren't the best, so occasionally the pressure was more of a slap than a soothing pat, but Gina knew the heart behind it.

❖

Eleanor stood under the hot shower and tried to relax her muscles. It had been another extremely long day at work. But this time, she had the added pressure that she was losing her mind.

Her brain insisted on reminding her of the hug she'd pulled Gina into that morning. For some reason, over and over again, her thoughts would turn to the hug. The feel of Gina, the pleasant sensation of being able to comfort her.

Eleanor opened her eyes and shook away the thought.

She didn't know why it lingered in her mind. But she did know that she needed to re-establish boundaries. Daydreaming throughout the day about how nice Gina smelt was not conducive to work. Why her brain was toying with her, she didn't know. Gina had somehow taken root front and centre in her mind.

She finished up her shower, got dressed, and headed to Gina's apartment for dinner. It felt strange to have not got Sophia up and dressed that morning. As if she'd forgotten to do something important. She trusted Gina, but she also knew that more and more of her motherly tasks were slowly falling away, and Gina was thankfully there to pick up the slack.

Gina opened the door and gestured down to where Sophia stood, holding on to the door. She was standing but only with the benefit of her grip on the wood. Her feet wobbled less than Eleanor had seen recently.

"We're close to walking," Gina said. "I hope you're prepared for some chasing."

"I'm really not," Eleanor admitted. She scooped Sophia into a hug and smiled.

The idea of Sophia starting to make a run for it at the drop of a hat wasn't appealing. But she'd been waiting for this moment for weeks, and now it was here, and she couldn't help but feel excited.

"I checked on your father again before I left. No change. Which has its good sides," Eleanor said.

"No worse, but no better." Gina understood.

"Exactly."

"Okay. Well, thank you for checking in on him. I really do appreciate that."

Eleanor smiled. She wished she could have done more. Anything to take the shadow away from behind Gina's eyes. She was smiling, but Eleanor could tell there was something weighing her down.

"While I was chopping carrots, she wouldn't stop screaming and pointing to them. Which is weird, because she can't see them from down there," Gina explained. "So I mashed up a bit of raw carrot on a spoon and she ate it. So the next time she complains about that luxury baby food you pay through the nose for, just remember that."

Eleanor laughed. "Seriously? She ate cold raw mashed carrot?"

"Yep." Gina returned to the kitchen to continue cooking dinner.

Eleanor looked at her grinning daughter in her arms. "You're getting that for breakfast every day from now on."

She walked around the apartment, enjoying the feel of Sophia in her arms and the sounds of Gina humming as she made dinner. The world had turned upside down and her home life was nothing like it had been just a month ago. But she found that she preferred things this way.

As much as she hated to admit that. The idea that any good could possibly come out of something as negative as COVID niggled at her. She logically knew that finding some silver lining in a dark cloud was a positive. But having any positive thoughts about what was happening seemed somehow wrong.

She sat on the sofa and moved Sophia to her lap, allowing herself to see Sophia's smiling face. There was no doubt that her daughter loved the time she spent with Gina. Eleanor had never seen Sophia so happy and bouncy with anyone other than herself.

She knew that Gina wasn't simply focused on watching Sophia but also helping her to grow. Gina knew the milestones Sophia was about to reach and worked with her to meet them. Sophia's standing was less wobbly, her speech was coming along, her sleep schedule was regimented to cause minimum friction in the evening. It was the perfect arrangement.

Not just that, Eleanor liked Gina. She looked forward to coming to Gina's apartment for dinner, and not just for the convenience of it. Gina was fun to be around and seemed to know that Eleanor needed to decompress after a day at work.

Gina's apartment had become a place of comfort, somewhere Eleanor hurried to after her decontamination shower at the end of the workday, and as soon as she was up and dressed in the mornings. A few extra minutes here and there with Gina seemed worth the hurry.

"Your dad thinks you should be an accountant," Eleanor said.

Gina stopped chopping and looked up with amusement. "Even in hospital he said that? To a stranger?"

Eleanor nodded. "Yes. Your drawing is just temporary. Why didn't you tell me? If I knew you had some hidden financial wizardry skills, I would have asked you to look over my water bill."

Gina chuckled. "He is so embarrassing."

"Surely you've explained to him what you do?" Eleanor bounced Sophia on her knee and enjoyed the little giggles that it produced.

"Multiple times. But they hear *games* and tune out. I used to walk around with a calc—"

"Calculator and a pencil behind your ear, I know." Eleanor grinned.

Gina laughed for real. Eleanor couldn't help but join in.

"Wow. My father, honestly. Can't take him anywhere," Gina said. "Did he say anything else? Do I even want to know what he's telling strangers about his daughter?"

"He seemed to think you were still figuring out your life," Eleanor confessed. "I told him you seemed to have everything figured out."

"Aww, thanks. Did it make the slightest difference?"

Eleanor shook her head. "Didn't seem to. I did try, though."

Gina continued cooking dinner. "It's okay. My parents are desperate to see me move job, settle down with a nice man, and start popping out kids."

Eleanor was confused. "Man?"

Gina paused. She bit her lip and looked up again. "Yeah, they sorta don't know I'm gay."

Eleanor knew shock was written all over her face, but she couldn't help it. Gina appeared so casual with her sexuality. To know that her parents didn't know the truth was bizarre to Eleanor.

"May I ask why?"

Gina let out a shaky breath. She raised a shoulder, attempting to appear casual about something that clearly bothered her greatly.

"They are quite traditional," Gina admitted. "I don't know what their reaction would be. And as I've never found someone to introduce to them, I never bothered telling them."

"I see." Eleanor really didn't see at all, but it felt like the right thing to say.

"I don't think they're virulently homophobic or anything," Gina hastened to add. "Well, I don't know. They're just…"

"Traditional?" Eleanor offered.

"Yeah." Gina continued cooking. "So if anything comes up when you're talking to my dad…"

"I'll not say anything," Eleanor promised.

Ordinarily, she didn't think that she'd be put in the position of potentially outing a patient's daughter. But Patrick Henley was chatty.

"I know it sounds silly," Gina said.

"Not at all. It's your decision and nothing to do with me."

"I'm proud of who I am. It just…doesn't seem necessary to tell them at the moment. Why rock the boat for no reason?"

Eleanor could think of a hundred reasons. She looked at Sophia and wondered if she would ever face similar difficulties. Would Sophia ever think there was something she couldn't tell her mother? Eleanor hoped not. Even if it was something terrible, which being gay most certainly wasn't, she would hope that Sophia knew her mother was a place of safety for her.

"You probably shouldn't spend too much time with my dad, anyway," Gina continued, a jokey tone returning. "He'll be asking you why you're not married. He's nosy like that."

"Family trait?" Eleanor asked playfully.

"Yep. We're all nosy. But my dad might be the nosiest of all of us."

"I'll tell him what I told you—I've just not found the right man." Eleanor lowered Sophia to the floor and encouraged her to stand and grip the edge of the coffee table.

"But have you tried lowering your standards?" Gina asked.

Eleanor laughed. "Oh yes, that's one of the first things I did."

"I don't know, maybe you're not trying hard enough," Gina replied jokingly.

"Do you think I'll need to get my diaries for the last three years to show your father the number of pointless dates I went on?" Eleanor asked.

"Evidence would be useful," Gina agreed. "What was the worst date you went on?"

Eleanor chuckled. "Oh, that would be mean to the person who took me to dinner."

"No, what's mean is that you didn't have to think for a second before you could pinpoint the worst date," Gina said.

Eleanor smiled. "Yes. That's true. It was awful, though. Online dating is something I'll never try again."

"Never?"

"Never. There's a lot of people who lie on their profiles. Some even use someone else's picture. It's the Wild West." Eleanor caught Sophia as her legs gave out and she started to fall. She picked her up and deposited her back into the playpen.

"No way," Gina said. "They just used someone else's photo? What do they say when you point it out?"

"Well, then they point out that it doesn't matter because it's superficial."

"Ah." Gina nodded. "By which time, you've already decided you want the date to end."

"Precisely." Eleanor walked into the kitchen area. "Can I help with dinner?"

Gina was just finishing layering the vegetable lasagne. "Nope. All done. We just need to put it in the oven. Did you use a photo of you on the dating websites?"

"Oh no, I found a photo of Kate Winslet to use."

Gina grinned. "Good choice."

Eleanor watched Gina putting the dish in the oven and marvelled at how quickly her mood had turned. She'd gone from exhausted and stressed to relaxed and even laughing. The little bubble they had formed was safe and comforting. And Gina was the glue that held it all together, whether she knew that or not.

"Is everything okay?" Gina asked, suddenly aware of Eleanor's staring.

She blinked and looked away. "Yes, just lost in my thoughts."

"Happy ones, I hope?"

"Actually, yes. For a change."

CHAPTER SEVENTEEN

Eleanor sat up in bed. Her heart was pounding, and her T-shirt stuck to her skin with sweat. But it wasn't like the other times she had woken from a dream. This wasn't a nightmare fuelled by events at work. This was a pleasant dream, the nature of which she couldn't recall experiencing for years.

She ran a hand over her face, trying to wake herself up and chase away the remnants of arousal.

The thrill of the dream quickly disappeared as the reality hit her. She felt guilty for having a dream about Gina, especially one of a sexual nature, even though she logically knew it was out of her control.

"You can't control your dreams," she whispered into the dark of her bedroom.

She knew that it was true, but it was also true that her subconscious must have taken its cues from somewhere. She could count the number of times she'd had dreams about sex and knew they had never included a woman.

Now she felt confused. On one hand, she'd been extremely turned on during the dream, but on the other she was ashamed now that she was awake. But whether that shame was rooted in the fact that Gina was a woman, or that Gina was someone she knew, she couldn't be certain. The whole thing felt inappropriate. Eleanor couldn't fathom why she'd had the dream or why she felt the way she did now.

She looked at the clock and was irritated to see that it was five thirty in the morning. Too early to get up, too late to properly fall back asleep again. Not that she imagined sleep would come.

Jolting awake meant she felt wide awake. She knew that feeling would not last for long. A couple of hours at work and she would be feeling every minute of lost sleep.

She climbed out of bed. A long shower might remove the lingering thoughts of Gina, or at least dream-Gina, from her mind.

❖

"Dr. Osborne?"

Eleanor was nearly at the exit to the COVID ward. She had one finger inside the folded lip of her rubber glove, ready to pull it off and begin the procedure of unwrapping herself from layers of protective gear.

She paused and turned.

A nurse was hurrying through the busy ward towards her.

"Dr. Osborne, Marissa said you were asking about Patrick Henley the other day."

Eleanor pulled her glove back on tight.

"Yes, that's right."

"He's taken a turn. Dr. Freeman is considering intubating."

Eleanor was already walking back into the ward.

"Thank you for letting me know," she said.

She hurried back through the wards. It had been a long morning. The number of patients coming in was growing every day, impossibly so. Every time she felt they couldn't possibly receive any more patients, more turned up. Every staff member was waiting for a levelling off that never came.

The death toll was growing, too. Eleanor had signed off more deaths in the last week than she had done in the last ten years combined. Every life was precious, but the man she barely knew, who she was now rushing to get to, was a different matter.

Without permission, Gina's smiling face from that morning

came into her mind's eye. She had barely been able to maintain eye contact with Gina after the dream. If Gina had noticed her discomfort, she hadn't mentioned it.

She arrived at Patrick Henley's bed to see Mark Freeman and a team of four nurses surrounding the bed in a hive of activity. Mark looked over the head of a nurse and looked questioningly at Eleanor.

"I know him," she explained. "Can I help?"

Mark shook his head. "We're getting him proned and maybe on a vent. He suddenly took a turn this afternoon."

The cruellest thing about COVID, to Eleanor's mind, was the unpredictability of it. Who it would hit and how it would hit them still remained a mystery. Some suffered for weeks with a minor cough before suddenly being hospitalised. Some caught the virus and were immediately bedridden. There was no pattern that Eleanor or any of her colleagues could discern. And no treatment. When a patient became unable to breathe, intubating them was the only course of action left.

She nodded towards Mark and stepped to the bedside to help. Proning a patient required a large team of staff to turn the patient to a position where the pressure on their lungs would be reduced.

Listening to the support team shouting vital statistics, she agreed with Mark's assessment. Proning would be the first step, and ventilation would probably be the second. That was all they could do for Patrick now. The rest was up to him.

❖

Eleanor entered the cardiology staff room wearily. Nigel looked up from his phone and gave her a tight smile. Even he had become worn down. His boundless good humour had been beaten by the seemingly hopeless situation.

"You okay?" he asked.

She shook her head. "I have to tell Gina that her father is on a ventilator."

Nigel's expression remained neutral. "I'm sorry."

Eleanor opened her locker and got her phone from her bag. She gestured towards the empty cardiology ward. "I'll just go and make this call."

She had rehearsed what she wanted to say the entire way from the COVID wards. Giving families bad news was the worst part of the job. When it was personal, it was so much worse.

The cardiology ward was empty, all the essential cases having been moved to a distant pop-up ward or another hospital. All scheduled procedures were on hold for no one knew how long. It was surreal to see the rows of empty beds and all the equipment having been removed.

She sat on the edge of a bed and held the phone in front of her as she FaceTimed Gina. Her camera activated and she could see just how drained she looked. Deep red marks from the PPE burrowed into her skin. As each day passed and things seemed to get impossibly worse, she tightened the mask and goggles. Some days she wondered if the bruising would be permanent.

Gina's smiling face appeared on the screen. "Hey!"

Eleanor hesitated. All words fell from her mind and clattered uselessly on the ward floor.

Gina's smile vanished. "Oh, right. This…isn't a social call."

"I'm afraid we've had to put your father on a ventilator." Eleanor quickly managed to find her tongue. She knew from experience that another couple of moments would lead Gina to think the worst.

Gina bit her lip and nodded rapidly. "Okay. Okay. So what does that mean?"

"It means he was struggling to breathe, and now the ventilator is doing that for him."

Gina swallowed and wiped at her eye. "Okay. So he…can't breathe?"

"It was a lot of strain for him to breathe. This takes some of the pressure off his body."

"Is he going to die?" Gina asked bluntly.

"I don't know," Eleanor confessed. "We're doing all we can. But I'm afraid there's not enough known about COVID to be certain of anything. I'm sorry."

Gina sucked in a deep breath, presumably to keep herself calm. "I'm sorry. I wish I had better news," Eleanor said.

"It's not your fault. I know you're dealing with a lot. I appreciate you calling me," Gina said. A hint of a smile tugged at her mouth. "Thank you, I really know you're doing all you can."

"I'll let you know anything else I find out," Eleanor promised.

"Thank you. I better go and call my mum. See you tonight."

"See you tonight."

Eleanor hung up the call. She placed the phone beside her on the bed and let out a big sigh. Gina had taken it well, but Eleanor hadn't. Seeing the flurry of emotions fly across Gina's face had been hard. She'd wanted to be there, so she could deliver the news in person and hold and comfort her.

The realisation that Gina was closer to her than anyone else hit her like a brick. She didn't know when Gina had taken the crown from Nigel or even her sister, but she had. It seemed bizarre that it had happened and in such a short space of time. Gina had gone from a neighbour and babysitter to the person Eleanor spent the whole day thinking about and rushing home to. The person Eleanor dreamt of. The person Eleanor felt the need to hold.

Eleanor flopped down on the bed and stared up at the ceiling. The world didn't make sense any more. She knew that she was happy to have Gina in her life, but it seemed somehow wrong to feel positive about anything that was happening as a result of a pandemic.

Logically, she knew she should take the positives where she could. There were precious few of them right now. But guilt nibbled at her. Did she deserve to find some kind of happiness in such terrible circumstances? And, most importantly, what was happening with her feelings towards Gina?

Chapter Eighteen

Gina opened the apartment front door and stepped to one side to allow Eleanor in. She imagined her eyes were still red from her intermittent crying all afternoon. She tried to look strong but knew she was failing by the sympathetic look Eleanor gave her.

"How are you?" Eleanor asked softly.

Gina handed Sophia over. "I'm okay. I can't really be anything else. There's not a lot we can do. My mum is freaking out—I wish I could go and comfort her. But we're all stuck dealing with this on our own."

"You have me," Eleanor said.

Gina smiled, her first genuine smile since she'd heard the news about her dad. She didn't know what she'd do without Eleanor. The pandemic had brought a lot of terrible things into her life, but it had also brought her the bright lights of Sophia and Eleanor. She didn't think she'd have been able to hold it together that afternoon if she hadn't had them both.

"Thank you." Without thinking, she leaned in and placed a soft kiss on Eleanor's cheek and then a matching one on Sophia's.

As she walked into the kitchen to start dinner, she realised what she had done and felt heat upon her cheeks. It was a casual kiss, the sort she would frequently share with her friends, a peck on the cheek to show friendship or gratitude. But she didn't know Eleanor that well and had no idea if they were at that point in their relationship. She'd moved purely on instinct, and now she was worried about Eleanor's reaction. She couldn't make eye contact with Eleanor and instead opened the fridge door and hoped the chill would take any residual redness from her face.

"I couldn't decide what to have for dinner," she called over, hoping to sound natural.

It was just a kiss on the cheek, but it felt different with Eleanor. Meaningful. Possibly dangerous.

"Would you like me to cook?" Eleanor sounded just as confused as she did, and obviously not because of the lack of dinner plans.

Gina reached for some plates. "No, it's fine. Leftovers and salad, I think. Use up some of this food. Does that sound okay?"

"Sounds great."

Gina started to prepare the food. Her mind was elsewhere, mainly thinking back to the phone call with her mum, who'd told her all kinds of things about people who went on ventilators. Basically, her mum explained that it was the end for her dad. Gina didn't know what to believe. She knew that the death toll was growing every day.

For the first time in a long time, she'd sat down and watched the news that afternoon. While Sophia slept in her arms, she listened to reports of hospitals overflowing with patients, the spread of the virus, the numbers of people sick and dying.

Old Gina would have turned the television off and put some music on to distract her. Anything to avoid the terrible news and pretend nothing was happening. Now she wanted to know.

She felt different lately. Still herself but not quite. She remembered when one of her party-loving friends fell pregnant. After the baby was born, she'd gone through an enormous metamorphosis over the course of under a week, from someone who had no idea how to even boil water to becoming a mum. At the time, Gina had mourned the loss of her friend and felt that she'd changed because circumstances had wrenched her old life away from her.

It was only now, while going through a change of her own, that Gina realised that change hadn't been placed upon her friend like a burden. A change in perspective and priorities had caused it.

Gina had never been able to understand how someone could change so much in such a short period of time. Until now. Now she saw her own change happening before her eyes. She'd stopped sulking about the cancelled music festivals and started understanding what was happening in the country. People were dying every day and leaving friends and families behind. The virus was leaving a scar across the nation, one that grew every day.

It wasn't just that her dad had become unwell—it was seeing Eleanor at the front line of this viral war every single day, seeing someone she cared about so deeply distressed when she arrived home every night, the bruising of PPE still clear on her face. The empty streets and the frightened looks from elderly people when she popped into the supermarket for supplies had slowly chipped away at her childish concerns about her own personal freedoms being taken away.

Gina understood now that her staying home meant that the virus spread less, and that meant she was doing her part. She couldn't join Eleanor in A & E, she couldn't drive an ambulance, she wasn't a scientist searching for a cure or a vaccine. But staying home and avoiding people was her assignment. Simple and soulless, but probably the most important thing that she could do.

"Eleanor, what might happen to my dad next?" Gina asked.

She wanted to be prepared. Her mum had already gone to the worst-case scenario. Gina had to know whether to prepare her mum for the worst or to soothe her and tell her that there was a chance. She'd never been in this situation before, never been the adult in the conversation. Her mum had never needed her to be that person.

"It's hard to say," Eleanor said.

Gina could tell that she was holding back. Eleanor had changed, too, over the days and weeks. In the past, her professional approach had been ice-cold and clinical, giving details Gina hadn't been prepared for. Now, Eleanor moderated her replies and took a moment to think about whether Gina needed to hear what she was going to say.

It had taken Gina covering her ears and shaking her head a few times when Eleanor explained how she intubated someone for Eleanor to realise Gina was too squeamish for that level of detail.

Gina appreciated the consideration. But now she needed to know.

"Eleanor, really, what might happen?"

Eleanor was holding Sophia's arms and walking her around the living room. She paused as she considered her words.

"His lungs are full," Eleanor said. "We'll do what we can to help him fight the virus. But it's taken hold of him. He's prone, on his stomach, to allow his lungs more space and energy to work again. The ventilator is breathing for him until we think he can take over. But he might not. It's really impossible to know."

"Do many patients on ventilators survive?" Gina asked.

"I don't know the statistics—it's too early to know for sure. But you can consider the fact that he is on a ventilator an indication of how serious his condition is."

Gina heard the warning loud and clear. She sucked in a shaky breath and continued with her dinner preparations. Her appetite was gone, but she knew that Eleanor and Sophia needed to eat. If they weren't there, she would have simply gone without an evening meal and maybe eaten some chocolate while kicking herself for all the times she hadn't seen her father when she'd had the opportunity.

Suddenly, Eleanor was next to her, taking her shaking hands off the Tupperware container that she was struggling to open as tears escaped down her cheeks.

"Let me deal with dinner," Eleanor said. "Go and sit down."

She didn't know how long she had been standing crying but she imagined it was a while considering Eleanor's tone and the fact that Sophia was back in her playpen.

"I'm sorry," Gina said.

Eleanor captured her arm as she tried to walk away. She softly spun Gina around to face her. She placed her hands on either side of Gina's face, cupping her cheeks and encouraging Gina to make eye contact.

"There is absolutely nothing to be sorry for," Eleanor said, her face centimetres away from Gina's. Her eyes bored into Gina, conveying care, warmth, and kindness.

It was all Gina could do not to cry again, but this time from relief and gratitude that Eleanor was there with her. She tipped her head in a tiny nod. Eleanor released her and turned towards the counter to prepare the food.

Gina watched her for a second. She was falling for Eleanor. It was becoming clearer to her all the time. She pushed the thought away. There was no room for that as well as the worry about her family. But she knew that soon she'd have to face facts.

Chapter Nineteen

Gina shouldered the phone as she poured frozen fruit into her smoothie maker.

"You're a fool," she told her friend of fifteen years with absolute seriousness.

"What harm will it do? It's only ten of us. We're all under forty. No one will know," Charlie explained.

"I cannot believe you're even considering having a party." Gina put the lid on the pitcher. She held the phone in her hand. "I'm serious. You're a fool."

"No one will catch us. We'll keep the music low. I mean, who's to know how many people are in a house? No one's paying attention."

"That's not the point. What if one of us is sick?"

"It's a cold—we'll get over it."

Gina gritted her teeth. She hadn't made a big announcement that her dad was in hospital. She didn't want to have to field a hundred questions from people or listen to their well-meaning words. People rarely knew what to say when something bad happened. In the end it was a wall of pep talks and assumptions that everything would be fine.

"And if we all get it and then we spread it to others?" Gina asked. She was barely able to contain her anger.

"What? They expect us to be locked up forever? This is illegal, you know. I looked it up online."

"Have you always been such a twit, or has the pandemic scrambled your brain?" Gina asked.

"Hey!"

"No, you listen to me. This virus is really serious, Charlie. I'm babysitting for a doctor, and you should hear about the things she's seeing every single day. They are seeing more patients die every day than you can even imagine. And every time someone dies, another ten people arrive a second later. It's relentless. This virus is spreading. Fools like you breaking the rules are helping it to spread. And you may be fine, but you might not be. There are twenty-year-olds in hospital right now, and before you tell me that they're obese or have an underlying condition, not all of them. And there's the chance that you, or me, or someone we know and love has an underlying condition that hasn't been diagnosed yet. Did you even consider that?"

"Gi—"

"No, I don't even want to talk to you. I know you'll go ahead and have this party. I know you'll lie and tell me you didn't, but I know you. And I'm really disappointed in how selfish you are."

"Gi, hold on," Charlie pleaded. "What's going on?"

Gina bit her lip. She didn't want to tell him. Didn't want to even talk to someone who was willing to put themselves and others at risk. But then she acknowledged that Charlie was *her* a few weeks ago. She'd changed. She'd seen and heard things that had made her re-evaluate what she thought she knew. Speaking to Charlie was like hearing an unflattering echo of her past.

"I've grown up," she said simply.

"Gi?"

"This pandemic has changed me, Charlie. I used to be like you, complaining about the shops closing, wondering when international travel would be back." Gina sat on a stool at her breakfast bar and rested her head in her hand. "But then I started to check my privilege. This doctor I know, you should hear what she goes through. She doesn't complain. But she's putting her life at risk every day. She's hoping she doesn't catch it, but she has to treat people who have it."

"I know it's bad," Charlie admitted.

"It really is. All we have to do is stay home. The more this thing spreads, the longer we'll all be locked up. You have a party with ten people and they all get infected, then who will those ten infect? And then who do they go on to infect?"

Charlie hesitated a second. "I know that, it's just—"

"Charlie, my dad is on a ventilator. I don't want everyone knowing. But that's where I am right now. It makes me feel sick that I would have attended this party a few weeks ago. But I know better now. Not just because of my dad, but because of what I'm seeing and hearing. Honestly, I'm different now, and I don't like how selfish I was. This pandemic, this virus, is really showing us that we have to care for each other. And it's really sad how many people can't do that. Don't have the party. Stay home and stay safe, yeah?"

Gina hung up the call. She blew out a breath and shook her head. She didn't know if she got through to Charlie or not. He was about as stubborn as she was.

She went over to her smoothie machine, the latest in her long list of pandemic purchases. She added some milk and switched it on, watching as the frozen fruit quickly turned into a mulch.

It was turning into a strange day. Eleanor had a day off from work, her first in a long time, and she was spending it at home with Sophia. Gina missed them both immensely and it was only mid-morning.

Nothing felt stable any more. Despite the fact that her job and home hadn't changed at all, she felt as if her world was shifting and there was little she could do about it.

She couldn't visit her family. Her father was in hospital and she wasn't sure she'd ever see him again. She was to stay in her apartment until the government decided it was safe for her to leave. Life was strange.

And yet, Gina's main thoughts were with Eleanor and Sophia just a few doors away. She wondered what they were doing on Eleanor's day off. She wondered if Eleanor had managed to sleep in.

Above all, she wondered when Eleanor had become such an important part of her life. When had she gone from the woman she was doing a favour for to the woman she spent most of the day thinking about? And why had she placed a kiss on Eleanor's cheek a couple of evenings ago?

She turned the machine off and poured the liquid into a glass. Thankfully, Eleanor was straight and wouldn't be interested in her. So all Gina needed to do was hold back and wait for whatever feelings she had to pass.

❖

Gina hadn't expected a knock on the door at four o'clock in the afternoon. No one knocked on her door these days unless it was Eleanor dropping off or picking up Sophia. But that didn't happen in the middle of the day. Although, judging from the loud cries from the other side of the door, it was Eleanor on the other side.

She opened the door. Eleanor was holding Sophia and grimacing. Sophia was bawling and hanging loosely in Eleanor's arms. Eleanor attempted to reposition her so she didn't fall, but that just caused Sophia to scream louder and flop backwards.

Gina took hold of Sophia and held her tight. She'd worked out a while ago that Sophia liked to be held very tight when she was upset, even though she initially acted like she wanted to be released.

"She's been like this for an hour," Eleanor said. "I'm so sorry to come here, but I was getting to the end of my tether. She's not had a nap. She's…she's—"

"Unsettled," Gina said. "She didn't know her daily routine was going to change. Come in."

Eleanor looked hesitant.

"Come in, before the neighbours think we're murdering your child," Gina said over Sophia's screams.

Eleanor stepped inside the apartment and closed the door. "I feel like such a failure. She would not stop crying for me. I would have thought that she'd tire herself out by now, but she just keeps going. If anything, she's gotten more upset rather than tired."

"She's stubborn," Gina said.

"And loud."

"Yes, she's pretty impressive all-round." Gina placed Sophia's head against her chest. She positioned one ear against her and covered the other with her hand and started gently swinging them both.

Gina could feel Eleanor's eyes on them. She looked defeated.

"She doesn't like change, you know that," Gina said.

"Yes, but I thought I'd be a constant in her life. That she might react badly to, I don't know, a new flavour. Or a cuddly toy which someone bought her. Not that I wouldn't be able to soothe my own child because we were in our home for a few hours together." Eleanor slumped on the sofa and watched Gina walk around the room with Sophia in her arms. "I wish I could turn back time. To think I would be able to do this was clearly madness."

"Don't say that," Gina said. "You don't mean it."

"I do. What kind of life is this for her? She spends more time with you than she does me. I don't know the little tricks to get her to calm down. And on top of all that, there's the lingering risk that I might infect her. What was I thinking?"

"Are you like this at work?" Gina asked. "One little bump and then you don't know what to do?"

Eleanor narrowed her eyes and glared at her.

"Thought not." Gina kept moving, knowing that the movement would distract and soothe Sophia, whose cries were lessening all the time. "Because life happened and this is where we all are right now. And that's not your fault. And it's not her fault. It's just the way life is at the moment. It's not great, but it's life."

"She's my child," Eleanor said. "I should be able to soothe her."

"That's toxic bullshit," Gina told her. "Honestly, there's this assumption that mothers are superhuman creatures who can do it all, and if they can't then they have failed. Just because you're Sophia's mum, that doesn't mean that you can always fix everything. It just means that you have to love her."

Eleanor looked as if she was about to counter with a reply but paused and looked thoughtful instead. Gina hoped that she'd gotten through to her. No one needed to drown in guilt, especially when it was guilt about being the perfect mother. Society constantly peddled that mantra, and it was wrong, damagingly so.

Gina continued walking around the room, bouncing Sophia and doing her best to distract her. After a few minutes, Sophia's constant crying broke into intermittent howls. Minutes later, she finally stopped and sagged against Gina in exhaustion.

Taking a seat next to Eleanor on the sofa, Gina continued holding Sophia and waited for her to fall asleep. If she'd missed her nap and had been crying for some time, then it was obvious that sleep would arrive soon. Gina just needed to wait.

Eleanor sat silently, just watching the two of them but saying nothing. Gina wanted to talk but knew that Sophia was drifting and there was a chance that she would wake again if disturbed.

They sat in silence, occasionally meeting each other's gaze. Gina couldn't recall when she had so comfortably shared silence with someone else. She used to fear silence, wanting to put music on or start a conversation instead. Now she was perfectly content to sit quietly, Sophia in her arms and Eleanor by her side.

When Sophia napped at Gina's, she slept in an armchair right in plain view of where Gina worked. Gina rarely used that armchair, so she left the temporary bed made up, with sheets and a protective pillow to stop Sophia potentially rolling to the floor.

Gina didn't want Eleanor to take Sophia back home. She'd missed them and was enjoying the company. So instead of handing Sophia back to Eleanor, Gina put her in the armchair, covered her with a blanket, and turned off the lamp in that part of the room.

The darker environment made it oddly romantic. Gina sat back on the sofa, not knowing what else to do.

"Tea?"

"No. Thank you."

"Any other beverage?" Gina tried again.

Eleanor shook her head.

They sat in silence for a while until Eleanor said, "I'm sorry. I shouldn't have come here. I was just at my wits' end."

"It's fine. It's not like I wouldn't be in. And I actually kinda like seeing you both."

"That's a relief," Eleanor said. "I didn't mean what I said. She is the most precious thing to me—of course I don't regret having her. I regret there being a pandemic, of course."

"I know."

"It's hard being a single mother," Eleanor said. "And that sounds so foreign coming from my lips because I have been told that a thousand times, and I knew it would be true. But the reality of it all hit me harder than I thought it would. I honestly thought it wouldn't be this hard. The things I thought I would struggle with came relatively easy. The things I thought would be easy, well..."

"You're a really good mum," Gina said.

"I don't feel it."

"That's because you're a good mum. You want to give her the world and make sure everything is as easy for her as possible. But life isn't always like that."

"You're very wise," Eleanor said. She leaned her head back on the sofa and smiled at Gina. "When did you get so wise?"

"Literally in the last few weeks," Gina said with a laugh. "I think this pandemic made an adult out of me."

"You were always an adult—look around you." Eleanor gestured to the apartment.

"Maybe. But I really feel like I've grown up recently."

"I think this situation has made a lot of people grow up. And a lot of people are taking a second look at their lives. Deciding what is important and what isn't."

"True. I think it's forced everyone to stop and really look at their choices." Gina thought of Kath and her change of outlook that was fuelling a full change of direction including looking at her home life, career, life goals. Kath had never been happier.

"Maybe, in many years, when all this is over, some people will look back and be able to see the positives," Eleanor mused.

"Probably," Gina agreed.

Gina had already come to terms with her thoughts about the

pandemic. She had decided that it was horrible and an opportunity in equal measure. People who survived would emerge from the pandemic with wildly different experiences.

She'd been very young when her father had sat her down and explained to her that it was entirely possible to like and dislike something at the same time. The example he had used was bedtime. Gina disliked it because she didn't want to go to bed, but she liked to feel rested in the morning. She'd taken the lesson with her, and the pandemic was turning into a good example of an experience both terrible and somehow brimming with opportunity, at the same time.

"I'm glad I met you," Eleanor said.

"I'm glad I met you," Gina replied.

"Not just for your babysitting services," Eleanor added.

Gina felt a pleasant shiver run up her spine. Sitting in the dim light, with Eleanor only centimetres away, it would be so easy to imagine them in different circumstances.

She was just beginning to enjoy the fantasy of their relationship being something else, something more, when Eleanor leaned forward and kissed her.

Gina's muddled mind rushed to catch up. Eleanor, straight Eleanor, was initiating a kiss. A very nice kiss that Gina had thankfully automatically responded to.

Just as Gina was relaxing into it, Eleanor sprang backwards and jumped to her feet.

"I'm sorry. I shouldn't have done that."

Gina stood, too. She was still reeling from the unexpected kiss and unable to form a sentence.

Eleanor was carefully lifting Sophia into her arms. "We should go."

"You don't have to," Gina said.

"I think we should. I'm so sorry. I shouldn't have done that. It didn't mean anything. My emotions were just running high."

"It's fine." Gina didn't know why she was claiming that it was fine when she felt anything but. She felt confused and a little hurt. Why would Eleanor kiss her if it meant nothing? Why would

Eleanor kiss her at all? It had come completely out of the blue, unless Eleanor was feeling the same way Gina had been feeling lately.

Whatever had happened, it was clear that she wasn't about to get an answer from Eleanor. She was already on her way to the front door to escape the tricky situation.

Gina rushed over to open the door for her.

"I'm sorry," Eleanor whispered.

"It's fine," Gina repeated. She wanted to kick herself for repeating her false claim that everyone was okay. It wasn't okay. She wasn't okay. But she was still too confused to know what to do.

Eleanor slipped through the door with Sophia in her arms and didn't look back. Gina closed the front door and leaned her back against it.

She didn't believe for a moment that Eleanor had meant that it was a mistake. People didn't just randomly kiss someone, even if emotions were running high. Which meant that there was a very real possibility that Eleanor felt something for Gina.

Gina pushed herself away from the door and paced the room.

She'd assumed that Eleanor might not be as straight as she thought, but she'd never considered that Eleanor might be interested in her. She remembered the times they had spent together and realised that they had become closer than friends would.

She sat on the arm of the sofa and stared into nothing. Eleanor said it meant nothing. But Gina didn't believe that. And Gina had already recognised and tried to bury the feelings she'd been experiencing for Eleanor. Now she needed to decide what to do next.

Was Eleanor going through some sort of sexual awakening? Was Gina the only available woman to test these new feelings on? Gina didn't think so. Eleanor didn't seem like the sort of person who would play the field or toy with someone else's feelings like that. Eleanor had been the woman searching for a serious relationship for years. It seemed unlikely that she would suddenly choose to jump into bed with anyone available.

Which meant, whether Eleanor was ready to admit it or not, the feelings she had for Gina ran deeper than either of them knew.

Which in turn meant that it was up to Gina to steer what happened next.

A kiss or more with Eleanor wouldn't be a casual fling. Eleanor and Sophia came as a package, and that meant a built-in family. If Gina was going to even consider a relationship with Eleanor, she had to be all-in.

A thought that didn't scare her as much as it might have once before.

CHAPTER TWENTY

Eleanor dialled the number she knew off by heart and held the phone to her ear. She sat at the dining table with a large glass of red wine and waited for her sister to pick up.

"Hey, Elle. How's it going?" Laura said.

Eleanor released a sigh at the soothing voice of her sister. Being so far away from her was usual after five years apart. Unlike her other friendships that had been suddenly torn apart by pandemic restrictions, staying close while being physically distant from Laura was their normal. And normal was something she craved at the moment.

"Rough," Eleanor admitted. "How are things there?"

"Pretty bad. But not as bad as it is where you are," Laura said, assuming Eleanor was talking about the pandemic. Eleanor couldn't blame her—it was all anyone was talking about. Why would anyone be starting a call off on any other subject with the way the world was at the moment?

"Yes, we seem to be getting it harder than many other countries," Eleanor agreed.

"Why is that?"

"We're not sure." She took a sip of wine. "There's a lot we're not sure about. We're an island with a huge population of people who travel, either for holidays or to see family. And we have an abundance of people who don't look after their health, something this virus seems to target. It exposes flaws and weaknesses. Going after older people, people with breathing difficulties, larger people."

"I bet work is insane."

"It is."

"Are you holding up okay?" Laura asked.

"I don't know." Eleanor took another sip of wine. "I don't feel like myself. But I don't know if this is the me I am in this situation, or if I'm losing my mind. It's hard to say."

"I know it's hard, but you've got to take care of yourself."

"I know." She took another sip of wine, preparing herself for what she knew she had to say. "Laura, I need a favour."

"Sure, anything."

"I'm on the front line. There's a possibility I might catch this thing, and we really don't know what that would mean. If something happens to me, if I die, I need you to take Sophia."

"Of course I will. But nothing will happen to you. You can't think like that," Laura said.

"I have to be practical. I wasn't very practical when I had Sophia. In fact, I was selfish. And now she might pay the price. There's a real possibility that she might grow up without a mother. Maybe… maybe I shouldn't have had her." Eleanor sipped some more wine. She hated to say that out loud, but she had to. The thought had been bouncing around her head for weeks. For all her planning, had she been oblivious to the reality that she had no safety net? Did she ignore the obvious signals because she really wanted a baby?

"Maybe you're stressed and tired and need to relax," Laura suggested.

"This was my day off. I spent it realising I don't know my daughter very well. She spent most of the day crying. I had to take her to the babysitter to get her to calm down. What kind of a mother is that?"

"Every mother who works," Laura said. "Sorry, Elle. That's just life. Kids get used to whoever they spend the most time with. If it's not you, then they'll take some adjustment in getting used to you. That's kids. In fact, that's people."

"Maybe." Eleanor stretched her neck to try to release some of the tension. "Thankfully, Gina is very good with her. You should have seen it. She had Sophia quiet in five minutes, asleep in ten."

"Good. I remember when you were worried about leaving Sophia with her. Now you're worried about…her being a better mother?" Laura asked.

"I'm not worried. I'm just…" Eleanor paused. "Well, yes, okay, I'm worried. What if Sophia prefers her?"

"She's a baby, she probably does. She doesn't have the higher emotional centre to make a distinction about who she prefers. She lives in the now. But if she started to spend all her time with you, then you'd be the favourite. Don't read too much into what you think Sophia prefers."

Eleanor stood up and walked over to the window. "That's not at all comforting."

"Maybe not. But it is the truth."

Eleanor looked down to the empty street below. It was still surreal to see so few people around. When she was at work, it was busier than she had ever seen it before. Teams were growing, incoming patient numbers increasing. And yet, outside work, there was hardly a soul to be seen. It was eerie.

"Just be glad you have a good babysitter—they are worth their weight in gold," Laura said.

"That's true." Eleanor recalled the unreliable people who had gone before. Sophia didn't adore them. Eleanor didn't want to kiss them.

She closed her eyes and turned away from the window. Embarrassment flooded through her. She had no idea why she had suddenly decided it would be a good idea to act upon her feelings and actually kiss Gina. It was as if she was possessed. One minute, she was thinking how wonderful Gina was with Sophia, and the next moment she was pressing a kiss to Gina's luscious lips.

"Elle?"

"Sorry, what?"

"I was asking if you're still having dinner with your babysitter."

"Yes. Yes, it makes sense. Rather than me rushing home. And she's lonely—it's hard for her to be locked up at home all day. She's used to going out. Seeing her friends."

Eleanor realised she'd provided a little more information than was required, something her sister would no doubt pick up on. She'd already suggested that she thought it was odd that Eleanor's babysitter was happily cooking her dinner every night.

It had seemed quite the normal thing until Eleanor had explained it to someone else.

"She seems really nice," Laura said. "Good with children, cooks dinner, reliable, fun to talk to. Wish I'd had that sort of a babysitter. Or that sort of a husband."

Eleanor bit her lip. She knew Laura was trying to coax more information out of her. Now that Eleanor considered it, she had been speaking a lot about Gina. Her feelings had obviously been bubbling away for some time to suddenly pop out. Laura had probably been aware of them without Eleanor really having a clue.

"How is he doing?" Eleanor asked, swerving the subject away from Gina.

She'd never gotten along with her brother-in-law, but she'd much rather talk about him than allow Laura access to any further information. Laura had a habit of simplifying everything. Eleanor was the sensible one, the one who analysed something from every single angle and even created pros-and-cons lists before a relatively simple decision was made.

Except she hadn't been sensible. She'd been strangely reckless, and she'd confused poor Gina. Eleanor hadn't even been able to look at Gina when she'd run away. When she'd first broken the kiss, she'd seen shock in Gina's gaze, and she hadn't known what it meant—didn't want to know what it had meant. All she'd wanted to do was run away. So she did. After issuing an apology and some nonsense about being emotional. As if she kissed just anyone when she felt overwhelmed.

But it had been the best she could do at the time. She just hoped no damage had been done. She didn't want to hurt Gina, and she certainly didn't want to take advantage of her. Just because Eleanor had experienced intimate dreams of Gina and started to question her own sexuality, that was no reason to drag Gina into her drama.

Gina who was kind, intelligent, and surprisingly hot.

Eleanor shook her head and tried to refocus on her sister's

conversation. But she couldn't. She'd brought back memories of the kiss. Memories of the dreams. Memories of the realisation that Gina was all the things Eleanor wanted in a partner.

On top of that, Gina was a good kisser. A fact that Eleanor wished she didn't know.

She tried again to push the feelings away. She couldn't risk her friendship with Gina. It wasn't right. She decided then and there that she would ignore the fact that the kiss ever happened and apologise again to Gina if it ever came up.

It wasn't right that someone of her age should be lusting over someone like Gina. And she certainly shouldn't be kissing them without their consent. Shame smothered her again and she sat down at the dining room table and winced. She didn't know what had possessed her. And she didn't know if she could ever apologise enough.

Chapter Twenty-one

Gina watched Sophia slowly work her way around the coffee table. She'd managed to pick up some speed and stability lately as long as she was holding on to something. She'd almost stopped crawling, willing to give all her attention to the next big leap in her growth.

Gina sat in the armchair, allowing Eleanor to have the whole sofa to herself. It seemed safer to keep some distance between them. Not that anything had happened in the two days since Eleanor had kissed her. Nothing except the initial apologies and then the silent agreement to never speak of it again.

The incident had left a strange atmosphere in the apartment, as if the air was charged with something ready to ignite. Neither of them mentioned it.

"So you just booked the flight there and then?" Gina asked.

In her attempt to start up conversation and break the silence, she'd asked Eleanor about her travels. Surprisingly, it seemed that Eleanor had at one point been very interested in seeing the world. Until work and obligation got in the way and she slowly stopped her adventures.

"Yes, I'd seen a documentary about the history of New Orleans and it seemed so interesting. I went online, found a flight leaving the next day, and booked it."

Gina smiled. "That seems so very unlike you."

"I can be spontaneous," Eleanor replied.

The smile on her lips vanished as she seemed to realise that they both had evidence of Eleanor's spontaneity, and it was the subject they were trying to avoid.

"Did you like New Orleans?" Gina asked, hoping to wrestle the conversation back on track and not have another evening peppered with long and awkward silences.

"I loved it. I wasn't so interested in the drinking and partying culture, that's not my thing. But the history, the music, the food, the people." Eleanor looked wistful as she remembered the trip. "It was such a culture shock. In a good way. Have you been?"

"No. It's on my list. If travel ever opens up again."

"It will. It may seem like a long time, but things will get back to some sense of normality. I'm sure of it."

Gina didn't know if Eleanor was just saying that to make her feel better or if she actually knew that there would be a time when things went back to the way they were. Whether it was true or not, Gina was going to hold on to the idea.

Sophia took a step away from the coffee table, ready to make yet another attempt at walking. Eleanor held out her arms, encouraging Sophia to come towards her. Sophia stopped, focused all of her attention on her goal, and then fell on her bottom.

Gina laughed. "She hesitates and her centre of gravity knocks her over every time."

Eleanor lifted Sophia up to her feet again. "You're right. She's psyching herself up too much."

Gina knelt on the floor in front of Sophia. "Don't think, just do. Just…run."

Sophia looked at Gina and giggled. Gina jumped to her feet and took hold of Sophia's arms and lifted her up so just her feet touched the ground. She started to race around the apartment, letting Sophia's feet mimic walking.

"I hope she doesn't end up walking that fast," Eleanor said over the sound of Gina's racing noises.

Eleanor's phone rang. Gina stopped making the noises and slowed down, allowing Sophia time to stop giggling and to move her legs in time with Gina's.

Sophia was tired from all the excitement, so Gina put her back in the playpen, where she immediately picked up a toy telephone and held it to her ear in an approximation of what her mother was doing. If Eleanor hadn't been so engrossed in her call, Gina would have pointed it out to her.

Whatever the call was, Eleanor was smiling from ear to ear as she took in the information she was being told. Gina smiled, too. It was nice to see Eleanor receiving some good news. It was nice to see Eleanor happy.

When Eleanor looked up at Gina, she had an expression on her face that Gina couldn't quite read.

"That's great, I'll let her know now. Thanks for calling." Eleanor hung up the call and stood up and walked over to Gina. "Your father is off the ventilator."

Gina felt her eyes widen and she covered her mouth in shock. She'd been preparing herself for bad news. The idea of even thinking about good news felt like she would be jinxing things.

"Seriously?" Gina whispered.

"He's breathing on his own. My colleagues think he's over the worst," Eleanor confirmed.

Gina launched herself at Eleanor, wrapping her arms around Eleanor's shoulders and jumping for joy.

"I thought I'd never see him again," Gina admitted. "I didn't let myself think that he'd get better, just in case he didn't."

Eleanor held Gina close. "I know. I know. But he's going to be okay. That was the duty nurse—he's really rallying."

On top of all the other information that flooded Gina's mind was the knowledge that Eleanor had instructed the duty nurse to let her know of any change immediately, despite her hundreds and hundreds of patients.

"Thank you," Gina whispered. "For everything."

The desire to kiss Eleanor swept over her. She knew she shouldn't do it, but she didn't care any more. The intensity of wanting was so high, she wasn't sure she could hold back even if she wanted to.

She cupped Eleanor's face and planted a kiss on her lips. There was nothing chaste about it. Gina wanted to express all her gratitude and overwhelming affection to Eleanor. The memory of the previous kiss had never left her. She knew they'd agreed to pretend it never happened, but Gina didn't want that. She wanted more.

And it appeared that Eleanor did, too. To Gina's surprise, Eleanor passionately returned the kiss. Eleanor's hand threaded into Gina's hair, holding her in place with her other hand splayed across Gina's back.

Gina didn't want the moment to end. But at the back of her mind was the memory of where this had led to the previous time. Sense returned to her. Gina pulled back a little. "Is this okay?"

"Yes." Eleanor resumed the kiss immediately.

Gina wasn't going to ask again. She gently walked Eleanor backwards towards the sofa without breaking the kiss. When the back of Eleanor's legs hit the sofa, Gina lowered her onto the cushion.

Eleanor shuffled to the side, allowing Gina to join her while not breaking a kiss that was becoming as important as air. Memories of the previous kiss and how it ended nagged at Gina. She remembered feeling confused and hurt, feelings that she didn't wish to repeat. She pulled away.

"I can't."

Eleanor looked stricken.

"If this is nothing," Gina clarified. "If this doesn't mean anything to you, then—"

"It does," Eleanor interjected. "It does."

"But—"

"I've been thinking about you. Thinking about this. I'm sorry I gave you mixed messages before."

"It wasn't mixed," Gina said. "It was a no."

Eleanor licked her lips nervously. "I...know. And I'm sorry. I've had a hard time with this. I have feelings for you, that much I know. But I'm trying to figure everything out."

"Like what?"

"My sexuality, for one." A blush touched Eleanor's cheeks.

"You think you might not be straight?" Gina asked.

Eleanor gestured between them. "I think the evidence is stacking up."

Gina couldn't be swayed by humour just yet. There was something that she needed to know. Something that could definitely end everything for them.

"Are you...testing these new feelings on me?" Gina asked. Her voice had turned into a whisper, and she hated how weak she sounded.

"Absolutely not," Eleanor promised. "I would never do that to you. I meant what I said—I have feelings for you. You're not part of some experiment. Just a part of this journey of discovery for me, if you'll allow it?"

Gina knew Eleanor couldn't make her any promises. Nor could she offer any in return. But Eleanor's reassurance was enough to convince Gina that maybe this was worth pursuing.

"This is all very new to me," Eleanor continued. "I've never even kissed a woman."

"You're pretty good at it," Gina said.

"Only pretty good?" Eleanor teased.

Gina kept her expression neutral as she teased in return. "Remind me."

❖

Eleanor couldn't remember the last time she was kissing on a sofa. She was fairly sure it was decades ago. When Gina had kissed her, all thoughts of stopping had promptly been thrown out of the window. It was as if she'd been given another chance, and she was going to grab it.

She was thankful she had. Even though she still had questions, she knew they wouldn't be answered simply. There was no easy answer to what her heart was telling her. No easy way to grasp that she'd been potentially barking up the wrong tree all her life.

She ran her hand along Gina's side, excited to learn more but also tentative in a way she had never been with a man. It was like a light suddenly flipped on for her. She was experiencing attraction in a way she had never done before. And she liked it.

She pulled away from the kiss to catch her breath.

"You're so young," she whispered.

Gina smiled. "Is that something you're worried about?"

"Everything is something I'm worried about," Eleanor admitted.

"Do you want to stop?"

"Absolutely not."

Gina grinned and leaned in to kiss her, only to stop at the sound of Sophia giggling.

Eleanor sat up on her elbows and looked at her mischievous daughter looking at them both from her playpen.

"Well, that's killed the mood," Gina joked.

Gina disentangled herself from Eleanor and the sofa and stood up. Eleanor watched her go, immediately feeling cold and alone. She didn't want to say goodnight to Gina just now. She didn't even want to be a few metres away from her.

She felt as if she had just discovered something, and now, she wanted to find out more, like when she was researching and pulled on an interesting thread and then proceeded to stay up all night trying to discover more.

Except this time, it was far more intense. Because Eleanor had never been one to be swept away by passion. That was something for films and novels, not for real life. Or so she'd thought until a few minutes ago.

She realised that she probably looked a complete mess, flopped on the sofa, hair and make-up mussed up. But she didn't care. She was happy. Very happy for the first time in a long time.

But real life was encroaching on their slice of paradise, and Eleanor knew there were things to be done before they could—hopefully—return to where they had been interrupted.

"You should probably call your mum," Eleanor said.

Gina looked at Eleanor in surprise before she darted over to her phone. "Oh yes, wow. I completely forgot."

"Partially my fault."

While Gina called her mum, Eleanor picked Sophia up from her playpen.

"You can't watch and giggle at us, you know," she whispered. "Although you did maybe stop us from doing something your little eyes shouldn't see, so maybe that's a good thing."

Her thoughts strayed. Would they have gone further if left to their own devices? Was Gina ready for such a leap? Eleanor was. In fact, she felt she might lose her mind if she didn't spend some more time, intimate time, with Gina very soon.

She walked with Sophia around the kitchen while Gina spoke to her mum. Eleanor could hear what was being said, but her mind was completely preoccupied with what had happened and, more importantly, what she hoped would happen next.

Gina hung up the phone. "Done. Thanks for reminding me."

"Is she okay?" Eleanor asked.

"Ecstatic. They are deliriously in love. I was really worried how Mum would cope without him. You know, if the worst happened."

Eleanor didn't know what to say to that. She wished she had experienced the feeling of being deliriously in love, but she hadn't. She was only recently feeling what she now understood to be real sexual attraction.

"So…" Gina said.

"So…"

"How are you feeling about…" Gina gestured to the sofa.

Eleanor felt her cheeks warm. "I don't regret it, if that's what you're asking."

"But last time—"

"I don't regret it," Eleanor asserted. "In fact, I'm hoping for a repeat."

A smile spread across Gina's face. She stepped closer and softly kissed Eleanor's cheek before tapping Sophia playfully on the nose. "Not with this nosy little one around."

"Well, it is her bedtime." Eleanor turned away under the pretence of walking Sophia around the room. She was working herself up to inviting Gina back to hers, and she couldn't believe she was doing it. Nor did she have any idea what Gina might make of that.

"It is getting late," Gina agreed.

Eleanor knew that Gina was leaving the door open for her to make the decision. She shouldn't have been surprised. Gina needed to know that Eleanor was serious. She needed to make the move, even if it was causing her stomach to churn with nerves.

"Perhaps you'd like to come back to the apartment with us," Eleanor said. She hoped Gina didn't detect the waver in her voice. She didn't fancy explaining that it wasn't born of nerves but rather desire.

"Sure." Gina's voice was upbeat and casual. No judgement, no expectations.

Eleanor knew that she needed to be a little more precise in order to get what she wanted.

"Sophia will need a bath before bed. And then maybe you could…stay?"

She turned to look at Gina, hoping that her meaning was conveyed in her gaze.

Gina smiled. "I'd like that. If you're ready?"

Eleanor felt she was so ready that she might explode. She simply nodded, not wanting to give away too much and frighten Gina. She knew it was sudden, but she also knew that she wanted Gina more than she wanted anything else.

They returned to Eleanor's apartment and prepared a bath for Sophia. They slipped into the comfortable co-parenting arrangement that had first surprised Eleanor but that demonstrated Gina's hidden depths. Each took turns holding and chatting with Sophia while the other prepared the bath. All the while, the tension between them grew and grew.

By the time Sophia was in bed, Eleanor was desperate for Gina to stay the night. She needed her touch. They slipped out of Sophia's bedroom, switching off the light and closing the door.

Eleanor looked at Gina, not sure how to say what she wanted to say. She'd never done this before and wasn't sure of her next steps.

She wanted to take Gina by the hand and lead her to the bedroom, but that seemed a little presumptuous.

"I can hear you stressing," Gina whispered.

Eleanor smiled. "I'm new to this."

"Sex?" Gina asked.

"No. Well, with a woman, yes. But I meant wanting someone this much."

Gina bit her lip and looked deeply satisfied with herself. Gina took hold of Eleanor's hand and gently tugged her towards the main bedroom.

"Let's see if we can reduce some of that tension, Dr. Osborne."

Chapter Twenty-two

Eleanor woke up to the unusual sound of someone else moving around the apartment. For a moment, she couldn't figure out why she could hear the kettle boiling and muffled conversation.

Then her memory helpfully provided her with a replay of the previous night's activities. She smiled and then giggled to herself in a way she hadn't done since she was a teenager.

Gina had guided her through her first sexual experience with a woman with the stable kindness that Eleanor had needed. It had been unlike anything she'd ever experienced before.

She'd never been that into sex, assuming that she was one of many women who didn't find it particularly fulfilling. Nothing could have been further from the truth, she now realised. She briefly mourned the loss of time that she had wasted through not exploring such an obvious avenue.

She shook the thoughts away, determined not to be too depressed and instead to enjoy the fact that she had found her way, with a partner she truly cared about, one who appeared to be in her kitchen. She got out of bed and wrapped herself in a dressing gown.

In the kitchen, Gina was preparing breakfast with Sophia attached to her hip. Sophia was happily giggling and chatting with Gina in her own way. Gina conversed with Sophia as if she understood what the baby was saying, sparking a conversation from the random sounds.

Eleanor held back in the doorway for a moment to enjoy the

scene in front of her. She didn't want to get ahead of herself, but it was impossible not to when near perfection was right there—a woman she was growing to love, and her daughter adoring that same woman.

"Going to stand there and watch us or are you going to help with breakfast?" Gina asked playfully, her back to Eleanor.

Eleanor entered the kitchen and pulled two mugs out of the cupboard, pressing a kiss to Sophia's cheek and one to Gina's lips as she passed.

"You should have woken me," Eleanor said.

"I'd planned breakfast in bed. Well, Sophia suggested it," Gina said.

"Oh, did she?" Eleanor chuckled.

"I think it was something like that."

Light embarrassment washed over Eleanor as her memories started to filter back. She'd been fairly forthright the previous night, something that didn't come naturally to her. But the desire for Gina had been so strong that she didn't think she'd be able to ignore it. Now, in the cold light of day, she felt a little uncertain.

"I'm sorry if I was a little…"

"A little?" Gina asked, the lopsided grin indicating she knew what Eleanor was referring to.

"You know."

"Sexy?"

Her cheeks heated. She enjoyed the idea of Gina thinking her attractive, but that didn't mean she'd become used to it yet.

"No. You know what I mean."

"I don't," Gina said. Mischief was clear in her eyes. "I had fun last night."

The comment hung in the air for a second, a hint of a question within it.

Eleanor realised that she'd woken up and immediately apologised for the night before, potentially giving Gina cause to think that she regretted events.

"So did I," Eleanor said. She stopped making drinks and turned to face Gina, wanted to reassure her with a look of confidence that she hoped she could fake. "A lot of fun. I hope we can maybe have more fun in the future."

The grin on Gina's face exploded into a full smile.

"I'd like that. I'd like that a lot."

Eleanor nodded, happy that she had somehow managed to navigate some tricky waters. Thoughts of the day and work trickled into her mind. She'd almost forgotten about work. Lately it was normal procedure for Eleanor to struggle with sleep and then wake early with her mind full of thoughts of work.

This morning she hadn't even thought of work until now, something simply unheard of. And she'd slept through the night, eventually. It felt like a very welcome reprieve from her usual day-to-day.

Nervous questions about the future lingered in her mind, but she pushed them back. She deserved to have a little fun. Especially now.

"I'm making pancakes," Gina said as she handed Sophia to Eleanor.

"Pancakes?" Eleanor knew that some people viewed pancakes as breakfast, but for her they were firmly in dessert territory.

"Yes, you have the ingredients, and I think this little one will enjoy them. And I think you might need the energy." Gina winked.

"I can't argue with that."

Sophia started to reach out for her mother, and Eleanor happily took her from Gina.

"Good morning," Eleanor said. "Did you sleep well?"

"I could hear her chatting to herself when I got up," Gina explained while she cooked breakfast. "I popped my head in, and she was wide awake."

Eleanor kissed Sophia's plump cheek. "An early start? That probably means you'll be grouchy this afternoon. I'm relieved I won't be here to see it."

Gina laughed.

Later, after breakfast had been eaten and Eleanor had showered and gotten herself ready for work, she found that she didn't want to leave. This time it wasn't because of what awaited her at work, but more what she was leaving at home. She'd always missed Sophia when she went to work, but now the pull to remain home was stronger than ever. She didn't want to leave her new family unit, but she knew she must.

"Would you like me to speak with your father and pass along a message?" Eleanor offered.

"Yes, tell him to stop being silly and get better and get home." Gina sat cross-legged on the living room floor, accepting building blocks from Sophia one at a time.

"I'll probably top and tail that," Eleanor said. "Anything else?"

"No, just, you know, I love him."

"I'll tell him," Eleanor promised. "He seems like a nice man. I look forward to getting to know him more."

Gina looked immediately stricken and jumped to her feet. "What? Why?"

Eleanor blinked. Gina's reaction was such a surprise that she didn't know what to say next. She thought they were on the same page, thought they were building something together. Nothing Gina had said or done led Eleanor to believe that Gina thought this was a temporary thing.

"Because of us," Eleanor said quietly, feeling suddenly tiny.

"I told you, I'm not out to them," Gina said. "That's not going to change."

Eleanor felt confusion and anger battle within her. "Then why on earth did you...did we? You suggested that you didn't want this to be a casual thing. Am I wrong? What changed? Is it me?"

"It's not you, and I don't want this to be a casual thing," Gina said. "I want to be with you. Both of you. But that doesn't mean I'm going to tell my parents about us."

Eleanor felt the breath leave her lungs. Her perfect little world was falling down around her ears.

"Let me get this right," Eleanor said. "You want to have a relationship with me?"

"Yes." Gina nodded.

"This isn't a fling or a one-night stand?"

"Of course not."

"But you don't want to tell your parents about us?"

Gina's expression hardened. "You can't ask me to do that."

"I think it's a perfectly reasonable thing to ask," Eleanor said.

"You don't know them."

"And from what you have told me, you don't know what their reaction would be either," Eleanor argued. "You've said yourself that you don't know how they would take the news."

"Exactly! I can't take that risk. What if they do disown me? You can't ask me to lose my parents."

"And you can't ask me to go back into the closet just after I came out of it," Eleanor said. "Is there…is there a time limit on this decision? What if we're together for three months? Would you change your mind then?"

Gina folded her arms across her chest and looked down at the floor.

"Gina?" Eleanor pressed.

"I don't want to tell them," Gina whispered. "I can't see a time where I would. I don't want to take that risk."

"I see." Eleanor didn't see at all. Her mind was spinning with questions. She couldn't see how Gina could possibly think that would be an option.

"I want to be with you," Gina said. She looked up. "We can still be together. It doesn't matter if they know or not."

"Of course it matters. You'd be living a lie," Eleanor said. "What happens when they ask if you're dating? Do you say no? Do you say yes and I change my name to Eric?"

"Don't be silly—"

"I'm not being silly. I'm trying to show you how impractical this is. And frankly, how hurtful this is."

"It's not about you, it's about me," Gina said.

"It's a little about me!"

"You know what I mean."

"I don't think I do. What happens when Sophia is older? How do we explain that to her? Does she have grandparents? What do we tell her?"

"I don't know!" Gina threw her hands up. "I don't know. I

don't have all the answers. I know that I want to be with you and I can't tell them, but that's all I know."

Eleanor let out a sigh and turned away from Gina. She realised then that she'd been foolish to think that Gina could suddenly grow up in just a few weeks. Yes, Gina had matured in some ways, but that didn't mean she would in all ways. She seemed to honestly believe that Eleanor would be satisfied living a lie. And as much as Eleanor wanted to be with Gina, to explore what they might have, she couldn't put herself in that sort of situation. She couldn't be complicit in a lie.

She turned back to face Gina.

"I can't do this."

Gina looked as though she was about to argue, so Eleanor raised her hand.

"No, Gina, I'm sorry. I've just discovered who I am, or might be, or...I don't know, something. But I can't explore that from a cage. And I can't risk Sophia growing up in the middle of a lie. I do have feelings for you, but I can't be your secret. I can't live a lie. I don't want to pressure you into doing something that you're not comfortable with, and I don't want to be a part of a lie. So we have to end this here and now."

"Eleanor, wait, we can talk about—"

"We can't," Eleanor said. "I'm sorry, Gina. There's nothing to talk about. Do you want me to find other arrangements for Sophia's care?"

"What? No! No, of course not."

Gina looked heartbroken, but Eleanor knew there were no other options. She couldn't live a lie, nor could she force Gina to come out to her parents. They were stuck in an impossible situation.

"If you're sure," Eleanor said. She looked at her watch and let out a frustrated sigh. "I...I'm sorry, I have to go to work."

"I'm sorry, Eleanor. Really, I am. I just...I can't."

Eleanor couldn't help but place her palm on Gina's cheek. She smiled sadly at her. "I'm sorry, too. It seems this just wasn't meant to be."

"Maybe we could—"

"No," Eleanor cut Gina off. "I'm not going to force you to do something that you don't want to do. And I can't live a lie. The sooner we understand that we've come to the end of this journey, the better for us both."

Gina looked devastated, but Eleanor knew she had to stand firm. She grabbed her bag and her bike helmet and hurried out the front door.

CHAPTER TWENTY-THREE

Gina sat at the breakfast bar in her kitchen and pushed the pasta around her plate with a fork. It had been three weeks since she'd ruined everything with Eleanor, and three weeks since she'd been eating breakfast and dinner alone once again.

Eleanor hadn't thought it appropriate to eat together after they had ended things. Gina tried to argue with her and tried to get things back to the way they had been, but Eleanor remained unmoved. At one point, Eleanor had confessed her fear they would slip back into their old patterns if they shared meals.

Gina had hoped that they would drift back together again, but she knew that wouldn't solve anything. All it would do was bring more pain to Eleanor, and that was something Gina refused to do.

She'd ruined everything and had no one to blame but herself. She'd known from the very first kiss that she wouldn't be able to tell her parents about her true self. She'd allowed things to escalate out of selfishness and lust, knowing full well that Eleanor would never agree to what Gina was proposing.

"Stupid, stupid, stupid," she muttered to herself.

She put the fork down, her appetite gone. She didn't know how it was possible to fall for someone so quickly, but she had done. Eleanor had crept into her heart and made herself at home, and there was seemingly nothing that Gina could do about it.

The pain wasn't going away. She felt as wretched now as she had done that morning three weeks earlier. But she did what she could to make Eleanor's days tolerable—that was the least she could do. She looked after Sophia, checked in with Eleanor when Eleanor requested it, and then left Eleanor to her own devices.

The times when Sophia wasn't with her were now lonelier than ever. From the moment she said goodbye to Sophia in the evening, time seemed to drag in a way she didn't think was possible.

On the bright side, her father was at home now. She'd FaceTimed her parents a few times in the last couple of weeks, trying to pretend that everything was okay as she made small talk with a broken heart. She couldn't be angry with them. She was the one who had made her decision. She was too used to the notion that they would always be there for her to risk losing them. Especially after coming so close to losing her father.

Her phone rang, Eleanor's name appearing on the screen.

Gina held the phone in her hand for a few moments and wondered why Eleanor would be calling her at nine o'clock at night. She knew there was only one way to find out.

"Hi?"

"Hello," Eleanor said, her tone soft but with a seriousness lurking. "I wanted to tell you that I've…Well, I've made other arrangements for Sophia."

Gina slipped off the bar stool and started to pace. "What? Why? We're doing okay, aren't we? Did I do something wrong?"

"You didn't do anything wrong," Eleanor replied. "It's just difficult to see you. And I can tell that you are having the same difficulties as I am. I'm sorry, Gina. You really have been wonderful with Sophia, and I appreciate all that you've done—"

"No, wait, Eleanor—please. You don't have to do this. Really, we can adjust our plans again. I could pick her up from yours. You don't even have to look at me. We cou—"

"Gina, I'm so sorry. It's just not working out. I wish I could see another way. I think a clean break is for the best."

"I…" Gina raised a hand to her head and tried to think. She couldn't completely lose Sophia and Eleanor, she just couldn't. "We can work something out."

"We can't," Eleanor said, her voice still soft and still determined.

Gina felt her world slipping out from under her. "Will we see each other again?"

"In passing, I'm sure."

A cold feeling caused Gina to shiver. She was losing Eleanor completely.

"When?" Gina asked, fearing the answer.

"From tomorrow."

Gina leaned against the wall and slowly sank to the floor.

"I'm sorry that it's not much notice," Eleanor continued. "I thought it might be best this way."

"I—I understand." Gina leaned her head against the wall, eyes squeezed tightly shut, willing herself to hold on until the end of the call before she lost control and burst into tears.

"I'm sorry," Eleanor said again.

"I'm the one who should be sorry," Gina whispered. "Good luck with everything. I hope you find the right person to be with."

She hung up the call before Eleanor could reply.

❖

Eleanor looked at the phone and realised that Gina had hung up on her. She wasn't surprised. In fact the call had gone slightly better than she thought it might. She felt like a coward for not giving Gina any notice or telling her face to face, but she really didn't feel as though she could have faced either prospect.

She called Nigel. As always, he had been her rock for the last few weeks of hell. She'd told him what had happened the moment she had gone into work after ending things. Things which had only barely begun.

At first, he'd tried to reason with her, to see if Gina could be convinced somehow to change her mind. But Eleanor didn't want to go down that route. Forcing Gina to choose and to come out to her parents could mean their relationship starting with a weight dragging them down. Would Gina forever blame Eleanor if she did lose her parents' love? Would Eleanor be able to live with the guilt if she was the person who had torn a family apart? And would they both remain in a relationship that didn't work simply to justify what had happened?

No, Gina had to make that choice. And she was adamant that she wouldn't. No matter how Eleanor looked at it, they were stuck.

"How did it go?" Nigel asked.

"As well as could be expected," Eleanor said. "She was clearly upset but took it well."

"It was the right thing to do," Nigel said.

"I know. But it still hurts so much." She stood up and paced the dimly lit living room. "I finally find someone who I want to be with, and this happens."

"I know. But you have to look on the bright side. You have a whole other avenue of dating prospects to look at now."

Eleanor scoffed. "I don't want to start dating again. I actually feel I'd be better off not knowing. You know, in all the dates I had, nothing ever hurt like this."

"The hardest part is over. You had to make that break. Seeing her every day was just prolonging the pain. Maybe in a few weeks or months you'll start to feel better about things. You'll probably find the perfect woman by the end of the year."

Eleanor couldn't imagine a time when she'd feel better. But she didn't want to say such a thing to Nigel. He'd already been a rock for her, someone she knew she could rely on, someone who she knew would guide her right. He didn't need to listen to her feeling sorry for herself.

"We'll see," she said.

"Get some rest. I've heard through the grapevine that the Oxford vaccine trial is progressing to phase two shortly. Who knows, we may have a deliverable vaccine later this year."

Eleanor wasn't so sure. Nothing seemed to be going right, and the prospect of a vaccine seemed almost too good to be true. But she had been following the vaccine trials with interest, crossing her fingers that everything would go smoothly.

"Let's hope," she said. "I'll see you in the morning."

"Take the day off," he suggested. "We can manage without you. Take some time for yourself."

"I'd rather work," she said. "Take my mind off things."

"See how you feel in the morning."

"I will. G'night, Nigel. And thank you."

"You're welcome. Night."

She hung up and tossed the phone onto the sofa. The peak of cases had thankfully passed. Numbers were dropping as the effect of the lockdown filtered through to hospitalisations, or lack thereof. It was a relief to see things finally getting back to manageable levels. A relief that Eleanor couldn't fully appreciate as it had coincided with a part of her own life crashing and burning.

She heard a noise and looked around the apartment in confusion. She walked towards where the sound was coming from to see an envelope being wedged under the door. She hurried over and looked through the peephole. She saw Gina stand up. She was wearing a coat and carried a rucksack, apparently heading out somewhere.

Eleanor opened the door as Gina hurried away.

"Gina?"

Gina paused, her back to Eleanor. "Sorry, I just wanted you to have a couple of things. I won't bother you again."

"Where are you going?" Eleanor asked.

"Out."

"Gina, there's a lockdown. You can't go out."

"I'll socially distance from people. I just have something I have to do."

"Gina, please, can't it wait until morning?" Eleanor took a few steps out into the hall. "It's late."

"I have to go now. Before I lose my nerve," Gina said.

"Where are you going?" Eleanor asked.

Gina turned around. She looked devastated but wore a half smile, presumably to reassure Eleanor. "It doesn't matter. I'll be okay, I promise. I just have to go and run an errand."

Before Eleanor had a chance to say anything else, Gina spun on her heel and entered the stairwell.

Eleanor worried her lip. She couldn't imagine what errand Gina needed to run this late at night. Not that it was any of her business any more. She returned to her apartment and picked up the thick brown envelope from the hallway floor.

In the dining room, she switched on the ceiling light and tipped the contents of the envelope onto the table. Sketches of her and Sophia fluttered out.

"Oh my," she whispered as she looked over each image.

Some were simple outlines, others more complex. She spotted a letter and picked it up with a shaky hand.

Eleanor,

I'm sorry to have caused you so much pain, it was never my intention. I honestly didn't consider what I was doing, didn't think about the impact my decision would have. I'm including these sketches as they belong to you more than they do me. Do what you wish with them. If you want to throw them away, then that's fine.

Thank you for opening my eyes to what I have to do but have been putting off for so many years. I know it's too late for us. I'm not doing this for us. I'm doing it for me. I'm going to tell my parents, and if the worst happens, then it will be on me. But I can't live a lie any more. I thought it was just hurting me, but I realise now that I was wrong.

Thank you for letting me watch over Sophia for you. It's been a privilege. Most of all, thank you for all the time we spent together. I'm sorry I couldn't be what you need me to be, and I really hope that you find happiness.

Gina

Eleanor swallowed and lowered the letter to the table. She picked up a sketch of Sophia and smiled, marvelling at how Gina had managed to capture her likeness as well as her personality.

She didn't like the idea of Gina heading out into the night to make the journey to her parents, but she also knew she didn't get to decide things like that for Gina. All she could do was hope that things went well. And be proud that Gina was making the right decision for herself.

Chapter Twenty-four

Gina waited at the bus stop for the night bus to arrive. It wouldn't take her all the way to her parents', but it would take her more than halfway. The walk on the other end would no doubt do her good. She'd need a few fortifying breaths of fresh air before she potentially ruined her family relationships for good.

She shook her head to remove those thoughts. She needed to stay positive. Or at least stay determined.

Her indecision had lost her a chance with Eleanor, a fact that hadn't really hit home until Eleanor had fully finished things. As long as Gina could see Eleanor every day, even if only for a few moments here and there, she felt there might be a chance.

But that had just been false hopes and certainly not rooted in reality. Like with so many things, Gina had buried her head in the sand and wished for the best. She was learning, too late, that wasn't a good strategy.

Too late for a chance with Eleanor but perhaps not too late for herself. There was only one way out of the hole she had dug herself, and that was honesty.

The bus turned the corner, and Gina put on her face mask, covered in a beautiful gothic damask print. She'd bought it online from a woman she'd found on social media. Another first for 2020, face masks on public transport. At first it had seemed like madness, but after a few moments, Gina had decided that she'd rather wear a mask and keep others safe than be locked up for weeks more. And then she'd purchased several to match her outfits.

She boarded the bus, tapped her travel card for the first time in weeks, and took a seat at the back of the empty vehicle. She unlocked her phone with her passcode rather than facial recognition, which was already becoming tedious, and looked at the map. The bus would drop her a forty-five-minute walk from her parents' house. Enough time for her to prepare what she wanted to say. Or panic the entire way and wing it, which was more likely.

She tried to keep thoughts of banishment from her mind, reminding herself that she didn't know what her parents would really make of her coming out.

With nerves building, she got her headphones out of her bag and put them on. Music would hopefully let the time pass quicker, and maybe even give her some much-needed courage.

❖

Gina stood at the end of the driveway and let out a breath she'd been holding. It was time. There was no going back now. She was pretty sure that the local curtain twitchers were about to report her to the neighbourhood watch committee if she didn't do something soon other than stare at the house.

She called her mum.

On the fourth ring, her very tired sounding mum answered. "Gi?"

"Hi, um, I'm outside."

"What?"

"I'm out the front. I'm going to come around the back. Can you and Dad go into the conservatory? I've got something I need to tell you."

"Is everything okay?" Her mum sounded panicked. Gina couldn't blame her. It was hardly normal behaviour, their daughter turning up in the middle of the night during lockdown and requesting they go to the conservatory for a chat.

"Yes, everything is good. Fine. And well...just come down to the conservatory. I'll keep back two metres. I just need to see you."

The light in her parents' bedroom switched on and Gina hung

up. She walked down the driveway. She threaded her hands through the metal gate and grabbed hold of the latch and the bolt at the same time to lift the gate mechanism clean over the bulky padlock, which was just for show. Walking down the rest of the drive to the wooden gate, she stood on tiptoe and reached over for the sliding bolt, opening the gate and entering the back garden.

It was dimly illuminated by the hallway light from the house, and she immediately felt a wave of memories of family parties, evening meals, and even sharing a glass of wine with her parents throughout the years.

The garden held a lot of pleasant memories, but she didn't know for how much longer. It might ultimately be the location where she lost her parents' love forever.

The light in the conservatory sprang to life and her father appeared in his dressing gown and slippers. He unlocked the door and opened it.

"You okay, love?"

She took a step back, wanting to make sure that there was no way she could infect either of them. She didn't know if she had COVID or not, so simply always acted as if she did. Better to be safe than sorry, she'd decided.

"I'm okay. I just needed to speak with you both."

The garden floodlight came on, and Gina winced under the bright light. Her mum stepped into the conservatory.

"There, we can see you now."

"Bit of warning would have been nice," Gina said, shielding her eyes.

"Likewise, I was just drifting off to sleep." Her mum pulled her dressing gown around her and smothered a yawn behind her hand. "What couldn't wait?"

Gina opened and then closed her mouth. She knew now was the moment, and she'd had plenty of time to prepare for it, but her brain was giving her nothing.

"I..."

She couldn't find any words. She could see her parents were beginning to panic. It was only a matter of seconds before her dad became his usual decisive self and marched out of the conservatory and wrapped her up in his arms as he always did when she was upset.

She held up her hand. "Don't come out here, Dad. We have to stay two metres apart."

"You're frightening me, Gi," he said.

"I don't mean to." She sniffed as tears started to fall down her cheeks. "I just, I just need to tell you."

"Tell us what, love?" her mum asked. "It's okay. You can tell us anything. Are you in trouble?"

"No."

"Pregnant?"

Gina laughed bitterly. "No."

"What is it then?"

"I…" Gina took a big lungful of air. "I'm gay."

She swallowed and took a couple of shaky deep breaths. It was done. Not in any of the ways she'd practiced, but the words were out there. Now all she could do was wait for a reaction and hope.

She watched her dad turn to face her mum. "Told you."

"You didn't. I told *you*, you daft thing."

"No, I definitely told you first. It was back when she had the purple hair."

"That was after I told you—"

Gina held up her hand. "Wait…what?"

"We've suspected for years, love," her mum said.

"Why didn't you say anything?" Gina demanded.

"*You* didn't say anything. We didn't think you were ready. Or maybe we were wrong. We didn't want you to think we'd judge you, so we didn't say anything."

Gina looked from her mum to her dad with shock. "You both knew?"

Her father shrugged. "We suspected for a while. But then you kept saying you were dating boys, so we thought you were bi, or the other one…"

"Pan," her mum added.

"That's the one," he said. "So you came here to tell us?"

They stood side by side, each with an arm wrapped around the other's waist, looking at her with mild confusion. Gina was more than mildly confused herself. She hadn't for a moment expected this reaction. She'd expected shock, upset, screaming, denials. This quiet acceptance was literally the last thing she would have planned for.

"I thought you'd be mad," she whispered.

Her mum frowned. "Why on earth would you think that?"

"You just never said anything. Not about me or about anyone. Any celebrity that ever came out as gay, you just ignored it."

"It's none of my business who people want to be with," her mum said. "I didn't say anything because it's not my place to say anything. Not because I think it's wrong. And I wanted to give you space to explore. I never said anything negative when you were experimenting with hair colour or clothing, did I?"

Gina watched her mother's confusion give way to worry.

"No. No, I just…I didn't know what you thought."

"We just want you to be happy, Gi," her dad said.

"But you go on endlessly about me finding a man and settling down," Gina pointed out.

"Only because you never told us you were interested in anyone else," her mum retorted. "If you'd said you were interested in both, I would have said find *someone* to settle down with. Or a woman to settle dow—Wait! It's the doctor, isn't it?"

Gina winced.

"I knew it!" Her mum took her reaction as confirmation. "And that little girl! Oh, Patrick, she's an adorable one. And she's a doctor. The one that spoke to you."

"Yes, I know," her father said, not as excited as his wife. "Is that right, Gi? Are you telling us now because you're in a relationship with Dr. Osborne?"

Gina bit her lip and shook her head. "Not quite. I'm telling you now because I ruined my chances with her because of this."

Gina felt new tears race down her cheeks. No longer was she

relieved that her parents didn't seem to harbour any ill will about her sexual orientation. Now she was furious at herself for leaving things for so long and now losing Eleanor because of her own stupid fears.

"This is because of that documentary, isn't it?" her mum asked her.

Her dad looked between the two of them in confusion. "What documentary?"

"Years ago, when she was a teenager, there was a documentary about kids coming out to their parents and being disowned. It was on the TV one evening."

Gina nodded. "You switched it off." She remembered it vividly. Up until that point, she'd never thought it was possible for a parent to hate their own child. That was when the fear had started to gnaw at her.

"Yes, because it's disgusting how some people will treat their own flesh and blood," her mum said. "It's no reason to kick your child out of their home, just because you don't like who they choose to fall in love with. It made me feel sick."

Gina closed her eyes and sobbed. She remembered that evening as if it was yesterday. The documentary had frightened her, and when her mother had turned it off without saying a word, she'd assumed the worst. She'd thought that her mum was on the side of the parents, not the kids. Now, over a decade later, she realised she'd been completely wrong.

"Oh, Gina…" her mum whispered.

She opened her eyes to see her mum trying to step out of the conservatory but her dad holding her back.

"Nope, come on, we have to stick to the rules," he said.

"Love, I'm sorry if I've ever given you the impression that I'd not love you no matter what your sexuality," her mum said.

"It's not you, I think it's me," Gina said. "I think I was ashamed, and I've transferred that to you. Read things into things that I shouldn't have. And now I've ruined everything with Eleanor."

"How come?" her dad asked.

"I told her that I wouldn't come out to you two because I was worried about how you might take it. I thought it might ruin things between us. And I didn't want to risk it. She didn't want to stay in the closet. We split up."

Her mum thumped him in the chest. "I told you we should have said something."

He held up his hands. "I know, I know. I just wanted to give her time to come to us. We might have been wrong."

"We weren't."

Gina wiped at her eyes. "What are you talking about?"

Her mum folded her arms. "I said that we should sit you down and ask you if you were gay—"

"Or bi or pan," he added.

"Because we suspected," she said. "But you seemed so adamant that you weren't. So I thought we should have a talk with you. But your father"—she smacked him again—"said we should let you come to us when you were ready."

He took a step away from his wife. "I just didn't want you to think that we were assuming because you couldn't get a boyfriend that you were gay."

"Or bi or pan," her mum added.

"You pulled away from us, Gi. When you were about twenty, you remember?" he said. "Not fully. But you didn't want to talk about your feelings any more. Or who you were seeing, where you were going. So we just kind of assumed you didn't want us to be a part of your life in that way. Or, well, many ways."

Gina remembered. Around the time she was questioning her sexuality, she'd stopped telling her parents everything she did, thought, and felt. She was starting to worry about how they would take the news and so started to ration the information she gave them to protect herself. From dates, to nights out, to work, and even to friends. She couldn't risk her secret coming out.

Except that plan had backfired spectacularly.

"Well, we all know now," he said as if nothing bad had happened.

"Dad, I've been in the closet for almost a decade. It's ruined one of the best relationships I've ever had," Gina said.

"You said you split up because you wouldn't tell us?" he asked.

"Yes."

"And now you've told us. Maybe with some grovelling you can fix this." He pulled his dressing gown tighter, clearly feeling the breeze from the open door in the middle of the night. "Maybe don't wake her up in the middle of the night, though."

"How are you going to get home, love?" her mum asked. "It's very late."

"Night bus," Gina said.

She shivered as if Gina had suggested she was going to hitchhike. "No, you should stay here."

"No, that's against the rules," Gina reminded her.

"But it's the middle of the night!"

Her dad put his arm around her mother's shoulders. "She's a big girl, don't worry."

Gina looked at her parents and smiled. They really were adorable. She'd always assumed that she'd never have what they did, but now there was a small possibility that she might be able to. If only she could get Eleanor to forgive her.

"I love you both," she said. "I wish I could hug you, but the government would hate that."

"We love you," they said in unison.

"We'll talk on the phone tomorrow," her mum promised. "But Gina, know that I will always love you and there will always be a place for you in my heart, okay, love?"

Gina felt tears building again. "Stop making me cry," she said. "And go to bed, it's late."

Her parents chuckled.

"Close the gate behind you," her dad called out.

"I'll call you tomorrow," her mum said.

Gina gave them one last socially distanced wave before she left, locking up again as she went. On the street, she looked up to her parents' bedroom window and waved goodbye to where she knew her mum would be watching her walk away.

She walked back towards the bus stop, thankful for the forty-five-minute journey which she would need to clear her mind. She'd been living in unnecessary fear for years. She'd possibly ruined one of the best things that had ever happened to her over nothing.

She took a few deep breaths and reminded herself that there was nothing that could be done. She couldn't turn back time. All she could do was move forward as best as she could, learning from her mistake.

And hoping that maybe, if she was extremely lucky, Eleanor would give her a second chance.

Chapter Twenty-five

Eleanor grabbed the piece of toast from the toaster and threw it onto a plate. She raced to the fridge and took out some raspberry jam and quickly made herself an almost passable breakfast.

It had been a fitful night with only some sleep and many nightmares. Sophia had woken up at three in the morning, causing Eleanor to bring her into her bedroom where they both stared at one another for thirty minutes before Sophia eventually drifted off to sleep again.

Now she was running late. The new babysitter, who came highly recommended and seemed to be a reliable sort, was a fifteen-minute walk away and Eleanor wanted to make a good impression. She'd discovered that babysitters were precious, rare creatures while single mothers who desperately needed childcare were very common. That meant it was important for Eleanor to arrive on time and give the impression that she was reliable.

She itched to text Gina to check that she was okay but knew that would give the wrong message. She was trying to maintain boundaries—the last thing she needed to do was confuse matters even more. Even if she really couldn't take her mind off Gina. Especially what had happened the night before. She hoped that Gina's parents had been understanding, but she feared the worst.

Twenty minutes later, she strapped Sophia into her harness and pulled the straps on over her shoulders. She liked having Sophia so close, exactly where she could see her, and it was considerably easier than a buggy. Especially when she had to hurry to the new babysitter. She opened the front door and took a step back in shock when she saw Gina sitting on the floor and leaning against the wall.

Gina jumped to her feet. "Hi. Sorry. I didn't know when you would be leaving this morning. I didn't want to miss you."

"Have you been there all night?" Eleanor looked at the coat, which had been used as a blanket, and the variety of snacks that surrounded the rucksack on the floor.

"Yes. I didn't want to wake you either. So I thought I'd just wait for you to leave this morning. Which, in hindsight, is probably a bit creepy."

If it had been anyone else, Eleanor would have found it creepy. But instead she was just worried about what had caused Gina to want to sleep in the hallway just to guarantee that she'd see her that morning.

"You could have called," Eleanor pointed out. "Or sent a text message."

Gina made a face that indicated she hadn't considered that option. Which made Eleanor worry all the more. From Gina's evening backpacking trip to sleeping in the hall, she couldn't help but feel concerned for Gina's wellbeing.

"Are you okay?" Eleanor asked.

Gina had picked up her bag and was rummaging through the contents.

"Gina?"

Gina looked up. Her eyes were glossed over with tiredness. "Hm?"

"Are you okay?" Eleanor repeated.

"Yes. Yes, I'm good." She looked in her bag again before bringing out an envelope. "I made you this."

"Gina…you've already given me those beautiful sketches."

"It's an invitation," Gina continued.

Eleanor sighed and put her bag on the floor. There was no chance that she would get to the new babysitter in time, so she would just have to call and say she was delayed and hope for the best. Eleanor wouldn't feel right until she was satisfied that Gina was safe and well.

Gina handed her the tatty envelope. "Sorry, I made it on the bus."

Eleanor was certain her confusion and alarm were written all over her face.

"I wore a mask," Gina added. "Not that anyone else was on the bus, anyway."

Eleanor looked at the envelope. "You made me this?"

"Yes."

"On the bus?"

Gina nodded.

"And it's an invitation?"

"Open it," Gina suggested.

Sophia reached out a hand to Gina, but Gina ignored it. She smiled and made a funny face, which caused Sophia to giggle. Eleanor was grateful that she wasn't using Sophia's connection to her to make matters more difficult.

She opened the envelope and took out a sheet of paper. On one side was a sketch of her, Sophia, and Gina with two people she didn't recognise. The man looked familiar, but she couldn't place him immediately.

She turned the piece of paper over and gasped at the beautifully calligraphed invitation. What Gina had done on a bus, Eleanor would never have been able to do in a year with all the appropriate tools and a desk.

"I don't understand," she finally said, not grasping why Gina was presenting her with an invitation to an event with a question mark instead of a date.

"It's an invitation to my dad's birthday party. It's been postponed, but when it happens, I'd like you to come along. With Sophia, of course."

Eleanor frowned. "As your...?"

"Girlfriend, if you'll accept my apology."

Eleanor's heart started to beat faster. She looked down at the invitation and turned it over to look at the sketch again. She now recognised the man as Patrick Henley, Gina's father. Presumably the woman was Gina's mother.

"Like I said in my letter, if you read it, I went to tell them last night that I'm gay," Gina explained. "I did it for me. Not because I expect you to take me back now that I've done it. I did it because you were right—it is ridiculous for me to think that I can live a lie forever. And if I keep lying to them, then they won't even know me. Why maintain a relationship with them if it's built on lies?"

Gina took a step forward and brushed a finger across Sophia's brow. "And I did it for her. Because she needs people like me to be brave in this world so it's easier for her generation. I was being a coward. I'd built it up in my mind to be something huge and frightening, and I'd convinced myself that I could live the lie forever. But that's unfair to my parents, unfair to me, and it was unfair to you. I'm sorry."

Gina stepped back. "I never would have"—she looked up and down the corridor to check they were alone—"let things happen if I'd really thought about it. It was wrong of me to put you in that situation and expect you to live my lie. I'd not thought it through, and I put you in a tough position, and I really can't apologise enough for that."

"How did they take it?" Eleanor asked.

"They suspected I was gay already." Gina blushed and looked down at her feet.

Eleanor wanted to say something but couldn't think of anything to say. Gina had dragged her through hell and back for nothing. But Eleanor knew that Gina's fears had felt real to her, and that was the main thing.

"Gina…" Eleanor tried to piece some words together.

"*Dee-na.*"

Eleanor looked down at Sophia in shock. She'd been close to talking a few times but never so clear as that. Her hand reached out in a grabby motion towards Gina, who was staring at her in equal shock.

"That's right," Gina said. "How about *mummy*?"

"*Mmm,*" Sophia said.

"Mummy," Gina repeated. She crouched down to see into the harness better. "Mummy."

"*Meemee*," Sophia said.

"That's the closest we've gotten so far," Gina said. She looked up at Eleanor and then took a step back. "I'm sorry. I don't want to confuse Sophia. I know we're not a thing any more and I shouldn't be—"

"You'd introduce me as your girlfriend?" Eleanor asked.

Gina nodded.

"To everyone?"

"Yes."

"You're out of the closet to everyone now?"

Gina nodded again.

Eleanor licked her lips nervously. "And you think that this could work between us?"

"I've never been more sure of anything," Gina said softly.

"Despite…" Eleanor let out a nervous breath. "No, no, we're too different. I'm a homebody and you like to party. And I'm so much older than you. What would your parents say?"

Gina cracked a smile. "Yeah, I like to party but not that much. Not any more. I'm appreciating the finer things in life like a good box set after a home-cooked meal. And you're not a homebody, you just forgot how much you like to travel. We could see the world together, us three. And I can take Sophia to festivals, with adequate ear defenders, while you have a weekend in bed if you want. It can all work out if we let it."

Eleanor had to admit, that sounded nice. It had already become very clear that Sophia was going to adore music. Even the slightest beat and she would immediately stop what she was doing and sway to the rhythm.

"And, yeah, you're older than me, but so what? My parents wouldn't say a thing. They just want me to be happy. I realise that now."

Eleanor looked down at Sophia, who was happily playing with the button of her blouse. Fear was clouding her judgement, she knew that. The hurt caused by the argument and the split was still raw. But just beyond that, she could see that Gina was right for her. Right for the both of them. She'd connected with them in a way that no one else had ever come close to.

"Think about it," Gina said. She picked up her belongings and threw them into her bag. "I'm sorry to be all creepy, waiting outside your apartment. I've not had any sleep, and I wanted to apologise for everything. And invite you to the party if there's even the slightest chance that you might give me a second chance. I understand if it doesn't make any difference to how you feel after these weeks. But I thought you deserved a proper apology and a thank you, whatever you ultimately decide."

Eleanor watched speechlessly as Gina walked away. She couldn't help but be impressed that Gina had only come to apologise. Not to convince Eleanor, and not to consider everything repaired by her actions. Just to apologise. A lesson had been learnt. And an understanding that things wouldn't be magically healed was obvious.

It was one of the most romantic things Eleanor had experienced. And it showed just how much Gina was growing and changing. Eleanor hurried after her. She caught Gina's arm and turned her around and kissed her. It was a quick peck, considering she had Sophia in the harness in front of her, but she hoped it conveyed just some of what she was feeling.

Gina looked momentarily confused before smiling.

"Come back to mine?" Eleanor asked.

"I thought you were heading to work?"

"I've worked hundreds of hours of overtime in the last couple of months. I can take the day today. Can you take some time off?"

Gina nodded quickly. "Yes, sure."

"I'd like to hear what your parents said. And hear more about this party I'm invited to." Eleanor smiled.

Gina smiled back. "So we're…?"

"I haven't decided yet." Eleanor knew that her grin was giving her away.

"Then I'll have to make it up to you," Gina said, a meaningful look crossing her expression.

Eleanor swallowed. "That would be…acceptable." She looked down at Sophia, who was looking up at her curiously. "Maybe we should have this conversation when I don't have a baby strapped to my chest?"

"Good idea."

They walked back towards Eleanor's apartment. Inside, Gina helped to remove Sophia from the harness and placed her in her playpen. Eleanor tossed the empty harness to the floor. They met in the middle of the room. Gina looked hesitant, but Eleanor knew exactly what she wanted.

She pulled Gina into a passionate kiss, one that she had been dreaming of ever since they split up. While she had known that ending things had been the right choice at the time, that hadn't put a stop to her desire for Gina. A desire she could now spend time attempting to satisfy.

Gina wrapped her arms around her and held her tight. The strength of feeling in the kiss was palpable. Gina pulled back for a second and peppered small kisses down Eleanor's neck.

"I'm sorry," Gina whispered between kisses. "So sorry."

"Don't be. It's all worked out." Eleanor closed her eyes and enjoyed the feeling of being loved and loving in return. "We'll work it all out. As long as we work together."

"*Mumma.*"

Gina pulled back, and they both looked at Sophia. She stood in the playpen, face pressed up against the soft white netting as she smiled.

"I've missed you," Gina said. She picked Sophia up out of the pen and stood beside Eleanor. "I love you. Both of you."

Gina looked at Eleanor with the most serious expression Eleanor could ever recall seeing from her.

"I mean it. I do," Gina said.

The final walls of worry and protectiveness fell within Eleanor. "I love you, too."

She placed a feather-light kiss to Gina's lips.

EPILOGUE

G ina watched her mum exit the conservatory with an armful of brochures.

"Mum, come on! You must be the only person in the world who still uses printed travel brochures. Go online like everyone else," Gina said, rolling her eyes.

"Quiet, you. I'm talking to Eleanor, not you," she said, waving her hand dismissively towards Gina.

She sat down at the patio table in the Henley family back garden and started to show Eleanor her top picks for holiday destinations. Eleanor eagerly took the brochures and read through the details.

Gina chuckled to herself. She just had to accept that her mum and her fiancée were both Luddites.

"Here we go!" Her father exited the house carefully with a full to the brim plastic bucket. He walked over to the paddling pool and slowly deposited the boiling water into the pool before swooshing it around with his hand.

It reminded Gina of when she was a child on a hot summer's day. She'd beg her father to get the blow-up paddling pool out and would then pout at how cold the water was. Her dad would bring freshly boiled kettles full of water out to the pool to top up the water and keep it just warm enough for her.

It seemed that he'd now discovered a quicker way to do that with his bucket. The paddling pool had been upgraded, too. While little Gina had made do with a small round pool that barely covered her legs when she sat down, Sophia had a large rectangular pool with a metal frame and even a ladder.

Sophia noticed what was happening and raced across the garden. She wore her favourite Disney Princess swimming costume and sunglasses, a gift from Gina's parents, who had decided upon first sight that Sophia was a princess who deserved the world.

He lifted her up and spun her around a couple of times before lowering her into the pool. Sophia laughed the whole while and started to splash him the moment she was in the pool.

"Get him!" her mum called out playfully from the patio.

He retreated to the patio table. Sophia stopped splashing and grinned at Gina.

"You want to come in?"

"Sure, but only walking," Gina said. She kicked off her shoes and stepped into the pool. The water came up to just below her knees and she walked around a little to enjoy the coolish water on the hot summer's day.

Sophia nodded over to Gina's parents and Eleanor sitting at the patio table, all engrossed in travel brochures. "What are they doing?"

"Planning our holiday," Gina said.

"Why are they not on a computer?" Sophia asked.

"I have no idea." Gina chuckled. Even the four-year-old thought the grown-ups were strange with their brochures. "Are you looking forward to our holiday?"

Sophia nodded hard.

"What are you looking forward to the most?" Gina asked.

"The pool," Sophia said without hesitation.

Gina smiled. Her parents had been showing Sophia holiday pictures of their previous villa trips, before the pandemic, whenever they babysat her. She'd come home stating that she wanted to go to Spain and have a barbecue by the pool the following weekend, leading Gina to a conversation about airplane journeys and the need to book holiday time from work.

As soon as pandemic restrictions had started to lift, Gina had introduced Sophia and Eleanor to her parents at a socially distanced gathering in the back garden. Back then she had no idea that for the next three years she'd be spending every other weekend visiting her parents with her fiancée and stepdaughter.

Eleanor and her parents had bonded immediately. After the first meeting, her mum had started nagging Gina to propose to Eleanor and showered Sophia with presents like any desperate grandparent would. A year ago, Gina got down on one knee during a weekend trip to Paris. Eleanor had said yes so fast that Gina had barely finished asking the question.

The five of them had been on a short break in the Lake District and had gotten on so well that they started talking about taking the plunge and going overseas together next.

"When we go on holiday…" Sophia started and then drifted off as if she was about to ask something.

"Yes?" Gina said in a sing-song voice.

"Will you take me to the beach?"

Gina nodded. "Absolutely. We're going to go to the beach, build sandcastles, swim in the ocean, and have ice cream. It's the law."

Sophia beamed. She held out her arms, closed her eyes, and angled her face towards the sun. Gina watched her enjoying the sun and smiled. She realised that Sophia had never been to the beach. The series of lockdowns that defined her toddler years meant she was behind on many experiences that Gina had already had at her age.

Gina had vowed to put that right.

"Time for a top-up," Eleanor said, appearing beside Gina with a bottle of sunscreen lotion.

Gina opened her mouth to call Sophia over to her.

"Not her, you," Eleanor clarified.

Gina noticed that little freckles had started to form on her arms. She took the factor fifty lotion—Eleanor wouldn't allow her out with anything less.

"Thank you. Have you picked a cave for us to stay in yet?" She squeezed some lotion into her hand.

"I'll assume that's a joke about us preferring brochures."

Eleanor held out her hand and Gina deposited another blob of lotion into it.

"Yep." Gina grinned.

"Well, we have picked somewhere, actually. There's a delightful villa with a separate guest house." She applied the lotion to Gina's neck and whispered, "Affords us all a bit of privacy."

Gina enjoyed the feel of skilled fingers massaging her neck. "Sounds good to me."

"Not bad for us old folks with our brochures," Eleanor said.

"Mummy, Gina's taking me to the beach to eat ice cream," Sophia said, wading over.

"That sounds like fun, can I come?" Eleanor asked.

"Sure. You can build sandcastles, too."

"I look forward to it."

Sophia walked away, chasing some of the floating toys.

Eleanor finished applying the lotion, and Gina groaned with disappointment.

"You can have more when I will clearly need to apply aftersun later," Eleanor said.

"Promise?" Gina waggled her eyebrows.

"I do." Eleanor placed a kiss on her lips. "I love you."

"I love you," Gina said.

Eleanor checked on Sophia. Gina watched the loves of her life and knew just how lucky she was.

About the Author

Amanda Radley had no desire to be a writer but accidentally turned into an award-winning, best-selling author. Residing in the UK with her wife and pets, she loves to travel. She gave up her marketing career in order to make stuff up for a living instead. She claims the similarities are startling.

Books Available From Bold Strokes Books

Before She Was Mine by Emma L McGeown. When Dani and Lucy are thrust together to sort out their children's playground squabble, sparks fly, leaving both of them willing to risk it all for each other. (978-1-63679-315-3)

Chasing Cypress by Ana Hartnett Reichardt. Maggie Hyde wants to find a partner to settle down with and help her run the family farm, but instead she ends up chasing Cypress. Olivia Cypress. (978-1-63679-323-8)

Dark Truths by Sandra Barett. When Jade's ex-girlfriend and vampire maker barges back into her life, can Jade satisfy her ex's demands, keep Beth safe, and keep everyone's secrets...secret? (978-1-63679-369-6)

Desires Unleashed by Renee Roman. Kell Murphy and Taylor Simpson didn't go looking for love, but as they explore their desires unleashed, their hearts lead them on an unexpected journey. (978-1-63679-327-6)

Here For You by D. Jackson Leigh. A horse trainer must make a difficult business decision that could save her father's ranch from foreclosure but destroy her chance to win the heart of a feisty barrel racer vying for a spot in the National Rodeo Finals. (978-1-63679-299-6)

Maybe, Probably by Amanda Radley. Set against the backdrop of a viral pandemic, Gina and Eleanor are about to discover that loving another person is complicated when you're desperately searching for yourself. (978-1-63679-284-2)

The One by C.A. Popovich. Jody Acosta doesn't know what makes her more furious, that the wealthy Bergeron family refuses to be held accountable for her father's wrongful death, or that she can't ignore her knee-weakening attraction to Nicole Bergeron. (978-1-63679-318-4)

Tides of Love by Kimberly Cooper Griffin. Falling in love is the last thing on either of their minds, but when Mikayla and Gem meet, sparks of possibility begin to shine, revealing a future neither expected. (978-1-63679-319-1)

Catch by Kris Bryant. Convincing the wife of the star quarterback to walk away from her family was never in offensive coordinator Sutton McCoy's game plan. But standing on the sidelines when a second chance at true love comes her way proves all but impossible. (978-1-63679-276-7)

Hearts in the Wind by MJ Williamz. Beth and Evelyn seem destined to remain mortal enemies but are about to discover that in matters of the heart, sometimes you must cast your fortunes to the wind. (978-1-63679-288-0)

Hero Complex by Jesse J. Thoma. Bronte, Athena, and their unlikely friends must work together to defeat Bronte's archnemesis. The fate of love, humanity, and the world might depend on it. No pressure. (978-1-63679-280-4)

Hotel Fantasy by Piper Jordan. Molly Taylor has a fantasy in mind that only Lexi can fulfill. However, convincing her to participate could prove challenging. (978-1-63679-207-1)

Last New Beginning by Krystina Rivers. Can commercial broker Skye Kohl and contractor Bailey Kaczmarek overcome their pride and work together while the tension between them boils over into a love that could soothe both of their hearts? (978-1-63679-261-3)

Love and Lattes by Karis Walsh. Cat café owner Bonnie and wedding planner Taryn join forces to get rescue cats into forever homes—discovering their own forever along the way. (978-1-63679-290-3)

Repatriate by Jaime Maddox. Ally Hamilton's new job as a home health aide takes an unexpected twist when she discovers a fortune in stolen artwork and must repatriate the masterpieces and avoid the wrath of the violent man who stole them. (978-1-63679-303-0)

The Hues of Me and You by Morgan Lee Miller. Arlette Adair and Brooke Dawson almost fell in love in college. Years later, they unexpectedly run into each other and come face-to-face with their unresolved past. (978-1-63679-229-3)